THE GREATER GLORY OF GALANTHUS

SUSAN ALEXANDER

Susan Alexander

Copyright 2021 by Susan Alexander

All rights reserved.

All characters in this publication are fictional.
Any resemblance to persons living or dead is purely coincidental.

Also by the author

The Snowdrop Mysteries:
The Ainswick Orange
The Snowdrop Crusade
A Remittance Man
The Heracles Project
St Margaret's
Beaumatin's Blonde
Hereford Crescent
Wolcum Yole
Gnat
And Only Man is Vile
Jersey Jones and the New World Order
Dies Dirae
Super Lucid
The Snowdrop Legacy
The Cotswolds Chronicler

The Eve Paxton Trilogy:
A Woman's Book of Rules
Hair and Maintenance
A Closet Romantic

Cover drawing: Galanthus reginae-olgae by Freda Cox

The Greater Gloucestershire Galanthus Group

For Freda and Joan

SUSAN ALEXANDER

The Greater Gloucestershire Galanthus Group

Dramatis Personae

The Cotswolds

Professor Margaret Spence Eliot (Maggie. Also Lady Raynham). Weingarten Fellow at Merrion College, Oxford.

Lord Raynham (Thomas). The twenty-eighth baron and Maggie's husband.

Mrs Cook. Beaumatin housekeeper.

Ned Thatcher. Beaumatin estate foreman.

Lady Ainswick (Beatrix). Friend of the Raynhams.

Lord Ainswick (Cedric). The eleventh viscount. Friend of the Raynhams and Beatrix's husband.

Chloe Symeon Osborne. The Ainswicks' daughter.

David Osborne. Chloe's husband and botanist in charge of the gardens at Rochford Manor.

William Conyers. Thomas' oldest son and heir to the barony.

Gweneth Conyers. William's wife and Lord Ainswick's niece.

Muriel Stonor. Gweneth's mother and Lord Ainswick's sister.

Clive Stonor. Gweneth's uncle and Muriel's brother-in-law.

Sir John Nesbitt. Friend of Thomas and Cotswolds neighbour.

Lady Nesbitt (Thalia). Wife of Sir John and head of the local Church Ladies Guild.

Dr Giles Sumner. A local surgeon.

Celia Sumner. Giles' wife and member of the Church Ladies Guild.

Dr Woods and Dr Perry. Dentists.

Deborah Mullins (Debbie). Dental hygienist.

The Greater Gloucestershire Galanthus Group

Jonquil Pilkington. Chair.

Iris Murtaugh. Vice chair.

Irma Swindon. Secretary.

Colonel Sebastian Aspinall. Treasurer.

Betty Mason. Membership.

Norman Weaver (Norm). Group website and newsletter.

Marjory Eaton. Snowdrop sales.

Mark Pilkington. Headmaster of Churn Valley College and Jonquil's husband.

Rosamunde Pilkington. Jonquil and Mark's daughter. Deceased.

Oxford

Stephen Draycott. Master of Merrion College.

The Greater Gloucestershire Galanthus Group

Laurence Brooks. Professor and head of Oxford's Institute for Global Development.

Anne Brooks. Laurence's wife and Maggie's friend.

Andrew Kittredge. Professor of Economics.

Chitta Kazi. Professor of Sociology.

Stanley Einhorn. US billionaire venture capitalist, founder of the Weingarten chair, and Chitta's husband.

Joshua Paley (Stone). Appleton Fellow.

Mrs Steeples. The Master's secretary.

Roger Bishop. A porter.

Jersey Jones. New media celebrity and TV personality and friend of Stephen Draycott.

Brooke Eliot. Oxford DPhil student in Chinese studies and Maggie's niece.

Mrs Royce. Hereford Crescent housekeeper.

Luke Fitzroy. A solicitor.

London and Dorset

James Conyers. Commodore in the Royal Navy and Thomas' second son.

Victoria Conyers. James' wife.

Malcolm Fortescue-Smythe. Owner of The Global Press, Maggie's publisher.

Lord Timothy Hillier. (Tim). Head of a shadowy government agency dealing with national security issues.

Paul Simmonds. Works for Tim.

Martin Hewitt. Works for Tim.

Fred Pilchard (The Fish). Works for Tim.

Lennox Archibald-Atherton (Crispin). Works for Tim.

Sarah Cartwright. Works for Tim.

Colby. BBC project manager for programme development.

Ced. Works for Colby.

Sir David Talbot. BBC Director of Programme Development and Malcolm's friend.

Lady Sarah Archibald-Atherton. Lennox's aunt.

The Trevelyans. Butler and housekeeper at Longview, Dorset.

Boston

Frances Eliot. Maggie's mother.

Samuel Eliot. Maggie's oldest brother and a neurosurgeon.

Ariadne Eliot. Samuel's wife.

Alice Hawkins. Professor of Sociology at Boston University and Maggie's tenant.

Patty Rizzoli. Sports coach at Simmons College, Maggie's tenant, and Alice's wife.

The Greater Gloucestershire Galanthus Group

Kevin Hegarty. An administrator at Simmons College.

Eamonn Dolan. A Boston police detective and Kevin's cousin.

Nick Holmes. A Boston police detective and Eamonn's partner.

Police

Detective Chief Inspector Tom Willis. Gloucestershire Constabulary.

Detective Sergeant Marcy Hickson. Gloucestershire Constabulary.

Detective Inspector Brenda Bartlett. Thames Valley Police.

Detective Sergeant Philip Dexter. Thame Valley Police.

The story takes place in the autumn of 2014.

Susan Alexander

Chapter One

"They can't do this to me!" Jonquil Pilkington shrieked as she stormed into the dining room. "I'll show them!"

Mark Pilkington frowned. He paused in the consumption of his dinner of liver and onions and said, "I'm sorry Jonquil. I wasn't quite following. Who did what to you?"

"The Snowdrop Society. Iris just called. They had elections of officers and Eunice promised she would support me for secretary if I supported her for chairman. But I lost. Lost. To that odious Olive. So I spoke with Sebastian. And he told me that Eunice and Pamela, who won the vice chair, were telling everyone to vote for Olive and not for me. That Olive would make a more positive contribution to the society. Can you imagine?"

His wife's voice had taken on the strident quality Mark found particularly unpleasant. He tut-tutted and turned his attention back to his dinner.

But Jonquil was not finished.

"I'll show them!" Jonquil repeated. "I'll form my own group. There are certainly enough galanthophiles out there. There were over a hundred people at the last society meeting. There was even a waiting list. Even so, we ran out of seats and some had to stand. They weren't happy about that."

Jonquil chewed on her lip.

"I'll call Iris back and tell her what I've decided to do. She can be vice chair."

Iris Murtaugh was Jonquil's closest friend. She and Iris had attended the same Cheltenham women's college where Jonquil had been bitterly disappointed that, even though her father was a fashionable dentist and her grandmother had been a Redfern, she had not been admitted into the inner circle of the more popular girls. Gentle Iris, who had struggled to meet the school's modest academic requirements and had no such ambitions, had bonded with the more dominant Jonquil over their unfortunate floral names.

"And I know what I'll call it. We'll be the Greater Gloucestershire Galanthus Group."

The Greater Gloucestershire Galanthus Group

Chapter Two

Professor Margaret Spence Eliot, Weingarten Fellow at Merrion College, Oxford, took a sip from her third mug of coffee of the morning and sighed as she surveyed her study.

It was not that there was anything displeasing about the room itself. It was tidy and clean. Immaculate, in fact. There was not a speck of dust on her bookshelves or the marble mantlepiece of the fireplace, and latticed windowpanes sparkled in the September sun.

It was a lovely room. She had decorated it herself. She loved the William Morris wallpaper in greens and rusts and cream that complemented the Victorian Gothic stonework of the windows. The over-sized sofa with its down-filled cushions that invited a nap. And, over the fireplace, the Dante Gabriel Rossetti painting of a woman brushing her long, curly auburn hair that was so like Maggie's own.

No. It was just that Maggie was jet-lagged, having only the previous day returned from a month's holiday on a beach in Maine.

It had been a wonderful month. She and her husband Thomas had flown into Boston and stayed at Maggie's Back Bay townhouse while they adjusted to the time difference and paid an obligatory visit to Maggie's mother. Then they had driven up to Kennebunk Beach where there was a beachfront house, a rambling, shingle-clad Edwardian lady that had been in Maggie's family for several generations. They had been joined by Thomas' sons William and James and their families. The children played on the beach while Maggie read mysteries on the porch and dispatched a multitude of lobsters.

But now she was back in England and facing the start of Michaelmas term, which was a mere two weeks away.

Before Maggie could settle at her desk and check her email, there was a knock on the door.

"Hello?"

It was Thomas, her husband. In his early sixties, he was still strikingly handsome and his vacation tan emphasised the brilliant blue of his eyes.

"My dear?"

He stood aside and two women entered the room.

Both were in their late forties, but there the similarities ended. The first woman was of medium height and thin, with dark brown eyes and brittle, chin-length hair dyed a harsh chestnut. An aggressive nose dominated a narrow face and a thin-lipped mouth was formed into an ingratiating smile.

Her companion was shorter, plumper, and softer, like a photo that was slightly out of focus. She had hazel eyes and fading, honey-blonde hair that was gathered back into an untidy bun.

"My dear, this is Mrs Pilkington and Mrs, er…"

"Murtaugh," supplied Mrs Pilkington.

"Mrs Murtaugh. Mrs Pilkington and Mrs Murtaugh, this is Lady Raynham."

Hands were shaken.

"These ladies are organising a snowdrop group. And they asked… Well, perhaps I should let them explain."

Behind them, Thomas grimaced.

"And now I'm afraid I must excuse myself. Estate business."

Thomas grimaced again, which Maggie interpreted to mean she was to act in her role of lady of the manor.

"Of course."

Thomas left.

"Won't you please sit down. And would you like some tea? Or coffee?"

"That's very kind, but..." began Mrs Murtaugh.

"Yes, please. Some tea would be most welcome."

Mrs Pilkington overrode her companion.

At that moment, Mrs Cook appeared bearing a tray with tea, coffee, and a plate piled with slices of her famous lemon drizzle cake. The housekeeper was a comfortable woman in her fifties, with curly grey hair and kind blue eyes.

"Tea, my lady?"

"Thank you, Mrs Cook."

Maggie indicated that the women should make themselves comfortable on the sofa while she poured tea and refilled her mug of coffee.

"So Mrs Pilkington and Mrs..."

"Murtaugh," prompted Mrs Pilkington.

"Mrs Murtaugh. How may I help you?"

"Well," began Mrs Pilkington as she wiggled further back into the sofa cushions and took a piece of cake. "Iris—Mrs Murtaugh—and I are spearheading an initiative to form a new group for snowdrop enthusiasts. Based in the Cotswolds, as not everyone wants to travel far afield and events sell out so quickly or they run out of space. Like this year's Snowdrop Society meeting. Even though they limited it to members who were ticket holders, some people had to stand. You can imagine the complaints!"

Mrs Pilkington paused for breath and to take a bite of cake.

"And we have attracted an excellent committee. I'm the chair, of course."

Mrs Pilkington gave a self-deprecating laugh.

"And Iris, Mrs Murtaugh, is the vice chair. Then we have Irma Swinford as secretary. She lives in a lovely cottage over in Duntisbourne Leer and is an ardent galanthophile. And Colonel Sebastian Aspinall is treasurer. You must know Colonel Aspinall. He has a wonderful garden over in North Cerney, with over two hundred varieties of snowdrops!"

"I'm afraid I don't..." Maggie began, but Mrs Pilkington rolled on.

"We're calling ourselves The Greater Gloucestershire Galanthus Group. Greater to include neighbouring areas. Worcester. Bath. Oxford. We already have more than thirty people who are interested in joining."

Maggie wondered where Mrs Pilkington was going with this. If she wanted to organise a tour of Beaumatin's gardens for her group, she could have asked Thomas. But Thomas had referred the woman to her.

The Greater Gloucestershire Galanthus Group

Mrs Pilkington decided to cut the cackle and get to the horses.

"So we, Iris and I..." Mrs Pilkington indicated her friend, who nodded. "We hoped you would be willing to serve as our patron."

"Patron?"

"Yes. Like the Royal Horticultural Society's patron is Her Majesty The Queen," Mrs Pilkington explained.

"I'm hardly a royal," Maggie protested.

"No, of course, we know that, but you are a member of the peerage. And Beaumatin does have one of England's finest snowdrop gardens."

Maggie thought quickly. The last thing she wanted—or needed—was another commitment beyond her work at Oxford and her marriage. She was already a reluctant participant in the local Church Ladies Guild. And she did not much care for Mrs Pilkington and her silent friend.

On the other hand, apparently Thomas wanted her to do this. He could get extremely cranky if he thought she was not living up to her responsibilities as Lady Raynham. And he was trying to commercialise Beaumatin's snowdrops.

"What would being patron involve?" Maggie asked.

"Oh, not a lot."

Mrs Pilkington waved a hand vaguely.

"If you could say a few words at the beginning of our first meeting..."

Maggie knew what saying a few words meant. She had opened a church fete a few months before where she had had to say a few words.

"Very well."

Maggie was aware she sounded resigned rather than eager.

"You'll do it?"

"Yes," Maggie confirmed.

Mrs Pilkington beamed.

"I told you, Iris. Didn't I tell you?" she nudged her friend.

Iris nodded and smiled.

"Well. And so…"

Mrs Pilkington looked Maggie over shrewdly as she took the last piece of cake.

"I wondered… Could we have our first committee meeting here, at Beaumatin? It would be so terribly kind."

"Here? At Beaumatin?" Maggie echoed while she mentally kicked herself for not realising what kind of woman Mrs Pilkington was. Give her an inch and she'd take a mile, as Maggie's mother would say.

"Yes. It would be so inspiring. So motivating. For our membership drive. And fund raising."

Uh oh. Fund raising. And Mrs Pilkington was looking so hopeful.

"Um. When would the meeting be?"

"The end of next week?"

Maggie reflected that Mrs Pilkington was not letting any grass grow under her feet, which was another of her mother's sayings.

"I'll need to check with the others. Would an afternoon around teatime suit?"

"Er…"

"Wonderful. How do I let you know…"

Maggie got up, went to her desk, found her visiting cards, and handed one each to Mrs Pilkington and Mrs Murtaugh.

Mrs Pilkington examined the card. It was on heavy cream stock with the Raynham coat of arms embossed at the top and the name *Lady Raynham* engraved in copperplate font. At the bottom were Maggie's mobile number and *Beaumatin GL52 7NP*. Thomas had had the cards made for her.

Apparently the card met Mrs Pilkington's expectations. She put it reverently in her purse and stood.

"I'll let you know when the date has been confirmed, then. Come, Iris."

Mrs Pilkington's companion smiled amiably and followed her friend to the door.

Maggie realised she should say something that expressed some enthusiasm.

"And I look forward to meeting the other members of the committee."

Susan Alexander

Chapter three

Maggie went to find her husband. As she expected, he was in his study. An accumulation of paperwork was piled beside his laptop.

"My goodness. That looks daunting."

Thomas leaned back in his chair and regarded his wife over the half-moon reading glasses that Maggie loved.

"Quite."

Maggie sat in one of the leather club chairs by the fireplace.

"They've gone. That Mrs Pilkington. And her silent friend. After consuming quite a few cups of tea and an entire lemon drizzle cake. Anyhow, I agreed to be patron of the snowdrop group they're organising.

"What?"

"It was what you wanted, wasn't it?"

"No, I didn't."

"You didn't?"

"No. Of course not."

"But I thought... You seemed to indicate..."

"I could hardly say anything outright."

"You mean I misinterpreted your grimaces? Great. Just great. I assumed you meant you wanted me to do the Lady Raynham thing."

Thomas began to take exception to Maggie's characterising her role as his wife as "the Lady Raynham thing," but decided not to be diverted.

"She asked me first, but I told her I was too busy. Especially in February. I suggested you thinking you would also plead the pressures of work."

"How was I to know?"

Maggie drank some coffee.

"Do you know Mrs Pilkington?" she asked her husband.

"She reminded me that we had met when she visited Beaumatin on a tour three years ago."

"So at least she is a galanthophile."

Thomas shook his head. His wife had no experience of women like Mrs Pilkington and was being naïve again.

"Well, I don't see how I can avoid doing it now. I'll have to wait until the end of snowdrop season. Then I'll get out of it somehow."

"Humpf."

"And I should warn you. Pilkington asked if they could have the kick-off meeting for their committee here. Sometime next week. I couldn't think of a good excuse why they couldn't, so I agreed," she said apologetically.

"The road to hell…"

"Is paved with good intentions. I know. I know."

"Just tell me when your meeting is so I'll be sure to be out."

"Right. And I'll let you get back to your accounting."

Thomas grunted.

Maggie returned to her study. She felt depressed. She wished they were back in Maine. Life was so simple in Maine.

She was contemplating refilling her coffee mug again when there was a knock on her door.

"My lady?"

It was Mrs Cook. Behind her was Lady Ainswick.

"Beatrix!"

"I was in the neighbourhood and thought I would welcome the travellers home in person."

Lord and Lady Ainswick were old friends of Thomas. Rochford Manor, their estate, was nearby and was also famous for its snowdrops. Beatrix was an energetic woman in her mid-sixties. She wore a long grey skirt and a jumper that matched her sky-blue eyes.

The women hugged.

"I'll bring tea and some more coffee," Mrs Cook offered as she picked up the tray from the Pilkington visit.

"Thank you, Mrs Cook."

"It looks like you've already had some guests," observed Beatrix.

"Oh that. Yes. Well, I should tell you."

"Yes?"

"These women. Two. Women. Appeared. They're organising a new snowdrop group and wanted a patron. They asked Thomas first, who declined. He brought them to see me and I thought he wanted me to accept. So I did. Except he didn't. Want me to."

"Jonquil Pilkington," said Beatrix disdainfully.

"Jonquil?"

"Yes. That's her name. The woman is a misery. She's married to the headmaster of Churn Valley College."

"Churn Valley College?"

"It's a boarding school, located between Rochford and Cirencester. You couldn't even call it a minor public school. And it's co-ed."

From her tone, Maggie concluded that Beatrix had reservations about co-education.

"Pilkington came to ask Cedric if he would be patron, but he declined. Then she asked me and I said no, because of Cedric's health."

"You think she's working her way down the ranks of the peerage?"

"It wouldn't surprise me. She's very pushy. In the end, to get rid of her, I agreed to give her group a tour of Rochford Manor at their meeting in February. Assuming she manages to form a group.'

"Well, it's too late now."

"Maggie, you're much too nice. People like Jonquil Pilkington take advantage."

"I am? Anyway, I agreed that they could have their committee kick-off meeting here next week. Besides Jonquil, there's her friend Iris... Iris Murtaugh. She's very quiet. Do you know her?"

"No."

"And another woman whose name I can't remember and a colonel... Colonel Aspinall?"

"Aspinall? He's all right. Pukka sahib, as my mother would have said."

"He has a garden..."

"Ten or twelve acres or so in North Cerney. With a nicely curated collection of Galanthus. He has a gift for coaxing some of the more temperamental varieties to flourish."

Mrs Cook came in with Earl Grey for Beatrix and more coffee for Maggie.

"Thank you, Mrs Cook."

Beatrix added milk to her tea, then asked, "How was Maine?"

"Wonderful. I discharged all my Eliot family obligations the first week, then William and James and their families came. The children were in heaven. The house is right on the ocean. Young Thomas took sailing lessons, Elizabeth took a course in marine biology, Harry learned tennis, and John added to his Spiderman collection. I engaged an au pair for the babies so Gweneth and Victoria could enjoy the Portland cultural scene and shop and I sacrificed quite a few lobsters. Then, at the end, Thomas and I had a week to ourselves and he relaxed, really relaxed, for the first time since I've known him."

Beatrix nodded.

"And the stables have been rebuilt and the horses can come back in the next few days which will also help."

The previous spring the Beaumatin stables had been set on fire by an arsonist. Two horses had burnt to death and Maggie had barely escaped the inferno.

"And Michaelmas term starts soon," Beatrix observed.

"Yes. In two weeks. I am hoping for a few uneventful months. I have my research project, a few lectures, and a couple of DPhil dissertations to supervise, but that's it."

Maggie was working on a book, *PeopleFlows*, which detailed patterns of human migrations through several thousand years of history. She hoped the perspective it provided would counteract some of the anti-immigrant feelings that were currently prevalent on both sides of the Atlantic.

"I hope you're right," said Beatrix dryly. In the time she had known Maggie, the woman had attracted trouble like a magnet.

Chapter Four

The following Thursday afternoon saw seven people sitting around the Beaumatin dining room table. In addition to Jonquil Pilkington, Iris Murtaugh, Colonel Aspinall, and Irma Swinford, whom Maggie had expected, there were Norman ("Norm") Weaver and Betty Mason.

"Betty is going to be in charge of membership and Norm has volunteered to do our newsletter and website," Jonquil explained.

While the committee debated the optimal amount for dues, Maggie studied her guests. They all conformed to what Maggie privately called the "snowdrop demographic." Anglo, middle aged or older, and prosperous, given that a single bulb of a rarer variety could set the buyer back a hundred pounds or more.

"Thirty pounds for an individual membership is good, but we need a special rate for couples. Maybe forty-five?" Irma proposed.

"Forty-five would work for Joan and me," agreed Norm.

The committee duly voted on membership dues.

"Now for the next item on our agenda. The date for our big meeting in February," announced Jonquil.

"We don't want it to conflict with the RHS Winter Show," said the colonel.

"Or another major snowdrop event, like Myddleton House or Shaftsbury," added Betty.

"Does anyone have a calendar of snowdrop events?" asked Norm.

"Should it be on a weekday or a weekend?" pondered Irma.

"And where should we hold it?" Jonquil mused.

Maggie, whose mind had been wandering, suddenly realised six pairs of eyes were fixed on her.

"I'm sorry. What?"

"It's about the venue for our meeting in February," said Jonquil.

"The venue?"

Again six pairs of eyes looked at Maggie expectantly.

Maggie knew what they were asking. They wanted to hold their meeting at Beaumatin. She frantically tried to think of a reason to decline. Her mind refused to cooperate.

"How many people do you expect?"

"Ah. That depends on our membership. Of course, the Snowdrop Society puts a limit on the number of tickets. It's first come, first served. Since their meetings are usually held in a village hall and Health and Safety determines the maximum capacity," Jonquil explained.

"And village halls are really cold in February," added Iris to everyone's astonishment, as it was the first time the woman had spoken.

"Aren't they heated?" asked Maggie, who had never been in a village hall.

"Well, they're heated enough to keep the pipes from freezing. But you have to bundle up if there's a meeting," Irma clarified.

"And that's why... why we sort of hoped... if it isn't too much of an imposition..." Jonquil began.

"You'd like to have it at Beaumatin," Maggie finished.

"Oh yes. It would be such a wonderful way to launch the group."

Maggie's mind raced.

"A marquee on the great lawn?" she suggested.

Silence.

"There are heaters. It would be quite cosy," she added.

Jonquil and the colonel exchanged glances.

The colonel cleared his throat.

"I remember coming to a hunt ball at Beaumatin. When the twenty-seventh baron was alive. It was a splendid do," Colonel Aspinall reminisced.

The ballroom. They want to meet in the ballroom, Maggie realised, and felt like she was being sucked down in a whirlpool.

"You think the ballroom would be appropriate?"

"Could we see it?" asked Jonquil hopefully.

"Um..."

But the group was standing.

Maggie reluctantly led the committee out of the dining room and across the great hall, oak panelled and hung with portraits of the barons and their families. She opened the door to the ballroom.

The enormous room was dim, as the curtains were closed. Massive crystal chandeliers were covered in sheeting, as was a grand piano. Neither Maggie nor Thomas played.

Maggie crossed the parquet floor and drew back a pair of heavy brocade curtains. Golden light from an autumn afternoon filtered into the room.

"We could put a dais along that wall. And a screen. Chairs could be in rows," Jonquil gestured.

"Do you have chairs?" she asked Maggie.

"No. They're rented when there's a dance."

"Oh."

Jonquil was clearly disappointed but ploughed on.

"And the Snowdrop Society lets members sell their own snowdrops. The Society gets ten percent from every sale. Do you think we could set up tables in the hall?"

At this Maggie balked. Enough was enough.

"No. There is a terrace. You could use that. But you would need to provide the tables."

"Speaking of tables, what do we do about lunch?" asked Betty.

"A buffet?" Jonquil began, but Maggie intervened.

"If you are going to Rochford Manor for a tour in the afternoon, there is the Rochford Inn. And a nice restaurant nearby called The Old Vicarage. The inn does lunches for Rochford Manor's study days and I am sure would be happy to organise something for you. As would The Old Vicarage."

Maggie was firm and Jonquil decided she had gotten as much from her ladyship as she could for the moment.

"So we are off to a good start. Next we have to set a date," Jonquil said.

"And confirm our speakers," reminded Irma.

"And continue recruiting members," added Betty.

"And set up a website," finished Norm.

And Maggie decided that it was a long time until February and perhaps Thomas did not need to know immediately that she had committed to having the first meeting of the Greater Gloucestershire Galanthus Group at Beaumatin. After all, they had not even decided on a date yet. And attendees would certainly want to buy some of Beaumatin's snowdrops.

Susan Alexander

Chapter Five

Maggie and Thomas were having dinner with Stephen Draycott, the Master of Merrion College, Maggie's friend Anne Brooks, Anne's husband Laurence, who was another Merrion colleague, and Malcolm Fortescue-Smythe, Maggie's publisher.

Stephen accepted another glass of Burgundy, sighed with contentment, and said, "Ah. I almost forgot. They've announced who's been appointed as the new Appleton fellow."

"Tell me it's not another fanatical Islamist," Laurence pleaded.

The last Appleton fellow had been a Saudi who had radicalised some students and subsequently had his visa revoked.

"No, I think they learned from that mistake. In fact, it's another Yank. You may know him, Maggie. Coming to us from Harvard. Name of Stone Paley."

Maggie, who had been taking a sip of wine, swallowed down the wrong way and choked.

"Stone Paley?" she asked in a strangled voice when she was again able to speak.

"Yes. Unusual moniker. But that's what I'm told."

Anne frowned. She thought she had heard her friend mention the name before.

"You know him?" Stephen asked.

Everyone was looking at Maggie curiously.

"Um. Yes. We were at Harvard at the same time. For five or six years. I left to come to Oxford. I guess he must have stayed on, then."

"So you do know him," Stephen repeated.

"Er, yes, I do. He'll be, um, interesting. He's quite a celebrity in the U.S. Hero of the left. Media darling. Tall. Good looking. Lots of charisma. But quite brilliant. He didn't get the academic standing he has because of his beaux yeux, beaux as they may be."

She paused.

"In fact, Malcolm, if we could convince him to contribute to one of your publishing lines, I've no doubt you'd have a best seller on your hands."

Thomas noticed Maggie was avoiding eye contact. And Anne had finally remembered when she had heard Maggie mention the man.

"Stone Paley," repeated Stephen. "Is that really his name?"

"No. He's actually Joshua Paley. But when he was at Choate—it's a distinguished prep school, a bit like your Eton—Paley became known as Palaeolithic, which got converted to Stone Age, which eventually became, simply, Stone. Well, you know how boys are with nicknames."

Thomas frowned. "It seems like…"

Maggie cut him off.

"He was a colleague. Our offices were on the same hall. Corridor. It's normal to know that sort of thing."

"Anyhow, we'll have some sort of welcome reception for the chap at the start of term," Stephen concluded.

After dinner, while they were having coffee in the drawing room, Anne cornered Maggie.

"Maggie. Stone Paley. Wasn't he your…"

Maggie looked over her shoulder nervously, but Thomas was occupied talking to Malcolm.

"Shh. Yes. My ex. And, as you know, our break-up was not without… I guess you could say, without its drama."

"And since then?"

"Not a word. Seen or heard."

"Then why? He must know you're still here."

"I don't have a clue. Looking for a new challenge? Mid-life crisis? He just turned fifty. I am surprised he's coming to Oxford, though. I would think one of the London universities would be much more his style."

"People change."

"Perhaps."

But Maggie looked doubtful.

"Are you going to tell…"

"His lordship? I don't think I have much of a choice. They're bound to meet. And he knows I had a couple of prior relationships with fellow academics. About which he's been remarkably uncurious. I suspect he imagines someone like Andrew Kittredge…"

Kittredge was a Merrion colleague whom Maggie had secretly christened "Dumpy." His wife Claire she thought of as "Frumpy."

"...who is nothing at all like Joshua."

Maggie smiled and, seeing her friend's expression, Anne decided she would google Stone Paley the moment she got home.

"In his own way, I expect he'll be as disruptive as his predecessor," Maggie continued. "Joshua tends to attract a great deal of female attention."

"He was attracted to you," Anne pointed out.

"Hm. Apparently. Lucky me."

Maggie changed the subject to the Brooks' recent summer holiday. The party broke up and everyone left for home except for Malcolm, who was spending the night.

Thomas was in his bedroom. He had taken off his tie and jacket and was in the process of removing his cufflinks when Maggie came in. He immediately noticed she was wearing what he called her "Bravado" costume, a long kimono of dark green silk brocade with a fiery dragon embroidered down its back.

Maggie felt her stomach go wobbly. She loved Thomas in his braces, which were the proper kind, with leather fasteners that attached to buttons inside his pants. She took a deep breath.

"Um... Thomas?"

"Yes?"

"Remember you once asked me if I had ever married?"

Thomas thought.

"Yes. And you said almost. Twice. But that you hadn't because it would have meant your taking his shirts to the cleaners, children to cello lessons, and bottles to recycling."

Maggie was always surprised at the things Thomas recalled.

"Yes. Well..."

Thomas was watching her closely, his face expressionless.

"Yes?"

"Well, um, one of those, er, twice. It was Joshua Paley."

"Paley? Really?"

Maggie nodded and realised she had no idea how she had expected Thomas to react to her revelation. He had a tendency to be jealous, whether or not it was justified, and it had caused them significant problems in the past.

"Is Paley's being at Merrion going to be an issue for you?" he finally asked.

"An issue? For me? No. No, I don't think so. No. Our relationship ended years ago. And he must know I'm here. And that didn't stop him from applying. So I wouldn't think there'd be a problem. It's just that I thought you would want to know. Since you'll doubtless meet him at faculty functions."

Thomas was still expressionless.

"Anyway, I imagine after all this time he's got a wife and two kids and I'm just another old girlfriend."

Thomas noticed that Maggie was still looking worried.

"It's all right, Papillon. And thank you for telling me."

Chapter six

Mark Pilkington took a sip of tea and reached for another chocolate biscuit from the plate on the table beside him. He ate the biscuit in four small, neat bites, then licked a smear of chocolate off a finger. Pilkington was a tidy man. Of medium height, with thinning dark hair, mild blue eyes, and a pleasant face, he was approaching fifty.

Pilkington was in the sitting room of the headmaster's quarters at Churn Valley College. In addition to the sitting room, the small apartment consisted of a dining room, a morning room, two bedrooms, two bathrooms, and a kitchen with a pantry. The headmaster was expected to dine in hall, his laundry was done by college staff, and he worked in the headmaster's study, a considerably more impressive suite with a small office for his secretary before his own room which boasted oak panelling, an immense mahogany desk, an antique oriental rug, a marble-fronted fireplace, and portraits of half a dozen previous headmasters.

Mark Pilkington enjoyed being the headmaster of Churn Valley College, which took boarding and day students from age six up to sixth form. After twenty years in the position, he had the job down pat. He got along well with his board and parents and was respected by pupils and staff alike.

He looked across at Jonquil, who was reading the latest Jilly Cooper. It was a secret vice, her taste in lurid potboilers. Had it not been the long vacation, she would have had what she considered to be a more acceptable tome within easy reach. William Thackeray. Virginia Woolf. The latest Booker Prize winner. Should an unexpected visitor appear, she would shove the trashy volume under the chair's seat cushion and quickly pick up the more respectable offering. Jonquil had always been very conscious of appearances.

Mark supressed a sigh. When he had met Jonquil, he had been a junior research fellow in modern history at Oxford's Merrion College. Jonquil had been working as a librarian's assistant at the Bodleian. He had long forgotten what they had seen in each other. Perhaps it was because they had both been lonely and neither was very gregarious.

They had married. Jonquil had great plans for her husband. A named chair. Even a college mastership. But then Jonquil had gotten into a feud with the Master's wife and Mark's research fellowship was not renewed. Jonquil blamed the Master's wife. Mark blamed Jonquil.

Mark was relieved when he landed a post at the University of Bristol. In his spare time, he penned a humorous treatise on the history of England from Ethelred to Edward VII. He found a publisher and, to his amazement, the book became a best seller.

While the celebrity he gained from his success did not help his academic career—scholars are an envious, spiteful lot—the name recognition helped with the trustees of Churn Valley College when Mark applied for the headmaster's vacancy.

Mark was attracted to the school's beautiful Cotswolds setting because, to his amazement, he and Jonquil had managed to produce a daughter.

Rosamunde was a delicate child with pale blue eyes and wispy dark hair. She was a good girl, quiet, compliant, and dominated by her mother, who decided her daughter should attend her own Cheltenham school rather than be stigmatized for being the headmaster's daughter at Churn Valley.

After an undistinguished academic career, Rosamunde astonished her parents by declaring that she wanted to attend Simmons, a women's college in Boston. Jonquil, of course, was opposed, but Mark privately thought it would do his daughter good to get away from her mother and, for once, put his foot down.

Rosamunde enrolled and seemed to be flourishing when, midway through her second year, her body was pulled from the Charles River. She had been three months pregnant and her death was ruled a suicide.

Mark was shattered but kept his grief to himself. Jonquil, however, refused to accept that her daughter had killed herself and decided that Rosamunde had been murdered by the father of her unborn child. As evidence, Jonquil pointed to the photos and newspaper clippings that had been found in Rosamunde's dormitory room. She had developed a crush on a local celebrity. Some Harvard professor. Jonquil convinced herself that the man was to blame for her daughter's death.

After weeks of listening to his wife's ranting and vows of retribution, Mark again took a stand and gave Jonquil a choice. Shut up or get out. Shocked by her husband's unusual forcefulness, Jonquil decided on the former, nursed her grievance in private, and waited for the chance of revenge that she was sure would eventually present itself.

Mark finished the last chocolate biscuit and opened the day's *Oxford Mail*, to which he subscribed both because he liked the publication and from a sense of "où sont les neiges d'antan." Mark had also once nurtured dreams of a distinguished academic career and held his wife responsible for the failure of his ambitions as well as for the death of their daughter. In fact, he loathed Jonquil with an intensity that would have astonished the woman and that was no less virulent for its being unexpressed.

On page five of the newspaper Mark read a headline and stiffened. His wife noticed.

"What is it, Lumpkins?" she asked.

Lumpkins was Jonquil's term of endearment for her husband. It was high on the list of reasons of why he detested her.

"Oh, nothing," he said and quickly turned to the next page.

"It's not nothing," countered Jonquil, who crossed the room and removed the newspaper from his hand.

She scanned the page and stared.

The headline read, "Merrion College Announces New Appleton Fellow."

Jonquil made a noise as though someone had stepped on a cat's tail, then crumpled the paper and hurled it into a corner.

"Jonquil!" Mark protested.

"How dare he! How dare he! He's taunting us! He's… If he thinks…" she panted.

"Jonquil!" Mark repeated.

"If he thinks he can just come over here… I may not have been able to do anything while he was in Boston, but if he's here…"

Jonquil gestured wildly and Mark jumped up and grabbed her hands. She yanked them away.

"No! No! He killed my Rosamunde. He killed my baby. My baby needs justice and I'm going to see he gets what he deserves!"

Jonquil burst into tears and rushed from the room.

Mark shook his head. He crossed to where his newspaper had landed and started to smooth it out, then gave up and let it fall back to the floor.

There was going to be trouble. He just knew it.

Susan Alexander

Chapter seven

Maggie was in her study, packing for her return to Oxford, when Mrs Cook appeared at her door.

"Mrs Pilkington and... some others are here to see you, my lady," she announced dryly.

Maggie sighed. Since the board committee meeting, Jonquil had made two other unannounced visits. "I was in the neighbourhood and just wanted to ask..." she would begin and then settle on the study sofa to drink tea, eat cake, and ask intrusive questions.

Jonquil Pilkington was a type of person Maggie had not encountered before. The woman's avid curiosity that bordered on the voyeuristic was new to her. She was used to dealing with sexist department heads, mean and jealous colleagues, and students who thought they deserved firsts even if they did not do the work to earn them. But Jonquil was something else and Maggie was conscious that if she offended the woman, it would be as Lady Raynham and not Professor Eliot.

"Very well, Mrs Cook."

"And you'll like tea, my lady?"

"Yes, please," Maggie began, then, "No. Wait. Let me find out what they want first."

Maggie knew from experience that, once tea was offered, Jonquil would stay and chat inconsequentially until the last slice of cake had been consumed. And Maggie had too much to do.

Jonquil appeared with Iris and a third woman Maggie did not know.

"Oh Lady Raynham," Jonquil gushed. "I hope it's all right our just turning up, but..."

Jonquil suddenly seemed to notice the piles of journals, stacks of books, and half-filled boxes.

"Oh. What are you... Are you..."

"I'm returning to Oxford tomorrow."

"Oxford?"

"Yes, Oxford. I'm a professor there. It's the start of Michaelmas term. Isn't Churn Valley College also..."

"Oh yes. Yes, of course. We already have some students..."

"And so?" Maggie asked.

"Oh. Oh yes. Lady Raynham, this is Mrs Eaton. Marjory Eaton. She is going to be in charge of sales. Plant sales. At our meeting in February. And she wondered if she could see where people would set up and how many tables were possible. People are already enquiring. I think you said we could use the terrace?"

From Jonquil's tone, Maggie realised the woman still had hopes of Beaumatin's great hall. But that was not going to happen.

"Of course. I'll be happy to show you. If you'll come with me?"

She herded the women out of the house and around the side to the terrace.

The women looked around. They seemed unimpressed by the large, flagstone-paved space with its elaborate balustrade and steps that led down to the great lawn.

Marjory Eaton looked up at the sky. It was overcast.

"But what if it rains?" she asked.

"We'll just hope it doesn't. And if it does, you can always put your sales tables around the walls of the ballroom. Or you can set up a marquee."

Maggie was firm.

Marjory was pacing off the terrace when Thomas came around the corner of the house.

Uh oh.

At any other time, Maggie would have admired the man in his riding clothes. But it seemed that she had been "caught with her hand in the cookie jar," as her mother would have said.

Thomas halted when he saw the group and looked surprised.

"Hello, Lord Raynham," Jonquil waved.

"Thomas, you've met Mrs Pilkington and Mrs Murtagh. And this is Mrs Eaton…" Maggie began.

Jonquil cut her off.

"Lord Raynham, Lady Raynham is showing us where we can set up the sales tables for our Galanthus group meeting," Jonquil gestured to the terrace. "Although we are a bit concerned about what we'll do if it rains. Or, even worse, snows. It will be February…"

If Jonquil thought that appealing to a higher power would help, she was mistaken, Maggie thought as she watched Thomas assume the frozen expression that meant he was angry.

"I am sure you can rely on Lady's Raynham's good judgement," said Thomas. "Now, if you would excuse me…"

He turned and walked off.

Rats. Rats and phooey.

As soon as Marjory Eaton had determined the terrace could accommodate at least sixteen tables, Maggie pleaded the pressure of having to pack and escorted the women to Jonquil's car, a grey Mini Countryman. She was not surprised when Iris climbed in the back, while Marjory Eaton sat in the front.

Maggie turned to go into the house but was stopped by Jonquil.

"Oh, Lady Raynham!"

"Yes?"

"I almost forgot. I wanted to give you the schedule for our meeting. We've been lucky to get Chester Cope as one of our speakers. He's a leading American galanthophile. Do you know him?" she asked.

"No," Maggie responded neutrally. Her experience with American galanthophiles had not been positive and included more than one murderer.

Jonquil looked disappointed as she handed Maggie a sheet of paper whose greyish tone and texture proclaimed its eco credentials.

"Toodle-pip," she warbled playfully as she put the car in gear and drove off.

"Bye," Maggie muttered and reluctantly turned towards the house, where she was sure Thomas would be waiting, fuming, and wanting an explanation.

She was right. Thomas was pacing in the hall, still in his riding clothes.

"Well?"

"Thomas, I..."

"I assume your little snowdrop club wants to have their meeting here?"

"It's not a little club. It's the Greater Gloucestershire Galanthus Group and they only want to have their first meeting here. In the morning. In the ballroom. Then they'll go to lunch and visit Rochford Manor."

"Humpf."

"They said otherwise they would have to hold it at some village hall. Which are reportedly cold in February. Are they? Cold?"

"I wouldn't know."

Maggie hesitated. She really needed to get back to her packing.

"You couldn't have asked me first?" Thomas burst out.

Now Maggie fumed. Thomas' daughter Constance's wedding festivities had been held at Beaumatin, which had meant hosting ten members of her fiancé's family as well as a formal dinner dance. And that spring, Thomas' son

William had had a ball at the house to celebrate his becoming a Queen's Counsel. Certainly no one had consulted her on either occasion.

"Do I seem like the type of woman who tells people that she needs to ask her husband's permission to do something? I thought you were trying to commercialise Beaumatin's snowdrops. This is a great opportunity. It's not like I invited a coven of Druids to dance naked on the great lawn to celebrate the solstice."

"You still should have asked me. It's my house," Thomas blurted out before he had time to think.

"Yes. You make that fairly obvious," Maggie said coldly. She turned, went into her study, and closed the door firmly behind her.

Maggie looked at what she had left to do and decided that, if she applied herself, she could be ready to leave that evening. And would not need to spend another night at Beaumatin. Her husband's house.

Thomas cursed himself. And then his wife. Damn the woman. He always got cranky when a new term began and it was time for her to return to Oxford. Although he had known that had been the situation when they married, at some level he had hoped that eventually she would resign her position and spend her time with him at Beaumatin, rather than be away for three or four days a week.

He had fixed up a townhouse on Hereford Crescent so they could be together when he could get away from the demands of the estate, but there was nothing for him to do there. Once he had caught up on reading, seen whatever was on exhibit at the Ashmolean, perhaps had lunch with an old classmate from Balliol, he had nothing to do until Maggie came home in the evening. He pushed the thought away that Maggie would be in the same situation if she were at Beaumatin full time when he spent half his day out on the property and the other half on estate administration.

Still, he should not have said what he did. Even if it were true. Beaumatin was his. And while he appreciated that Maggie's intentions were good when she had gotten involved with that silly snowdrop club, he still felt he should have been consulted.

Thomas turned and went up the grand staircase. He needed to change out of his riding clothes, shower, and then continue to deal with the seemingly endless administrative tasks required to manage the estate and the other Raynham holdings.

Susan Alexander

The Greater Gloucestershire Galanthus Group

Chapter eight

Maggie put the last journal on the appropriate stack and sighed with contentment. She had finished unpacking and still had a day to enjoy some leisure before the start of Michaelmas term.

She surveyed the room with satisfaction. It had the requisite old oak panelling, mullioned windows, and elaborately plastered ceiling of one of the older Oxford colleges, but was otherwise decorated for comfort rather than to impress. There was a large wooden desk where she worked, an oak refectory table with sturdy wooden chairs for seminars, and two wingback chairs on either side of a fireplace for cosier talks. A door led to a small bedroom and bath.

Bookshelves were full but not so full as to leave no space for mementoes from her work. Some Mexican pottery. Some African figurines. And framed photos of Maggie with presidents, prime ministers, and other heads of state of countries to whom Maggie had consulted on issues relating to immigration policy.

Over the fireplace was a portrait by George Romney of Caroline, the second wife of the fifteenth Baron Raynham. Thomas had presented it to Maggie and insisted that she hang it in her rooms. Maggie quite liked the look of the middle-aged woman in an elaborate dress and powdered hair. She seemed intelligent and no nonsense. Maggie reminded herself she should check out the woman's story the next time she was at Beaumatin. She was sure the library there would contain some record.

She poured herself a fresh mug of coffee, sat down at her desk, and began to open her mail. Some conference flyers she binned after a cursory glance. Maggie had no time to attend conferences at which she was not a speaker. A subscription renewal form for a scholarly journal. She checked. She still had eight months to go. What were the publishers thinking? That got binned as well. A plethora of administrative memos she had also received as email attachments. She made sure she had seen them all, then consigned them to be recycled with the rest.

That left an envelope. Greyish, its colour and texture proclaiming its environmental correctness. She absently opened it and removed a single sheet. Unfolded it. Bold block capitals in an unusual font proclaimed:

STONE PALEY IS

A VILE SEDUCER AND A MURDERER

Good grief. An anonymous letter.

Maggie looked at the envelope. Addressed to Professor Eliot, it had been mailed in Oxford the previous day. No return address, for obvious reasons.

Her phone sounded. It was Mrs Steeples, Stephen's secretary.

"Professor Eliot? The Master asks if you could come to see him. As soon as possible."

"Immediately?"

"If that's convenient."

"I'll be right there."

Maggie took a plastic folder out of a drawer and, careful to touch them only by the edges, slipped in the letter and envelope. She put the folder in her purse and walked over to the Master's Lodge.

The Greater Gloucestershire Galanthus Group

"Professor Eliot. Go right in."

Mrs Steeples was a brittle blonde who had served the Masters of Merrion College for three decades. Cool and efficient, she was a fierce gatekeeper but seemed rattled at the moment. Maggie thought she could guess why.

She found Stephen pacing and holding a sheet of greyish paper.

"Maggie! I'm glad you're here. Look what I just got."

He thrust the paper at her.

It read:

STONE PALEY IS A MURDERER

WHO SEDUCES YOUNG GIRLS

"I got one too," said Maggie, reaching in her purse and removing the plastic folder.

"You did? Really? I wonder who else may have received one."

"You could check with Roger."

Roger Bishop was the porter.

"That's a good idea. Why didn't I think of that?"

Stephen buzzed Mrs Steeples, who appeared almost instantly.

"Mrs Steeples, can you please ask Roger if he remembers who else may have received an envelope like this? Besides Professor Eliot and me. And if any are still in the mailboxes, please bring them to me here."

He picked up an envelope from his desk and handed it to the secretary.

"Certainly, Master," said the woman and hurried off.

Stephen sat down behind his desk and brandished the sheet of paper.

"You know Paley. I assume there's no truth in this?" he asked.

"Joshua? A murderer? No. No, I'm sure not. As for the seducer bit... While he has, or had, a bit of a reputation, it was always graduate students. Or post docs. Never girls. And never from Harvard. His motto was, 'Never shit where you eat.'"

"So I don't have to worry about having to deal with another Gordon Ross?"

Gordon Ross was a former colleague who had been discovered trading recommendations and research fellowships for sex.

"No. No, not Joshua."

"Really? How can you be so sure?" Stephen demanded.

"Er, because I knew him rather well," Maggie admitted. "And I believe he's married."

"That didn't deter Ross," Stephen reminded her. "Besides, I understand Paley's divorced."

"Oh."

Before they could discuss Paley further, Mrs Steeples returned. She carried several of the grey envelopes, holding them out from her body by her fingertips as though they were toxic. Which in a sense they were, Maggie reflected.

"I have ones for Professor Kazi, Professor Kittredge, Professor Enderby, and Professor Brooks," she announced as she laid them on the Master's desk.

"Only senior faculty?" Stephen asked.

"Roger said those were the only other ones. The junior faculty did not receive any."

Stephen looked relieved.

"As long as none went to the Provost. Or the Vice Chancellor. Or the Appleton people," Maggie felt compelled to point out.

Stephen groaned.

"Why did I ever think it would be fun to be Master? Alastair made it look so easy."

Alastair Carrington was the previous Master of Merrion College.

"Did Alastair ever get poison pen letters?" Stephen asked Mrs Steeples.

"No, he certainly did not!" said Mrs Steeples, to whom the memory of the former Master was sacred.

"Well, let's see what these say," said Stephen.

"Be careful how you handle them. In case there are fingerprints," Maggie warned.

Stephen flexed his fingers, paused, then looked at the women.

"Maybe one of you should open them."

Mrs Steeples took a step backward, so Maggie concluded it was up to her.

"Do you have a letter opener?"

"I'll get mine," said the secretary.

Holding the envelopes by the edge with a tissue, Maggie slit them open and teased out the contents. They were all essentially the same. Stone Paley was a seducer and murderer.

"Well!" said Mrs Steeples.

"It's not true," Maggie assured her.

The woman looked doubtful.

"Truly. I knew him at Harvard. We were, er, close friends."

Maggie turned to Stephen.

"So what are you going to do?"

Stephen threw up his hands.

"Should I do anything? This is obviously some crank. Someone who resents Paley's appointment. Or disagrees with his views. Or wants to cause problems for the college."

"Are you going to show them to Joshua?" Maggie asked.

"No. I don't think so."

"Maybe he's gotten one as well. Or had the same problem at Harvard."

"Hm. No. I think I'll just hold on to these for now. If Paley mentions them, then of course…"

This was typical Stephen, wanting to avoid unpleasantness, Maggie thought.

"So, Mrs Steeples, please put these in a folder, with the other confidential files. Tell Roger that if any more come in the post he should bring them to you immediately. We'll see if anything further occurs."

With a moue of distaste, Mrs Steeples picked up the letters and carried them off.

"We'll just have to hope this is the end of it. We have the reception for Paley on Friday."

Maggie wished she were as sure as Stephen that this was the last they would hear from the anonymous author. There was something about the letters that was niggling in the back of her mind. But perhaps that was because she had also been the victim of some anonymous letters the previous spring. Yes, that was probably it.

Maggie returned to her rooms. She had work to do.

Susan Alexander

Chapter nine

Thomas was dressed and waiting for Maggie. He heard footsteps and watched her descend the stairs of the Hereford Crescent townhouse.

She was wearing a dress of deep green satin that matched her eyes. It was long sleeved and high necked and showed off her slim figure. He was also pleased to see she was wearing the emerald earrings he had given her as a wedding present. And her wedding and engagement rings, also emeralds.

"You look very nice," he said approvingly.

"Er, thank you," said Maggie, distracted by Thomas in his dinner jacket and by her own nervousness about the evening ahead.

Stephen Draycott had arranged a cocktail party in the Senior Common Room to welcome the new Appleton fellow. As the latest Master of the college, which had recently received a generous endowment, he had expanded the bar offerings from the traditional sherry to include whisky and gin and some decent wines.

"We are hardly going to attract the top talent if all we're serving is Amontillado and soft drinks. It is 2014, after all," he explained to Maggie and Anne.

"You won't get any objections from me," Maggie assured him.

"Me neither," agreed Anne.

Maggie and Thomas were talking to Anne and Laurence when Thomas noticed Maggie's wine glass was empty.

"Let me get you a refill."

"Thank you."

He took the glass and walked off to the bar.

Thomas had replenished Maggie's Chardonnay and his own whisky when he turned around without looking and bumped into someone. Some of Maggie's wine splashed on the arm of the man's dinner jacket.

"Oh. So sorry..." Thomas began, then stopped abruptly. There was only one person this could be.

"No problem," said Stone Paley, flicking away the droplets.

Maggie had been right when she had told Anne that Thomas had a false image of the man. But now Thomas was confronted with the reality. Paley was tall, a bit over Thomas' height of 6'2". He had the slim, wiry physique of a rock star and, with high cheekbones, a sensuous mouth, and arresting, grey-green eyes, the good looks of one. His dinner jacket fit perfectly and he wore it easily, as though he were accustomed to formal dress. But his most striking feature was his hair, which he had styled in long dreadlocks, a tangled mass of blond and light brown. On another man it might have looked ridiculous, but Paley carried it off.

Thomas also saw that Paley was at least a dozen years younger than his own sixty-three years.

"Stone Paley."

Paley held out his hand.

"The new Appleton fellow," he added when Thomas hesitated.

Thomas shook hands. Paley waited.

"And you are…"

"Er, right. Raynham. I'm Raynham."

"Raynham. Is that your first name or last?"

Thomas looked at Paley without expression.

"Last," he said finally.

"So your first…" prompted Paley, thinking Thomas was unusually awkward, even for an aging academic. But he was trying to create a positive first impression for himself, so he persisted.

"Lord," Thomas finally said, while he tried not to grit his teeth.

"Lord," Paley grinned. "I've known of Dukes and Earls and Princes, so why not Lord? And I'm Stone, so… What's your field?"

"Military history, but I'm not a don," Thomas admitted.

"Oh? So you're a guest?" asked Paley, losing interest.

"I'm, um, married to one of the faculty."

Thomas glanced across at Maggie, who had her back to him and was still chatting with Anne and Laurence. Paley followed Thomas' gaze.

"Elle," he said to himself, then looked back at Thomas. "Don't tell me you're married to Elle? Elle got married?"

63

He sounded incredulous and the "to someone like you" was unspoken but obvious.

"Elle?"

"Elle. As in Eliot. The ever so distinguished and highly controversial Professor Margaret Spence Eliot. I call her Elle. Never did like Maggie. Reminded me too much of your Prime Minister Thatcher."

Paley looked at Thomas curiously.

"How long have you been married?" he asked.

Normally Thomas would have stared down Paley's intrusive questions, but for some reason he felt compelled to answer.

"Two years."

"Well, Lord, I wish you luck. Elle's a handful. Stubborn. Independent. Elusive. Never lets you know what she's thinking until it's too late. At least until it was too late for me. She…"

Paley was interrupted by the appearance of Chitta Kazi and Stanley Einhorn. Chitta was a beautiful Bangladeshi scholar and Maggie's closest friend on the faculty. Her husband Stanley was physically unremarkable except for his nearly colourless eyes.

"Thomas!" Stanley greeted his friend.

"Hello, Thomas," added Chitta.

Paley looked at Chitta appreciatively, then noticed that she and Stanley were holding hands.

Thomas made the introductions.

"Stone Paley? I've read your work," said Stanley.

Paley looked pleased.

"Yes? What did you think of it?"

"I considered the reading to be in the nature of opposition research," Stanley said pointedly.

Paley was momentarily disconcerted, then said, "Wait a minute. Einhorn. Stanley Einhorn. Are you that Stanley Einhorn?"

"If you mean Stanley Einhorn, high-tech venture capitalist multibillionaire, then yes. That's me."

Modesty was not one of Stanley's virtues.

"Really. And why are you at Merrion? Teaching a course on how to succeed at hostile takeovers? Or ten things you need to know before you price your IPO?" asked Paley derisively.

"No. Like Thomas here, I'm married to one of the faculty." Stanley indicated Chitta. "But I've also contributed significantly to Merrion's endowment and funded the Weingarten chair that Professor Eliot now holds. Her taking that position provided an opening for a new Appleton fellow."

"Yes, after they got rid of that nutjob, bin Abdulaziz," said Paley.

Everyone looked at him.

"The Appleton committee briefed me," Paley explained.

Stanley was about to say that it seemed they had just appointed another nutjob in his place, but Chitta nudged him. So instead he said, "If I understand what you've written, you'd like to relieve me of my billions and divide them up among the planet's poorest five percent."

Stone grinned. "Unfortunately, I'd need more than your billions to make an appreciable difference to the bottom five percent. But it would be a start."

Paley glanced across at Maggie again. He removed the glass of wine from Thomas's hand and, before the man could protest, said, "Tell you what, Lord. Let me take this over to Elle before it gets warm."

Maggie was listening to Anne describe her middle son's latest girlfriend when she was handed a glass of wine. Assuming it was Thomas, she was about to say thank you when she noticed Anne was gaping. A warm hand was placed on the small of her back and a voice she knew said, "Hello, Elle."

She looked up at Paley and her eyes widened. Then she said matter-of-factly, "Joshua. You changed your hair."

"And yours is still the same, I see," he responded. "Although I'm surprised to find after a decade at Oxford you're still a fashionista. I expected a long skirt, a twin set, and pearls."

Maggie supressed an eye roll and just smiled enigmatically.

"And I met your husband. Lord."

Joshua said this with an edge to his voice.

"Lord?"

"Yeah. At least he said he was your husband. And that his name was Lord."

"Oh," Maggie laughed. "That's not his name. That's his title. He's a baron. You address him as Lord."

Joshua thought about this.

"You mean he was awarded a title? Launched a successful chain of supermarkets? Gave money to the right political party?"

"No. He inherited his title. He's the twenty-eighth baron. The Raynhams go back to the Conquest and the barony to the thirteenth century."

"Huh."

Joshua projected unimpressed.

Maggie decided to change the subject.

"So, Joshua. Oxford? I'm surprised. I wouldn't have thought this would be your thing."

She gestured at the oak-panelled walls on which hung the portraits of centuries of college Masters.

"Well, Harvard had become rather same old, same old. I felt like I needed a change and thought this would be interesting."

"New worlds to conquer?"

"Something like that," he admitted and grinned.

Thomas observed Paley and Maggie. They were talking easily, like old friends. Paley said something and Maggie laughed. He stood close to her. The hand which he had resting on her back strayed up to touch a curl. Thomas's innards curdled.

Stanley was watching Thomas watching Paley talk to Maggie.

"Thomas, if you grip your whisky any harder, you're going to break the glass."

Thomas looked down and realised Stanley had a point. He moved the glass to his other hand and flexed his fingers.

"What's the story with Paley? Does he know Maggie?" Stanley asked.

"Apparently they had a... a relationship at some point. While they were both at Harvard."

"Oh. Really?"

Stanley was surprised. He watched the pair talking.

"Well, if you read their body language, Paley may be trying his moves on Maggie, leaning in towards her, putting his hand on her back, touching her hair. But look at Maggie. See how stiffly she's standing? And she's holding her glass of wine in her left hand, putting it between herself and Paley to create some distance. Usually she holds her glass in her right hand."

Thomas regarded Stanley in surprise.

"I took some training in this stuff. It really helps when you're having to decide whether to give millions of dollars to someone you don't know very well. People say what they think you want to hear, but you can usually tell if they're bullshitting by the physical cues they're giving off."

Thomas was grim.

"So Paley's not just flirting? You think he's…"

"Oh, I wouldn't worry, Thomas. Maggie's true blue. As we both have reason to know," he added pointedly.

Thomas tried to unclench his stomach as well as his fingers.

"You're right, of course."

Susan Alexander

Chapter ten

It was a mild evening and Thomas and Maggie walked back to Hereford Crescent in companionable silence. Once they were inside, Maggie moved towards the stairs, but Thomas stopped her.

"No. We need to talk. Wait in the library. I'll get you some wine."

Maggie wanted to say she had had enough wine, but since she was quite certain she knew what the subject of their conversation was going to be, she did not argue.

Thomas returned with a wine glass and a bottle of Puligny Montrachet in a cooler. He poured some wine for Maggie and a Laphroaig for himself. He took off his dinner jacket, undid his tie, and sat, not next to her on the sofa as she had expected, but in an adjacent chair. He took a sip of his whisky, then said, "Tell me about your relationship with Paley."

Maggie looked at Thomas. He did not seem frosty. He had used the same tone he would have if he had been asking her about pending U.S. immigration legislation. So she said, "We lived together for five years when we were both teaching at Harvard. It ended when I accepted the Appleton fellowship and moved to Oxford."

"You lived together?"

Thomas had not been expecting this.

"Yes."

"And you didn't keep in touch?"

"No. No emails. Or exchanges of Christmas cards. Or Facebook friendships. I had no idea Joshua had applied for the Appleton fellowship, and been selected, until Stephen announced it at dinner the other night. Today is the first time I've seen him for a decade."

Thomas sat back, crossed one leg over the other, and steepled his fingers.

"That's not enough, my dear. Especially since your friend Stone still seems interested in you. You need to tell me a bit more."

"He's not..." Maggie began to protest. Then stopped. She supposed if they were going to encounter the man on a regular basis, it was normal that Thomas would want to know about their shared past.

"All right. Well, I had already been at Harvard a few years when Joshua arrived..."

"Joshua? You don't call him Stone?"

"Stone?" Maggie laughed. "No. No, never. Anyway, when he came, it was a big deal for Harvard. To have lured him from away from Berkeley. He was already a darling of the left, with his ideas about the redistribution of wealth. And a guaranteed minimum income. And his support for reparations for slavery. He was more like a rock star than an academic. Well, you saw how he is. Except back then he had a ponytail and not dreadlocks.

"Anyway, his office was a few doors away from mine and we'd bump into each other. After a few weeks he asked me out for coffee. Then for dinner. We began, I guess you could call it, to date. I was flattered. He was charming and the master of the romantic gesture. And he was invited everywhere, not just to the usual Harvard parties. He got tickets to concerts and sports events and would be asked backstage and into the locker room.

"He kept scrapbooks of press clippings of him with the Patriots' star quarterback and the Celtics' forward and Senator Kennedy and Matt Damon and Bruce Springsteen. And there I was as well. Heady stuff. After about six months he asked me to move in with him. I agreed.

"He had a wonderful duplex apartment overlooking the Charles River. Views of the Boston skyline. He paid for it through a trust fund he kept a secret to preserve his lefty credentials. I only knew about the trust because I happened to see a bank statement he'd left lying on a table. The place was minimalist. Very edgy. Black leather furniture and abstract expressionist art and high-tech kitchen appliances he never used. But the thing about minimalist is, the look is spoiled if you leave your underwear on the floor. Or pizza boxes on your coffee table. Or toothpaste smears on your designer porcelain.

"By the time we'd been living together for a few months, I had learned that when he wasn't lecturing to adoring undergrads or having his picture taken with a candidate for national office, Joshua was self-absorbed and moody and expected always to be the centre of attention. He took no interest at all in my own work and was unhappy when I went off to speak at conferences or consult. But he liked that his girlfriend was an Eliot. He called me Elle just to call people's attention to that, I think."

Thomas frowned. Maggie had mentioned being an Eliot before and he had meant to find out what she meant. But hadn't.

"Anyhow, whenever I'd go away, he would react by... Well, his worshipful groupies were always around and even though Harvard was off limits, that still left Boston College and Tufts and Wellesley and Brandeis and... There are a lot of schools in the Boston area. Even Dartmouth and Yale and Smith were close enough to... And Harvard has just as many unhappy faculty wives as Oxford. I would find evidence when I'd return that he'd had company. It wasn't blatant, like he meant for me to know, but it was there. Stray hairs, lipstick stains on a coffee mug, that sort of thing.

"I became unhappy with the situation. Eventually I told him it wasn't working and that I intended to move back to my own place. But he didn't really listen to what I was saying and jumped to the conclusion that I was upset about a lack of commitment on his part and he proposed. Marriage. Which came as quite a shock. And was not at all what I wanted. Well, you know what I feel about..."

Maggie stopped abruptly. Then hurriedly continued.

"The day before he proposed I had learned about the Appleton fellowship and decided to apply."

"So you turned him down."

Maggie looked away.

"Er, no. He had taken me to New York City. It's where he was from. He introduced me to his mother, who was very sweet. His parents had divorced when he was twelve. His mother had remarried some wealthy Wall Street type and his father had died a few years before. Joshua was being his most charming self again and I... I suppose I just lacked the courage to refuse. It's not something I'm very proud of.

"Then I made the Appleton short list and they flew me over to Oxford for an interview. I didn't tell Joshua why I was going and he wasn't particularly interested, as I said. But when I got back, I found a pair of bikini briefs that had been overlooked beneath the bedsheets. He hadn't noticed them. Or maybe whoever it was had left them there on purpose. I still remember what they looked like. They were turquoise lace. Inexpensive. Frequently washed.

"A month later..."

"Wait. You stayed with him, even though..."

Maggie shrugged.

"You slept with..."

"Like I said, he was self-absorbed. It wasn't as though... It wasn't like..."

Maggie stopped abruptly. Pressed her lips together.

Finally she said, "If that's all?"

"No. No, I'm sorry. I shouldn't have interrupted. Finish the story."

Maggie sighed.

"So the Appleton people offered me the position and I accepted. I gave notice at Harvard but made my department head swear to keep it confidential. I had to get through the next couple of months before the fellowship started. I was under constant pressure from my mother to set a date for the wedding so she could reserve a venue, have the invitations engraved, hire an orchestra..."

"You didn't say anything?" Thomas was incredulous.

Maggie shook her head.

"I know it was terrible of me. Awful. I'm embarrassed just talking about it. Beatrix would say I was exhibiting LMF—low moral fibre. But I was afraid that

Joshua and my mother... That they would have worn me down.

"Joshua left to spend a month in Paris to teach a seminar at one of their grandes écoles. Sciences Po, I think it was. It was perfect timing. I got all my things out of the apartment, sorted through the stuff I had decided to ship over here and sent it off.

"I'm truly ashamed. But I felt so trapped. Like I had been imprisoned in your dungeon for months, then found that someone had accidentally forgotten to lock the door. Anyhow, I left the apartment keys, the engagement ring, and the bikini briefs on a table in his hall. I left a letter, saying what you'd expect. And that I felt the break would be easier if we were not both at Harvard, so I had accepted another position.

"But he came back a day earlier than planned and tracked me down at Logan Airport just as I was about to go through security. He launched into a charm offensive. Then began to beg. Plead. When he realised that wasn't going to work, he exploded. There was a terrible scene. And you know how I hate scenes. And am not very good with anger. And Joshua is very recognizable. Someone took pictures which made the papers the next day. My mother sent them to me. She adored Joshua. Was over the moon when we got engaged.

"He began screaming that I was an ungrateful c... Anyhow, the airport police came. They escorted him away and I made it through security and got on the plane. I was completely shattered. But I didn't want to be someone's career accessory because I had the right name. Or be a handmaiden. Or look the other way about his infidelities. I wasn't that desperate to be in a relationship. To be someone's wife.

"My mother kept sending newspaper clippings. Joshua wasn't shy about telling his version of events to the press. I was a jilt and had broken his heart. Then, a year later, Mother sent me another set of articles. Joshua had gotten married. To a Harvard teaching assistant. An attractive brunette in her late twenties. She stuck on a Post-it note on which she'd written, 'This should have been you!' But by then I had settled in at Merrion and was just relieved to be free again.

"So now you know."

"Were you in love with him?"

Maggie thought.

"I don't know. I cared, certainly. But 'in love'? I had never really been in love at that point, so I had no means of comparison…"

Thomas looked at her and she avoided his eyes.

"Then tell me. If that's the way you feel about marriage, why did you marry me? Was it because you lacked the courage to refuse?" he asked.

Maggie stared at him. She certainly was not going to tell him that, having met him, the idea of her life's going on without him was so painful to contemplate that she considered marriage a small price to pay.

Instead she said, "You don't leave your underwear on the floor. Or empty pizza boxes on the dining room table. Unless you do, and Mrs Cook is covering up for you."

Thomas' mouth twitched.

"No. Really. I'm curious."

Maggie pretended to think about her answer, then came out with, "I had gotten accustomed to falling asleep with your arms around me at night. And knew that, for you, marriage was necessary for that to continue."

"Paley also called you 'elusive.'"

"He did? And so do you. So perhaps I am. I suppose it's... protective."

"Having regrets?"

Maggie gave a startled laugh. "Regrets? About Joshua? Good heavens no. I only wish I'd been more brave about how I ended the relationship."

She sensed Thomas was still waiting.

"Regrets about our marriage? Why would you... But no. No, none. Even though you have presented some challenges."

She paused.

"Although I realise that I have presented some challenges to you as well," she added thoughtfully.

"But speaking of sleep...."

Maggie put her untouched glass of wine down on the coffee table.

Thomas moved and sat beside her. He grasped both of her hands and fleetingly wondered whether his daily preoccupation with what Maggie liked to call "pie, sheep, and the History channel" made him just as self-absorbed as Paley.

"Just so we're clear. That I'm never going to find a letter from you saying it hasn't worked out and you've left to accept a position at Stanford."

Maggie stared at him.

"At Stanford?" she finally said. "Of course not. You know I don't care for California."

Thomas laughed, then gripped her wrists. Hard.

"Thomas! Ow!"

"I want you to promise me that you'll never do something like that. Like what you did to Paley. Just leave. Without talking first. Without giving me a chance to..."

"Thomas! You're hurt..."

"Promise me."

"All right. All right. I promise. I do. Now please..."

He decided he would believe her.

"Oh. Sorry." He loosened his grip but still held her wrists.

"I guess... Well, Paley... I had no idea... Had never imagined..."

"What? You thought our relationship had been more casual? Or that he'd be more like Andrew Kittredge?"

"Well, er, maybe not quite like Kittredge, but... No. I guess I just didn't think. Well I don't like thinking about your being with..."

He paused.

"And your other academic?"

"Who?"

"You said you'd had two relationships. Who was the first?"

"Oh. That was at Princeton. Hunter. His name was Hunter. We had both just finished graduate school and were trying to find our feet in academia. We kind of bonded together for mutual support. And comfort. After a while we both felt more self-confident, were on the tenure track, and realised we really didn't have a lot in common. So we moved on."

"Where is he now?"

Maggie sighed.

"My second year at Harvard, Hunter was helicopter skiing in the Canadian Rockies and fell into a crevasse. I'm not sure they ever found his body."

Maggie trailed off and Thomas reproached himself for feeling relieved that it was only Paley he had to worry about, then.

"All right, Papillon. Time for bed."

Some hours later, Maggie woke up. Thomas seemed to be sleeping. She began to ease out of bed, out of his arms, but his hold tightened.

"Thomas?"

"Don't go. Not yet."

He pulled her to him. He kissed her and his cheek was scratchy from a day's growth of beard. He smelled of sleep. Of last night's love making. And, best of all, of

The Greater Gloucestershire Galanthus Group

Thomas. Maggie decided that she was incredibly fortunate and happier than she had ever imagined she could be.

Susan Alexander

Chapter eleven

Thomas entered the stairwell where his wife had her rooms. He had been in her 'hood, as Maggie would have said, and decided to drop by. They could walk back to Hereford Crescent together. If she had more work to finish, he could continue exploring her book collection.

At the door he heard laughter. Maggie's and someone else's. He knocked.

"Come in," Maggie called gaily.

Thomas stopped dead on the threshold. Maggie had her feet up on her desk, with a loafer dangling from one foot and a glass of wine in her hand. Joshua was lounging in one of her wingback chairs, holding a tumbler of whisky.

"Hello, Thomas," Maggie smiled.

"Hi there, Lord. Come and join the party," Joshua gestured with his glass.

Thomas pressed his lips together and Maggie felt the blast of frost. Oh dear.

"Joshua is catching me up on some Harvard gossip. Isn't it wonderful that people mostly get what they deserve if you can just be patient?"

"If you sit on the banks of the river long enough, the bodies of your enemies come floating by," Joshua offered.

"Well, I'm not sure I'd call Foster an enemy, or want to see his body float by, but still. Sacked for falsifying research results. Sweet," she grinned.

Joshua noticed that Thomas was looking like he wanted to tear out his heart and eat it raw. He stood, emptied his glass, and put it on the desk.

"Well, back to sorting books and papers," he smiled at Maggie.

He glanced at Maggie's bookcases. "Although I suspect mine will also look like this in a few months, despite my good intentions."

"Thomas says I should set up a database so I know what I have and where things are. But I told him it would soon be as disorganised as my shelves. And trying to remember where I left a particular volume is a good way to make sure I'm not becoming senile."

"No danger of that," Joshua laughed. "Take care, Elle."

He said the words like a caress.

"See you around, Lord."

He swaggered from the room.

Maggie decided Thomas was considering ways to expedite Joshua's body floating by. And Oxford certainly had its share of rivers.

She stood.

"Thomas, sit down" she said sharply.

She pointed to the chair Joshua had just vacated.

Thomas crossed the room, looked at the seat with a grimace, and sat in the adjacent chair.

"Good grief. What, you think the chair has Paley cooties?"

Thomas looked confused. Maggie got him a tumbler of whisky and handed it to him.

"Now I want you to listen to me, Right Honourable Thomas Hugh Allardyce Baron Raynham Number Twenty-eight," she said sternly.

"You're about to jump to a wrong conclusion about my relationship with Joshua. I can tell. Since at this point I've certainly had enough experience. And then things will be extremely unpleasant until you realise you've made a mistake. And tell me you've been an idiot. And say you're sorry. Again. But I've had quite enough sorry's from you. So I'd prefer to, er, nip this in the bud.

"Joshua is a colleague. Just a colleague. I like to be on good terms with the people with whom I work. Especially as he's right upstairs..."

"His rooms are on your staircase?"

"Yes. He has Ross' old rooms. Above Chitta's."

Thomas scowled. He had agreed that when he was at Beaumatin, and Maggie was in Oxford, she could stay in her rooms at Merrion rather than at Hereford Crescent. But if Paley were going to be that close by...

"Thomas, you're going to have to trust me. You're simply going to have to. Any feelings I have for Joshua... Well, they're no different than the feelings I have for Stephen. Or Laurence. Or Stanley. There's nothing at all, er, romantic..."

"And what about Paley's feelings for you?" Thomas interrupted.

"Feelings for me?"

Maggie sounded surprised.

"Yes. You can't deny…"

"Oh. He's just… playing. It doesn't mean anything. And I think he enjoys winding you up. You make your feelings fairly obvious."

Thomas stared at his wife.

"I think you're being naïve," he said finally.

"Am I? Well, you've said that before. And you've been right. So perhaps I am. Being naïve about Joshua. But that doesn't change what I feel. And I hope I know how to take care of myself."

Thomas reflected that he very much doubted that Maggie knew how to take care of herself as far as someone like Paley was concerned.

"Yes, you're probably wishing you could lock me in your dungeon. Except it's now a storeroom and Mrs Cook is busy filling it with jams and preserves."

Thomas' mouth twitched. Then he became serious.

"All right, Papillon. But until… I know I agreed you could stay in your rooms when I'm not in Oxford, rather than at Hereford Crescent. But…"

Maggie sighed. She had figured Thomas would say this. She held up her hand.

"You want me to stay at Hereford Crescent. Because of Joshua. Well, all right. If I agree, though, I want you to tell me you'll also try to get a grip. Really. You think gossip is bad in the Cotswolds, but that's nothing compared to

Oxford. If anyone saw you reacting to Joshua the way you just did, it would be all over Merrion by evening, and all over the University the next day. And human nature being what it is, people would soon be saying there's no smoke without fire and… Anyhow, I'd like to avoid that. And I'm sure you would as well."

Thomas frowned. Finally he said, "Very well. I admit, you have a point. But just so we're clear…"

Maggie held up her hand.

"I think you said you came by so we could walk back to Hereford Crescent together. Then why don't we."

Susan Alexander

Chapter twelve

Maggie got a call from Stephen.

"Maggie, there's been another set of those letters. Can you come over to the lodge, please?"

"Of course. Right away."

Mrs Steeples desk was deserted. Maggie found her in Stephen's office. She looked like she had eaten something disagreeable.

"We've had more of these... these..."

Mrs Steeples was too upset to find the words. Anonymous letters were not supposed to happen at one of Oxford's oldest colleges.

"This never occurred when Dr Carrington was Master," she finally said.

Maggie remembered of some of the things that had occurred when Alastair was Master, but thought it more tactful simply to say, "I understand how unpleasant you must find this."

Mrs Steeples was about to tell Maggie exactly how unpleasant she found this when the phone in her office rang. She made a growling noise and stalked off to deal with the caller.

"Whew," said Stephen. "I've never seen Mrs Steeples so distraught. Except when Alastair died. But that was different."

"Yes, it was," Maggie agreed.

"So can I see the letters?" she continued.

"Yes. Same people as the last time. Senior faculty. I hope only Merrion people got them."

"And not the Vice Chancellor."

"Definitely not the Vice Chancellor. But I'm hopeful. If he had, I'm sure we would have heard by now."

Maggie pulled the letter addressed to Professor Eliot from the stack.

"May I?" she asked and opened it. She read,

STONE PALEY SEDUCES INNOCENT YOUNG GIRLS

AND THEN MURDERS THEM

"Well, at least we know it's the young girl Joshua's supposed to have murdered," Maggie commented.

"That makes it better?"

"It narrows it down."

"Humpf."

Maggie stared at the greyish, recycled paper with its eccentric font and suddenly realised where she had seen it before. Or where she thought she had seen it. She would have to check.

"Stephen, may I keep this?" she asked.

"All right. But why? I don't want anyone else besides Mrs Steeples, you, and me to know about this."

"I won't show it to anyone else, I promise. It's just… I had an idea about who might be sending these. Although it doesn't make much sense."

"You do? Who?"

"I'd rather not say. Not until I check. It seems so improbable. And it's no one you know. No one at Oxford."

Stephen seemed unconvinced, but finally nodded reluctantly.

"All right, then. But tell me as soon as you figure it out."

Maggie assured Stephen that she would and returned to her rooms.

She found her niece Brooke just turning away from her door.

"Oh hi, Aunt Maggie! There you are!"

Brooke Eliot was a pretty brunette who was a good head shorter than her aunt. She had just begun to work on a doctorate in Oriental Studies focussing on modern China.

"Brooke! How are you? Settling in all right?" Maggie asked as she unlocked her door.

"Yes. Christ Church is great. I have a nice room at St Aldgate's. I'm still meeting people and trying to figure out how to get around. I'm not sure how I'd do on a bicycle."

"Neither am I, even after a decade. I'm safer on two feet."

They entered Maggie's rooms.

"Sit down. Would you like some coffee? Tea?"

"No, thanks. I'm good."

"How is the family?"

Brooke was the daughter of Maggie's middle brother, Lyman, who lived in Manhattan and ran a private equity firm with a partner. Priscilla, his wife, was a high maintenance fashionista and active on the boards of a range of civic institutions and charities. Brooke's brother Lawrence was finishing an MBA and seemed destined to join his father's company.

"They're fine. And at least they let me come over here, even though Mom wasn't exactly enthusiastic. But she finally gave the okay in the hope that I would meet some earl and become an... an earl-ess?"

"A countess."

"Oh. Right. Anyhow, she said that if even you were able to catch some guy with a title, I should be able to as well. Oops. Sorry. Forget I said that."

Maggie decided to laugh.

"That's all right. And if that's what really interests you, I'll keep my eyes open. Although I'll think you'll find you'll have some stiff competition from some oligarch's daughter."

"I'm not afraid. Dad's a billionaire now too, you know."

"He is?"

"Yeah. At least that's what he says."

There was a pause, then Maggie asked, "Brooke, I don't care what your mother thinks, but I hope you don't believe I married Thomas just because he had a title."

"Nah. I'm sure the stately home helped too."

"Brooke!"

"Of course I don't, Aunt Maggie. I really like Uncle Thomas."

"Good. And speaking of Thomas, if you don't have any plans for the weekend, why don't you come visit us at Beaumatin. He would be very pleased to see you."

Brooke considered.

"I'd like that. I think my social calendar is clear," she admitted.

"Good. I'll figure out transport as soon as I have a better idea of my own plans."

"Super. And let me know if you're inviting any bachelor earls or their heirs, so I can reassure Mom."

Maggie hurled a journal at her niece.

Susan Alexander

Chapter thirteen

The following afternoon, Maggie was working on *PeopleFlows* when there was a knock on her door.

"Come in."

A perfectly groomed vision of gorgeousness appeared. Blonde hair fell in silky curtains down a slim, straight back, blue eyes sparkled, and pink lips exactly matched a cashmere sweater.

"Are you busy?"

It was Jersey Jones. Jersey was an American new media celebrity whose success had led to her being given her own show on British television. Maggie had met her when Jersey had been interviewing Stanley Einhorn.

"Hi, Jersey. Not too busy for you. What brings you to Merrion?"

"Stephen invited me up for the weekend," Jersey grinned.

"Really? How nice. If it's not too short notice, and Stephen doesn't have you fully booked, you should come out to Beaumatin for dinner tomorrow night. My niece Brooke, whom I think you met, is coming too."

"That would be great. I'll ask the Steverino. Who's tied up in a meeting. So I thought I'd come over and bother you."

The women smiled.

"How are you finding London?"

"Killer. I've never actually lived in a big city before. First the Jersey burbs, then Palo Alto, and then travelling the byways for the show, you know? There's so much to do in London. Although commuting on public transport... Well, I'd give that a pass if I could.

"And my show, *On the Edge with Jersey Jones*, is getting good reviews. And ratings. And for everyone who posts 'I hate you. You should die, bitch!' I get a dozen that think I'm better than ever. I guess I've still got a lot of Jersey Junkies out there following me, although they were pretty unhappy when the New World Order series ended, and they needed to be satisfied with the odd selfie and tweet and YouTube re-run."

"You can't please everyone," Maggie pointed out.

"Actually, it's not the fans who are the main problem. It's my new colleagues. I had no idea broadcasting was so vicious and cut-throat. Compared to the New World Order...." Jersey paused. "Well, I guess that got cut-throat too. Literally. But for different reasons."

Maggie nodded.

"Anyhow..." Jersey began when there was a knock at the door.

"Come in."

Joshua entered, then stopped dead when he saw Jersey.

"Jersey Jones?"

"Stone Paley?"

"I see I don't need to make introductions," commented Maggie dryly.

Jersey and Joshua looked each other up and down and Maggie decided that if she had not been present, they would have been down on her carpet, rolling around, and tearing off each other's clothes.

Jersey recovered first.

"How do you know..." she began to ask Maggie.

Maggie decided to keep it simple.

"We were colleagues at Harvard."

"What is Jersey Jones doing at Oxford?" Joshua demanded.

"Stephen Draycott invited me down. Or I guess it's up, for the weekend."

"Huh. How do you know Stephen?"

"Well, long story short. I did an interview of Stanley Einhorn. You know who he is?"

"I do," Joshua said grimly.

"Stanley introduced me to Maggie and Thomas, and I decided it would be fun to do a mini-series called *Jersey Jones and the Old World Order*. Which we did. Mostly at their place. Guess you didn't see any of the episodes?"

Joshua shook his head.

"I'm sure some are on YouTube. Anyhow, I met Stephen when he came to Beaumatin for a visit and... Oh, hey. I have an idea. Maggie's invited Stephen and me for dinner on Saturday. Maggie, could Stone come too? You really have to see this place, Stone. It's absolutely Downton Abbey. Well, they don't have a butler. That was a disappointment. But otherwise. Maggie, would it be all right?"

Both Joshua and Jersey were looking at Maggie. From Joshua's amused expression she assumed he was thinking the same thing she was. How was Thomas going to react?

Well, it was her home too, kind of, and it would give Thomas a chance to practise being civil to Joshua without the entire Merrion faculty looking on.

So she smiled and said, "Of course. And plan to spend the night as well if you like. Although... Jersey, does Stephen have an alternative to the Miata? Something a little bigger? So you could bring my niece too, as well as Joshua?"

Stephen loved his bright red sports car, but it only seated two.

Jersey wrinkled her perfect nose. "I'm not sure. I'll ask. We could always rent something."

"I have a car. In fact, it's a Rolls. We could take that if you like. As long as someone acts as navigator," Joshua offered.

"A Rolls? Won't that tarnish your image as being a man of the people, Joshua?" Maggie teased. At Harvard, he had driven a lovingly maintained Volkswagen Beetle circa 1970.

Joshua shrugged.

"It's only leased. I thought it would be a goof. Just let me know when we should leave."

He left and Maggie noticed Jersey watching him.

"Wow. He is so hot. I don't think I'd be able to get any work done, knowing he was so close by."

"Jersey?"

Jersey sighed.

"Jersey, sit. Have something to drink. There are some things you should know."

"Like what? That's Stone's married with twins?"

"No, he's divorced, apparently. No. Just… Red? White? Water? Tea? Whisky? Gin and tonic?"

"Red, if you've got some."

Maggie returned with a glass of red wine for Jersey and a glass of white wine for herself. She sat in the chair next to Jersey.

"I think you should know. Joshua and I. We lived together for five years. In Cambridge. Massachusetts. We were engaged. I broke it off and came here. It was not a very elegant breakup. It was ugly, in fact. It's no secret. It was in all the papers, Joshua being who he is."

Jersey looked incredulous.

"You and Stone were a couple?"

"Yes."

"You were engaged?"

"Yes."

"He gave you a ring and all?"

"Yes. A large and lovely diamond. I returned it when I left."

"Wow. And then you came here and wound up married to his lordship?"

"It was eight years later, Jersey. It wasn't a rebound sort of thing."

"But Stone. He's just so ridiculously fabulous. Completely edible. And he's a celebrity. A-list."

"You're flabbergasted."

"Well yes. How could someone resist Stone?"

Maggie sighed.

"Jersey. Remember when you talked about your experience with Faisal bin Abdulaziz? You said... I believe the way you put it, was that you found him self-absorbed?"

"You can say that again."

"Well, that's how I found Joshua."

"Really?"

"At least as far as I was concerned."

"Oh."

Maggie watched Jersey processing this information. Maggie thought she looked disappointed.

"This isn't you just being some dog in the manger, is it?"

Maggie laughed. "No. Absolutely not. But there is one other thing."

"Yes?"

"Stephen. Did he tell you about Kitty, his wife?"

"That she was killed? Yes. Sad."

"Did he tell you anything else?"

"No. What else is there to tell?"

"Well, if you're going to spend any amount of time at Merrion, someone is going to mention it. Kitty had a reputation. Although I hesitate to use the term, she was known for being, er, promiscuous."

"Really?"

"Yes."

"Poor Stephen."

"Please don't tell him I told you any of this."

"I won't. I know you may think I'm a total Miss Blabbermouth, but I can be discrete."

"Good. So I know you may think it would be cool to make Joshua another notch on your bedpost. And he has certainly accumulated a great many notches of his own over the years…"

"That's not surprising."

"No. But…"

"Yes?"

"I know your relationship with Stephen is none of my business. But if it's more than casual. Or if you'd like it to be more than casual... It's just that.... I don't know how he'd react if you and Joshua...

"I'm sorry. I know I'm sounding like someone's mother. But Merrion is a hotbed of gossip. It's nearly impossible to keep anything secret. And someone would be certain to find out. And it would be sure to get back to Stephen. And after Kitty, I'm not sure how he'd react. But I have to think he wouldn't be very happy about it. And as the Master, he does have to consider his reputation."

"How very old school."

"Oxford is about as old school as it gets, Jersey."

Jersey sighed. "I really am very fond of Stephen. I certainly wouldn't want to hurt him, so... Thanks for telling me all this."

She smiled.

"It should be an interesting weekend, then."

"Oh?"

"You. Stone. His lordship. You can tell Stone still likes you."

"You can? Oh dear."

"Anyhow, Stephen should be out of his meeting by now."

Jersey stood.

"Thanks for the wine. And the history lesson. And the advice."

Not five minutes after Jersey had departed there was another knock on Maggie's door. A knock she knew. Strange, after so many years, she thought.

"Come in."

"Sorry to interrupt. I was going to ask, but I got, er, distracted by Jersey. She really did a series on you and Lord?"

"Well, not just us."

"I'll have to check it out. Anyway, Elle, I had a question. About these tutorials...."

Maggie explained how the system worked.

"Do you give tutorials? Could I sit in on one?"

"In fact, one of the reasons I resigned the Appleton fellowship was to cut back on tutorials. And seminars. And faculty meetings. Reduce my schedule. I'm doing some doctoral and post doc supervision and some research. And serving as an editor for a book series. And organising a conference."

"Nice work if you can get it?"

"Yes."

"Well, thanks for the info."

Maggie walked Joshua to the door. Suddenly he turned, grabbed her, and kissed her.

Maggie had three thoughts simultaneously. The first was how familiar Joshua felt. And how familiar he smelled. She was surprised she remembered so exactly, given she had not really thought about him much for years.

The second was that she did not feel at all the same being kissed by Joshua as she did when she was kissed by Thomas. There was no sensation that she was going to melt into a puddle on the floor.

And thinking of Thomas reminded her that the man himself was due to arrive in her rooms at any moment, so her third thought was that it would be really, really bad if he found her like this with Joshua.

She began to pull away, but Joshua hugged her to him and rested his cheek on the top of her head.

"God, I've missed you. A day hasn't gone by when I haven't wanted you back."

Maggie was speechless. Then she said, "But you got married."

"A terrible mistake. I missed you every day of my marriage too."

"Your poor wife."

"Yes. Meredith called me an egocentric, manipulative bastard."

"Well, she was right about that."

"Probably."

He kissed her again.

"Joshua, I can't. I..."

"Can't? Of course you can."

"No. I mean... I'm married..."

"Yes. To Lord Fubsy Face Umptieth Baron Hayseed."

"That makes me Lady Hayseed, thank you very much."

"Do you really care about all that? Is that why…"

"No! Of course not."

"Then why…"

"I… I'm not going to discuss that."

"All right. Don't."

He went to kiss her again, but she thrust him away.

"Joshua, I'm sorry. I know I behaved very badly when I just ran off. I can't tell you how guilty I feel."

"Yes. I couldn't believe you did that. You were always so prim and proper."

"I'm so sorry. Really."

"Well, now's your chance to put things right."

"Joshua!"

He looked momentarily annoyed. Women did not say no to Stone Paley. Then he shrugged.

"All right. For now. But I want you back, babe. So don't think for a moment I'm giving up. And how convenient that my rooms are right upstairs," he grinned.

He gave her a last quick kiss, then left.

Maggie closed the door, then leaned against it.

Oh dear. This wasn't good. And she had no idea what to do about it.

Someone tapped on the door. Thomas.

"Hi."

"Are you ready? Am I early?"

Thomas looked at Maggie closely. She seemed flustered. Her hair was in disarray, which in itself was not unusual, but...

"No. No, let me just gather my things..."

She started towards her desk, but he took her arm.

"Wait. Your hair clip's come loose."

He turned her around and began to fix her hair. He paused. He caught a whiff of scent. Something musky. Not his aftershave. Or Maggie's scent, warm with spring flowers. He scowled. He remembered where he had smelled this before. Paley. How had Paley been near enough to Maggie that he could smell the man's scent?

With her back to him, Maggie noticed that Thomas had paused, but she could not see his face.

"Thomas?"

"There." He secured her curls.

Chapter fourteen

Thomas proposed they return to Beaumatin that evening and have a late dinner. Maggie agreed.

After they had enjoyed some boeuf bourguignon accompanied by an excellent Burgundy, Maggie plucked up her courage.

"Er, Thomas?"

"Yes, my dear?"

"You remember that Brooke is coming on Saturday?"

Thomas frowned.

"I did send you a text," Maggie reminded him.

"All right. That will be nice. I like Brooke."

"And I've asked Stephen and Jersey Jones as well."

"Stephen? And Jersey?"

"Yes. Stephen invited her to Merrion for the weekend."

"All right."

Maggie decided to rush her fences.

"Jersey and I were chatting in my rooms when Joshua came in and... Jersey invited him to come along."

Thomas, who had been about to sip some Burgundy, stopped abruptly.

"Paley's coming here? To Beaumatin?"

"Yes. With Stephen and Jersey. And Brooke."

"You couldn't have made up some excuse?"

"No. It would have been too awkward. And obviously false."

"Humpf."

"I knew you'd be unhappy…"

"Unhappy? To have that man in my home?"

His home. Maggie decided now was not the moment to address that.

"Well, it's done. They are coming in the afternoon on Saturday and leaving after breakfast on Sunday. I'll try to invite some other people for dinner to, er, dilute Joshua's presence for you. But it's short notice, so if you'll excuse me, I'll go make some calls."

Maggie got up and left. She wondered how many people she would need to invite to dinner Saturday night to distract Thomas from Joshua. And she would have to warn Mrs Cook. Thank goodness the woman took such things in her stride.

Chapter Fifteen

While Thomas was sulking, Maggie managed to enlist twelve more people for Saturday night, making it eighteen for dinner.

There would be the Nesbitts, Sir John and Thalia. Sir John was a neighbour and an old friend of Thomas, while Thalia was the head of the local Church Ladies' Guild, in which Maggie reluctantly participated. Anne Brooks had been sympathetic and said she and Laurence wouldn't miss it. Although the Ainswicks declined, Beatrix suggested that her daughter Chloe and husband David Osborne might like to come, while she and Cedric babysat their young grandson.

Maggie called Thomas's son William and asked if he and his wife Gweneth could attend. William told her that Gweneth's mother Muriel and Muriel's brother-in-law Clive Stonor would be visiting, so Maggie invited them as well, even though she knew Muriel disliked her. Finally she invited Giles Sumner, a surgeon, and his wife Celia, who was another member of the Church Ladies Guild, and friends with William and Gweneth.

And if that weren't enough people to create a buffer between Thomas and Joshua, then tough tuna, Maggie concluded.

She went to confer with Mrs Cook. Together they decided on a menu of potted shrimp, which Maggie disliked but knew was a favourite of Thomas, a venison stew, and trifle for dessert.

"I'll get the potted shrimp from Waitrose and make the stew this afternoon. It will taste even better tomorrow. And I have the raspberry jam I made for the trifle."

"That sounds wonderful, Mrs Cook," Maggie assured her.

They discussed rooms for the overnight guests.

"And if I give you the guest list for dinner, would you figure out the seating and make place cards?"

"Of course, my lady."

That was a relief. Mrs Cook was expert at the rules of protocol that determined who should sit where. Rules whose finer points Maggie was still trying to grasp. But she thought it would mean Thomas would sit between Lady Nesbitt and Muriel Stonor, while she would be between Sir John and Stephen. Or William. Or perhaps Clive. At any event, Joshua would be somewhere in the middle of the long table, far enough away from Thomas and surrounded by attractive women so he would be less tempted to flirt with his hostess.

Because despite what he had said, Maggie was sure that that was all it was. Flirting. And if Joshua could be sidetracked, he would leave her alone and not create further problems for her with her husband.

Chapter sixteen

Thomas was still avoiding Maggie on Saturday when, at three o'clock, she heard tyres on gravel.

Maggie went out to welcome her guests.

It was a perfect autumn day with deep blue skies and trees just beginning to turn. Beaumatin's golden Cotswold stone glowed in the sunlight and she felt the estate was looking its best.

But goodness gracious, she thought as she caught sight of the metallic grey Phantom.

It pulled up in front of the great house and stopped.

Car doors opened and Stephen, Jersey, Brooke, and Joshua emerged.

Jersey nudged Joshua.

"See! Didn't I tell you?"

While Stephen and Brooke were continuing a discussion about China's urban planning policies, Joshua was trying to look unimpressed at Beaumatin's eccentric architectural mix of Elizabethan, Jacobean, Georgian, and Victorian Gothic styles.

"Everything you see, it's all the estate. It's huge," Jersey enthused and gestured at the great lawn that rolled down to an elaborate fountain and beyond to distant slopes where sheep grazed.

Joshua looked at Maggie curiously.

"This is where you live?"

"When I'm not at Oxford."

"What do you think?" Jersey prompted.

"It's all right, if you like the Downton Abbey sort of thing."

"Yeah. Too bad there's no butler."

Mrs Cook came out.

"Joshua, this is Mrs Cook, our housekeeper. Mrs Cook, this is Professor Paley. You know Jersey and Stephen and Brooke. If you guys get your bags, Mrs Cook will show you to your rooms."

While Brooke and Jersey greeted Mrs Cook enthusiastically, Joshua pressed a button on his keypad and the lid of the boot slowly opened.

Just then, a Mini Countryman came up the drive.

Oh dear. It was Jonquil Pilkington.

A man Maggie did not know was behind the wheel.

Jonquil climbed out and bustled over.

"Lady Raynham, Lady Raynham, I'm sorry to just drop by, but I wanted to give you the programme for our meeting and the latest membership list. We're now up to ninety-five people!"

"That's nice," Maggie responded vaguely.

The driver got out and stood beside the car. Jonquil waved him over.

"Lady Raynham, this is my husband, Mark. Mark, this is Lady Raynham."

The Greater Gloucestershire Galanthus Group

Maggie shook hands with the headmaster of Churn Valley College. He looked like she would have expected a husband of Jonquil to look. Balding, mild-mannered, and unremarkable.

Maggie remembered her manners.

"Oh, Jonquil. And Mark. These are some friends who have just arrived from Oxford. This is my niece, Brooke Eliot, who is working on her doctorate. And Professor Draycott, who is the Master of Merrion College. And Jersey Jones, whom you may know from her television show, On the Edge. And this is…"

"Stone Paley!" Jonquil gasped.

"You're Stone Paley!" she repeated. Her face flushed a mottled mauve.

"Yes, I am," Joshua smiled. Pleased at being recognised. Practised at being gracious to a fan.

He extended his hand.

Jonquil stared at it as though it were a cobra, hood unfurled and ready to strike.

"No. No."

Jonquil thrust the papers at Maggie and backed away. Then she turned, race walked back to the Mini, and clambered in.

"Come, Mark," she ordered as she slammed her door shut.

Embarrassed by his wife's behaviour, Mark muttered, "Pleased to meet you," and got back in the Mini.

He carefully turned the car around and retreated down the drive.

"Strange woman," commented Joshua. Jersey and Stephen nodded in agreement.

"You have no idea," Maggie concurred. "I felt obliged to agree to be the patron for a snowdrop club she's forming. Thomas had turned her down and expected I'd do the same, but I misread his cues and accepted. Well, I'll wait until it's launched and then plead the pressures of work."

"You mean you'll cut the ribbon to open a snowdrop fair and have potato sack races on your lawn?" asked Jersey.

"It's not quite that bad," Maggie protested.

"Anyhow, please take your bags and come inside. Mrs Cook will show you to your rooms."

Maggie noticed Joshua looking up at the stonework on the façade.

"That's the Raynham coat of arms. And their motto. Numquam cede. Never yield. Or we never give up."

"Humpf."

In the great hall, Joshua again paused and took in the checkboard marble floor, linenfold oak panelling, Elizabethan settees, and ancestral portrait gallery.

"You should get Maggie to give you a tour. She knows all about the history of the barons," Jersey recommended.

"I'll bet."

Joshua was still projecting unimpressed.

"Is this really your thing?" he murmured and gestured at a painting of a long-faced man wearing a wig from the period of Charles II.

"No, not at all," Maggie admitted.

"But neither were your minimalist Cambridge digs," she added.

"Yeah. Well, the Ex changed all that."

"She did?"

"She preferred pastels."

He moved closer.

"And if that's what was bothering you…"

"You know what was bothering me."

Joshua grimaced.

"You never said anything…"

"I assumed some things didn't need saying."

"You were wrong. I assumed you didn't care."

"Not care?"

"Hey Aunt Maggie, is Uncle Thomas here?" Brooke interrupted.

"Er, he's probably out on the estate. Unless he's in his study."

"I'll go see."

Maggie noticed Mrs Cook waiting patiently.

"Um, Brooke? How about you let Mrs Cook show you to your room first."

"Oh. Ok. Sure."

The visitors followed the housekeeper up the grand stairway and Maggie retreated to her study.

Was Joshua right? Should she have said something? And if she had, would it have made a difference?

Did people really change?

She thought about Thomas.

She had known he was difficult. Volatile. Inclined to jump to conclusions. Often erroneous conclusions. She had married him anyway. She had let her heart rule her head.

With Joshua...

With Joshua her heart had not been engaged the same way it had been with Thomas, so it had been easier to let her head rule.

Head or heart, she faced a difficult twenty-four hours before her guests departed. She would just have to tough it out.

The Greater Gloucestershire Galanthus Group

Chapter seventeen

Maggie had just come downstairs when the first of her dinner guests arrived. It was William and Gweneth, accompanied by Muriel and Clive Stonor.

William looked much like his father at his age, Maggie had decided, while pretty, blonde Gweneth resembled his mother, Harriet. Thomas' first wife had died of cancer, and he had mourned her for years before marrying again. Gweneth's mother Muriel was Lord Ainswick's sister. A widow in her seventies, the thin, elegantly dressed woman disapproved of Maggie for reasons she did not understand. Muriel shared a house in Woodstock with her brother-in-law Clive, who liked Maggie quite as much as Muriel disliked her. Clive had an antiques shop in Oxford and Maggie invited him to dine at Merrion regularly.

Next to arrive were the Brookses.

"Anne! Laurence!" Maggie greeted them.

"Laurence, I don't know what has delayed Thomas, but would you mind playing bartender until he arrives?" she asked.

Maggie suspected Thomas' uncharacteristic tardiness was due to Joshua's presence, but she could hardly admit that, even to her friends.

The four houseguests appeared. Brooke and Stephen came in first, deep in an academic discussion. Brooke said something in Chinese, and Stephen laughed. Jersey entered, looking dazzling in a clinging, sapphire blue dress. She was smiling and looking over her shoulder at Joshua, who was behind her.

The man paused in the doorway, waiting to be noticed. He wore a severe black suit and a silky grey knit turtleneck. His dreadlocks were tied back with a black ribbon, and he wore black snakeskin cowboy boots that added a couple of inches to his height.

"Rock star," Maggie thought and was struck by how out of place he looked in Beaumatin's formal drawing room, a space that was bigger than her entire Oxford apartment. It had half a dozen seating areas, inlaid floors covered by Aubusson carpets, crystal chandeliers, and a Constable landscape that hung over a massive marble-fronted fireplace.

Muriel was the first to notice Joshua. Maggie thought that if she had had a lorgnette, she would have used it, the better to express her disapproval. She nudged Clive, who turned and raised his eyebrows at the spectacle.

Before Maggie could begin to make introductions, the Nesbitts came in. Sir John was plump and jolly and reminded Maggie of a Toby jug. Lady Nesbitt was a stout, formidable matron with short, battleship grey hair and a hatchet nose. Maggie wondered what her friend would make of Joshua.

The Nesbitts were followed by Giles and Celia Sumner. Giles was a good-looking surgeon and Celia was a sporty blonde whom Maggie knew from the Church Ladies' Guild.

Where was Thomas? Maggie wondered. She pulled Brooke aside.

"Brooke, could you check to see if Thomas is in his study and remind him people are here? If he's not there, perhaps tell Mrs Cook and she could look upstairs for him."

"Sure, Aunt Maggie," said Brooke, unaware of why her uncle-by-marriage might be avoiding his guests.

Last to arrive were Chloe and David Osborne.

"I'm sorry we're late, Maggie," the pretty brunette apologized. "But young Cedric was unhappy about its being his bedtime and I didn't want to leave Mother with him until he settled down.

"He's become a little monster," added his father proudly. David was a botanist who had taken over responsibility for the gardens at Rochford Manor when he married.

"He's started the terrible twos ahead of time," Chloe agreed.

Brooke reappeared, accompanied by Thomas. Maggie thought he looked exceptionally elegant.

Thomas went and thanked Laurence for undertaking bartender duties. He then greeted his guests. When he got to Joshua, who was talking to Stephen, he nodded briefly and then went on to chat with Giles Sumner.

As Paley watched Thomas move away, his eyes narrowed. Then he shrugged and, as Maggie looked on, launched into a charm offensive. He questioned Thalia about the work of the Church Ladies Guild and described to Celia Sumner watching Serena Williams win that year's US Open at Forest Hills. He spoke to Clive Stonor knowledgably about American silver of the late eighteenth century in comparison with Georgian craftsmanship and had just started to query William about being a Queen's Counsel when dinner was announced.

Anne came up to Maggie as they moved into the dining room and murmured, "Your old beau is making quite an impression."

"Thomas was just short of rude. Joshua's trying to make a point."

"He's certainly succeeding."

She indicated Joshua's taking Thalia by the arm and escorting her into the dining room, to the woman's obvious satisfaction.

Oh dear.

Chapter eighteen

To Maggie's relief, dinner went smoothly. She had Sir John on her right and Stephen on her left. Sir John reminisced about his time at Oxford and quizzed Stephen on how the University had changed since he had been an undergraduate, which allowed Maggie to be a passive listener and keep an eye on how things were going at the rest of the table.

At the far end, Thomas was bookended by Thalia and Muriel Stonor, who seemed to be relishing a good gossip about mutual friends and acquaintances, thus relieving their host of the duty to make conversation.

After dinner, everyone moved back to the drawing room for coffee and brandy. Thomas played bartender while Maggie served coffee. She noticed Joshua and Jersey talking together, then quietly leaving. Maggie located Stephen to see if he noticed, but he was busy talking to Giles Sumner.

Maggie had just poured a second cup of coffee for Laurence when Jersey burst into the room.

"Hey you guys, you've got to come. You've got to see this."

She grabbed Stephen and pulled him out the door.

Maggie stood. People looked at each other, hesitating.

Jersey reappeared.

"Come on," she urged.

Maggie followed the crowd across the hall and into the ballroom. While the two massive crystal chandeliers were still shrouded in sheeting, light came from gilt and crystal wall sconces that Jersey had turned on. In a far corner, the cover of the grand piano had been removed and Joshua was sitting at the keyboard, playing an old Elton John song.

Maggie had forgotten that Joshua was an accomplished pianist, had a fine tenor, and loved to perform.

"Go ahead, Stone. We're waiting," Jersey encouraged.

Joshua looked at his audience, who were trying to seem enthusiastic while hoping they were not going to be embarrassed.

"Shall I?" he grinned.

He played a long glissando, then launched into "I'm Still Standing," another Elton John hit.

Maggie, who had hung back, watched as people began to relax. Soon they were smiling and nodding.

Joshua finished and everyone applauded.

"Come on, Stone. Don't stop," Jersey urged.

He looked pleased and started to play "Crocodile Rock."

"Come on, Stevie. Let's dance," Jersey commanded.

Jersey grabbed Stephen and started to dance. The Sumners and, to Maggie's surprise, the Nesbitts followed. Even Anne and Laurence succumbed.

In moments, they were joined by William and Gweneth and Chloe and David. Clive asked Brooke to dance, while Muriel watched, smiling grimly.

Maggie noticed Thomas was missing. She returned to the drawing room and found Thomas was standing alone, holding a nearly empty glass of whisky, and brooding.

"Very Heathcliff," she said tartly. "Thomas, you really have to come and listen to this."

"Do I?"

"Yes, you do. You're the host."

She took his hand, yanked to create some momentum, and led him to the ballroom.

To give his audience a chance to catch their breath, Joshua announced he would switch to the other side of the pond and began to play "Walking in Memphis."

Something new in his repertoire, Maggie thought.

Then he segued into "I Guess That's Why They Call It the Blues," and the dancing began again. Thomas remained immobile.

"Oh. I forgot. You don't do contemporary," she murmured.

Thomas tightened his mouth. Maggie felt like they were chaperones at a high school prom.

The song ended and Brooke and Clive came up.

"Dance Uncle Thomas? Please?" Brooke pleaded.

Maggie stifled a laugh as Thomas allowed himself to be led off.

"Do you mind if we sit this one out?" Clive asked.

Joshua was playing a Mike and the Mechanics hit. "Over My Shoulder." It was a song about lost love, when everyone had told him she was leaving, and he was the last to know.

Clive observed Maggie watching Joshua.

"An old beau?" he asked her shrewdly.

"How did you…"

"It's a small world and you both come to us from Harvard. And after that magnificent Burgundy, I can't imagine any other reason why his lordship should be scowling."

"We were engaged to be married. Then I… I changed my mind."

Maggie paused, then added, "Thomas knows. I told him."

"And you prefer our dour baron to this charmer?"

"Yes. And I told Thomas that too. But I'm not sure he believed me."

"Oh dear."

"Yes."

"Well, dear heart, you know where I am if I can offer a sympathetic ear."

"Thank you, Clive."

Thomas decided he had suffered enough, and Brooke apparently agreed.

"Wow, Aunt Maggie. I never knew you were such a celebrity magnet. Jersey Jones and Stone Paley?"

Maggie gave a self-deprecating shrug.

Muriel Stonor came up, accompanied by William and Gweneth. She gave Maggie a frosty glare and then smiled at Thomas.

"Come, Clive. It's late."

"As you wish, Muriel."

He turned to his hostess.

"Thank you for a lovely evening, my dear. You too, Thomas."

Thomas went to show the Conyers and Stonors out. He returned, took Maggie's arm, and murmured, "Can't you put an end to this?"

Joshua finished a song, glanced across at Maggie, and launched into "Yesterday," when all his troubles seemed so far away because he thought she was here to stay.

Maggie could feel Thomas stiffen. He might not know Marc Cohen or Mike and the Mechanics, but he apparently knew his Beatles. His grip on her arm tightened to the point she was sure she'd have bruises.

"Thomas!" Maggie hissed.

The song died away. Then, without missing a beat, Joshua launched into Billy Joel's "Piano Man."

Maggie had forgotten Joshua's Piano Man. In her opinion, it was his best number. Plus she loved the song. With Jersey's and Brooke's encouragement, people joined in on the chorus.

Maggie felt herself being sucked in, then took a deep breath. This was Joshua, master of manipulation. She was sure every song had been chosen deliberately to either evoke a memory or play on her guilt. Or what he supposed was her guilt.

At the end, everyone clapped, and Jersey hooted. "Whoo-hoo!"

Joshua stood, gave a mock bow, and began to close the lid to the keyboard.

"Oh no, Stone. One more. Please," Jersey pleaded.

"Encore, encore," chorused some of the others.

Joshua pretended to hesitate, then shrugged and sat down.

Maggie glanced at Thomas. His face was expressionless, but his eyes were glinting.

Oh dear. This was so not good.

"All right. Just one more."

He did another Billy Joel. "Just the Way You Are." He plaintively asked what it would take till she believed in him the way that he believed in her?

Maggie sighed. She really didn't need this problem. She would have to talk to the man.

At the end, Joshua said, "I see my whisky is finished and it's always good to quit while you're ahead."

The Greater Gloucestershire Galanthus Group

"Stone, that was awesome," said Jersey.

"I can see I should look into having a piano installed in the Senior Common Room," agreed Stephen.

As people drifted back into the drawing room, Joshua came up to his hosts.

"You have a marvellous instrument, Lord. Do you play?" he asked.

"No. That's something that's usually left to the ladies," Thomas finally responded in a tone of indifference.

Oh dear, thought Maggie. Joshua had thrown down the gauntlet and Thomas had promptly picked it up.

"Shall we join our guests, my dear?" Thomas asked, then took Maggie's arm and guided her back to the drawing room. Joshua, looking amused, followed them.

Thomas was refilling glasses with whisky and cognac. Celia, Thalia, and Chloe surrounded Joshua.

Anne pulled Maggie aside and murmured, "Remind me again. Why was it you didn't marry Paley?"

"Et tu, Brute?"

Then Maggie sighed.

"If it comes to pistols at ten paces, do you think Laurence would act as a second for Thomas? I'm sure Stephen would act for Joshua."

"That bad?"

"Well, Thomas may not know Billy Joel, but he definitely knows the Beatles."

"Yesterday?"

Maggie nodded.

"Joshua couldn't have been more obvious."

"Yes, I noticed. I think Thalia did too."

"Oh dear."

Maggie glanced across at Thomas, who was talking with Giles Sumner, Sir John, Stephen, and Laurence. Joshua was still surrounded by the ladies and obviously enjoying the attention.

"On Thursday Joshua came to my rooms. He became physical and indicated he still had feelings. Even though I had made it clear that I had none. Thomas showed up only a minute after he left. If he'd come just a little earlier…"

Anne looked concerned.

"Can't you avoid him at Merrion?"

"I try. But he has Gordon Ross' old rooms. Right above Chitta's. Which are right above mine. I hope it will be easier once he finds his own place. At the moment he's living there as well and pops down half a dozen times a day to ask questions. All of which are perfectly legitimate for someone new to Oxford. It's just that… Well, I'm beginning to be afraid that I'm the real reason he's shown up here and not the chance to be the Appleton fellow. Which really is a lateral move for him in terms of the chair he held at Harvard."

"Chasing the one that got away?"

Maggie nodded.

"And you know Thomas and I had agreed that I would stay in my rooms when he's not in Oxford. Since I've never really been that comfortable at Hereford Crescent. But now, of course, Thomas insists I not stay at Merrion as long as Joshua's around. And I like my rooms. I'm productive there. And it's not as though I can avoid being at the college altogether."

Maggie took another sip of wine.

"Sorry about whinging."

"No. It sounds like you've got a problem." Anne thought. "Could you ask Stephen if he could move Paley to some other rooms?"

"And what reason would I give? I've been fortunate to avoid becoming gossip fodder as it is. And Gordon's old rooms really are splendid. Joshua was quite pleased when he saw them."

Anne looked thoughtful. "Well, girlfriend, I'm here if you need me. And I have to be in Oxford on Wednesday. Want to have lunch?"

"I'll need to double check, but as far as I remember I'm free."

Finally good nights were said and the guests who were spending the night went off to their rooms. Maggie had had Mrs Cook put Joshua at the end of the guest wing and as far away from her own room as was possible. She had given Jersey and Stephen rooms next to each other. Whether they slept together or apart was not her concern.

Maggie was in her bedroom, dithering. She had drunk too much wine in reaction to the stress of the evening.

She had just put on her night gown when the door opened abruptly and Thomas came in. He had removed his jacket and tie but otherwise was still dressed.

Normally he would knock. She wondered if he had expected to find her with Joshua.

He crossed to her and grabbed both her upper arms. He smelled of whisky.

"Tell me why you married me again. And not Paley," he demanded.

"Because I wasn't in love with him," she said simply.

"But you lived with him. Became engaged…"

"Yes, but in the end I didn't. Marry him. I married you."

"And you're not regretting your choice?"

"Oh for heaven's sake, Thomas," she said, jerking away.

"I am not the issue here. You are. And you are giving Joshua far too much power."

Thomas thought about this.

"You have to trust me. Is that really so hard for you to do?"

He did not answer, but asked, "Tell me. What was he like?"

"What was he like? I told you. Moody. Self-absorbed…"

"No. That's not what I mean. I mean…"

Maggie realised what he was asking.

"Oh no. Really, Thomas."

"Tell me. I don't want to keep imagining…"

"I don't discuss those things with anyone."

"I'm not anyone. I'm your husband."

"I would never think of asking about you and Harriet…"

"That's good because I certainly would not tell you."

"Yet you want me to…"

"Harriet's not in a room a few dozen yards from here."

"It was years and years ago…"

"Nevertheless, I have to know."

Maggie went over to the window. Parted the curtain. There was nothing but darkness outside.

"He was… predictable. And often….." she broke off.

"He…" Thomas began.

"No. No. That's enough. Enough." Maggie felt her face get hot.

Thomas saw her flushed cheeks and decided she hadn't said what she had just to placate him and that he could believe her. And felt the rush of relief he got when Maggie had made him crazy and he found his concerns were unfounded.

Thomas crossed to her and wrapped his arms around her.

"No, Papillon, that's not enough," he murmured and he kissed her.

Chapter Nineteen

Maggie's alarm clock was going off.

She groaned and was about to turn over and go back to sleep when she remembered.

She had houseguests.

She rushed through a shower, threw on jeans and an oversized sweater, and hurried down to the kitchen, where Mrs Cook was busy scrambling eggs.

"Am I late?" Maggie asked anxiously.

"No, it's all right. No one is down yet. Oh, and his lordship said to tell you he's out on the estate so would you please make his apologies if he's not back when people leave."

Maggie understood this to mean that her husband was avoiding Joshua.

Mrs Cook handed Maggie a mug of coffee. Then she deftly spooned the eggs into a silver chafing dish and headed to the dining room.

The housekeeper put the dish of eggs into its stand on a massive Georgian sideboard that was loaded with the other items she considered essential to a proper breakfast when the Raynhams were entertaining. These included three types of juice, smoked salmon, bacon, several varieties of sausage, scrambled and boiled eggs, baked tomatoes, sautéed mushrooms, and toast made from her homemade bread. With jam and marmalade, also the woman's own.

"My goodness. You've outdone yourself. As usual," Maggie commented.

The housekeeper smiled, then departed.

Maggie sat down at her end of the table. She needed more coffee before she could possibly think about eating anything.

Brooke came in.

"Hi, Aunt Maggie," she said brightly.

"Good morning, Brooke."

Brooke was looking extremely pretty in a deep red silk blouse and black wool pants. Ruby stud earrings echoed the blouse, while subtle makeup was expertly applied.

Maggie realised this was not the little girl whom she had cuddled while they read bedtime stories together. Or the teenager she had mentored through the ups and downs of adolescence. Her niece was a woman. When had that happened?

Stephen entered.

"Morning."

While Maggie poured tea, Stephen helped himself to eggs, bacon, and sausages.

He sat down beside Brooke.

"Hey Brooke. Did you read Philpot in the latest issue of *Oriental Studies*?"

Maggie noticed Brooke was blushing. Oh dear.

"Yes. And I thought his conclusions were rubbish."

There followed a very technical discussion about why Philpot was wrong and why it was absurd that his piece should have been published at all. It did not help that the man was from Cambridge.

An image of loveliness appeared in the doorway.

Stephen stood and Maggie felt a twinge of sympathy for Brooke.

Jersey Jones was spectacular in a turquoise angora sweater and tight jeans. Lips that were a luscious rose gleamed, blonde hair fell in a flawless swathe to her shoulders, and thick lashes framed sky blue eyes.

"Hi, everyone."

Jersey sashayed over to the sideboard, contemplated what was on offer, and selected some salmon and toast.

She gave Stephen a kiss on the top of his head and sat down on his other side.

Conversation became general.

Joshua was the last to appear. He was all in black, from his turtleneck to his signature black snakeskin cowboy boots.

"Please help yourself, Joshua."

Maggie gestured to the sideboard.

"Wow. I guess this is what you guys call a full English breakfast."

Maggie poured him coffee. Unless he had changed, he drank his black.

Brooke excused herself.

"I should get ready. We're still departing around noon?"

Joshua nodded.

"All right. Don't leave without me. I have an appointment with my advisor first thing tomorrow morning."

Stephen got up and went to serve himself seconds.

Jersey smiled across at Joshua.

"Hey, Stone. Did you get to visit the gardens yesterday?"

"Uh, no."

"They're really spectacular. Want a tour?"

Joshua studied Jersey.

"Sure," he smiled.

He got up and gave Maggie a quick hug.

"Great breakfast, Elle."

Joshua followed Jersey out of the room.

Stephen watched the pair leave.

"Stephen?" Maggie asked in concern.

Stephen sighed.

"It's all right, Maggie. Jersey and I had a talk yesterday and... we decided we had better just be friends."

Friends with benefits? Maggie wondered.

"With the demands of our jobs, and all," he explained.

"And you're all right with that?"

Stephen shrugged.

"It wouldn't have worked. Beyond casual. If we'd tried for more than that… There would be disappointment. Hurt. And drama. And I don't want drama. Kitty provided enough of that for a lifetime."

Stephen helped himself to another cup of tea.

"Did you find out anything about the anonymous letters? You had an idea…"

Maggie grimaced. With all the issues surrounding Joshua's visit to Beaumatin, she had forgotten about them.

"Have there been any more?" she asked as a diversion from Stephen's question.

"Yes. On Friday. You had already left for Beaumatin. Same paper and envelopes. Same recipients. Same message about seduction and murder.

"I don't understand it. I know Joshua has his detractors, but murder? Seduction? Have you mentioned them to him?"

"No. No, I hope that won't be necessary. That whoever is sending them will get tired when nothing happens and stop."

Stephen stood.

"Well, I had better get ready to go."

Maggie nodded.

She poured herself a third mug of coffee and savoured the warm, creamy liquid while she gathered strength. She was crossing the hall when she met Stephen coming down the stairs, carrying an overnight bag.

"I'll put this out by the car."

"I'll be in my study."

Maggie had just sat down at her desk when Stephen reappeared. He was pale and looked upset.

"Stephen?"

"There's… there's a body. In the boot. In the boot of Stone's Rolls."

Maggie doubted that she had heard correctly.

"A body?"

"Yes. A body. In the boot."

"A body in the boot?"

"Yes."

"A dead body?"

"Yes."

"In Joshua's Rolls?"

"Yes, yes, yes."

"Show me."

They went out and Stephen gestured.

The lid of the boot was up. Maggie looked in and saw the body of a woman. She had been strangled. A tie was wrapped tightly around her neck. But even with her distorted features, Maggie recognized the brittle hair and sharp nose. It was Jonquil Pilkington.

"It's Jonquil!"

"You know her?"

"Yes. But what is she... Was the car unlocked?"

"Yes. Well, I guess. The boot opened when I tried it."

Joshua and Jersey appeared from around the corner of the house. Jersey seemed very pleased with herself and Joshua had the look of a man who had been "Jerseyed," as Maggie called it.

"Joshua!" she called.

The pair came over.

Maggie pointed at the corpse.

"Holy shit!" exclaimed Jersey.

"What the..." Joshua exclaimed!

"Did you forget to lock the car?" Maggie demanded.

"No, I... Well, I don't know. Maybe. With everyone getting their bags. I might have..."

"Do you know her?"

Joshua took another quick look and turned away.

"No. Although it's hard to tell. With her face so..."

"Good god!"

It was Stephen, who had taken another peek at the corpse.

"What?"

"That tie! It's a Merrion repp tie!"

Maggie took her mobile from a pocket and dialled 999.

Chapter twenty

Detective Chief Inspector Willis surveyed the group who were assembled in the drawing room.

"Well isn't this a happy little reunion. I know you, Miss Eliot. And you, Professor Draycott. And you too, Miss Jones. And of course I know you," he indicated Maggie.

With grizzled hair and hooded grey eyes, the police detective was in his late forties but looked older. Maggie noticed that he had lost weight since she had last seen him the previous spring and he was wearing a new suit that was not in need of pressing, which was usually the case.

"So who is this?" he pointed at Joshua.

Maggie performed the introductions.

"This is Professor Paley. He is Merrion College's new Appleton Fellow. Joshua, this is Detective Chief Inspector Willis, of the Gloucestershire Constabulary."

"And that's your Rolls?"

"Yes. Well, it's leased," Paley explained.

"And you expect me to believe you left a car worth half a million pounds unlocked?"

Paley shrugged.

"You just left it sitting out there on the drive, waiting for someone to dump a corpse in the boot?"

"I assume that's a rhetorical question?" Joshua responded irritably.

Willis turned and scowled at Maggie.

"And you say you know who the victim is?"

"Yes. Jonquil Pilkington. The wife of the headmaster of Churn Valley College."

"And how do you know this Mrs Pilkington?"

"I only met her for the first time a few weeks ago. She is, she was organising a group of snowdrop fanciers and I agreed to be involved. She was very enthusiastic and had gotten into the habit of dropping by to keep me informed about progress. They, the group, are having their first gathering here at Beaumatin in February. I say they are, but I don't know what will happen without Jonquil."

"More murderous galanthophiles," Willis muttered.

A woman came in. She was tall and athletic-looking and had grey eyes and blond hair pulled back in a French braid. Maggie recognized her and stood.

"Marcy!"

Marcy stared.

"Maggie?"

Willis' frown deepened.

"You know Detective Sergeant Hickson?"

"Yes. From a case in Oxford a year ago," Maggie explained.

"Humpf."

"And Detective Sergeant Proudfoot?" Maggie asked Willis.

"Has been relocated to Portsmouth."

Maggie was relieved. Proudfoot hated her and had tried to have her charged with multiple counts of murder the previous spring. She made a mental note to avoid Portsmouth for the foreseeable future.

"Sir?"

"What."

"The pathologist would like a word."

Willis turned to go.

"Just a moment, Inspector Willis."

It was Stephen.

"Yes?"

"Professor Paley, Miss Eliot, and I need to get back to Oxford. And Miss Jones has commitments in London."

Willis glowered.

"And I'll need my car," added Joshua.

"Out of the question. Until it's been thoroughly processed."

"Then how are we to get back?" Stephen demanded.

"I'll arrange that, Stephen," Maggie reassured him.

The drawing room doors banged open and Thomas stalked in.

He surveyed the group, then addressed his wife.

"My dear, why are there police at Beaumatin?"

"Jonquil Pilkington's been murdered."

"Indeed? I admit the woman was a nuisance, but I fail to see what her death has to do with us."

"Her body was found in the boot of Joshua's car."

Thomas closed his eyes and took a deep breath while he controlled himself.

"I see. Then I trust you've told Mrs Cook she may have to put back lunch."

Lunch. Maggie had forgotten. It was Sunday and there would be the inevitable roast. And it seemed they would be having company. Again.

"Willis." Thomas acknowledged the detective with a nod, then turned and left.

Marcy looked her question at the DCI.

"Lord Raynham," he said succinctly.

"Whoa."

There was a pause. Then Stephen repeated, "So, Inspector Willis?"

"I understand the four of you travelled here from Oxford together. In the Rolls."

"Yes."

"Then I want your fingerprints. For elimination purposes. I will also need each of you to give a statement to DS Hickson about what you were doing from the time you arrived here yesterday until the moment the body was discovered. Which was around eleven this morning. Is that right?"

Maggie and Stephen nodded.

"I want your complete contact information. And I'm warning you, you're to be at the addresses you've given us. In Oxford. And London."

"Oh, I say," protested Stephen.

"Until you have been cleared as suspects." Willis continued. "Or you can remain here."

Uh oh. Thomas would have something to say about that, thought Maggie.

"But none of us had ever met the woman," Stephen grumbled.

"Um, that's not completely accurate," Maggie felt compelled to point out.

"What's this?" Willis's irritation changed to interest.

"You at least saw her."

"We did? When?" Jersey asked.

"Yesterday. When you first arrived. You were getting out of the car. Getting your bags. And a woman drove up in a grey Mini. You must remember. You were introduced."

"That was her?" Brooke asked.

"Yes."

Jersey shook her head.

"I must not have been paying attention. Oh. Wait. Now I remember. She wasn't very happy to meet Stone."

"She wasn't?"

Maggie saw Willis had on his "case face." That wasn't good.

"She seemed startled by Joshua. But then, his appearance is extraordinary," Maggie clarified.

"That was her? I thought she was a fan at first," he explained to Willis.

"A fan?" Willis was puzzled.

"Joshua has a lot of admirers. Not only in academic circles," Maggie explained.

"Humpf. So why was Mrs Pilkington here?" Willis asked.

"I told you about this snowdrop group. For which I rather unwisely agreed to be the patron…"

Joshua snickered.

"Jonquil was the primary organiser and she had taken to dropping by to share the latest developments. She appeared yesterday just when the others had arrived. And her husband was with her. He was driving. I introduced her and, when she saw Joshua, she became, well, agitated. She thrust the papers she had brought at me and left."

"The papers Pilkington gave you. Do you have them?"

"Yes. Probably. On my desk somewhere."

"Would you get them?"

"All right."

"Sir, the pathologist…" Marcy reminded Willis.

"Right. Go get the papers," he told Maggie.

"And you stay here with these people," he ordered Marcy.

Maggie went to her study. There they were, a small pile beside her laptop. She had been too busy since the arrival of her guests to put them in the file she had made for the Greater Gloucestershire Galanthus Group.

She stared at the pages. There was something familiar...

It was the paper. The greyish recycled paper. And the font. Not Times Roman. Not Arial. Something more idiosyncratic.

She opened her briefcase and took out the anonymous letter she had brought with her from Oxford and laid it beside Jonquil's pages.

STONE PALEY SEDUCES INNOCENT YOUNG GIRLS

AND THEN MURDERS THEM

There was no doubt. The paper and the font of the anonymous letter were the same as the documents from the Galanthus group.

So it seemed Jonquil had written the poison pen letters. But why? What did she have against Joshua? How did she even know him? He had certainly not known her. Or he had pretended not to know her, a voice in Maggie's head sounded.

No, she would believe Joshua.

Then she wondered why Jonquil would send her poison pen letters when the woman was also showering her with Galanthus group materials. Surely she would realise Maggie would note the resemblance between the font and paper. Jonquil wasn't that stupid, was she?

Then Maggie realised that Jonquil knew the patron of the Greater Gloucestershire Galanthus Group as Lady Raynham. She had not connected her with Professor Margaret Spence Eliot of Merrion College. Since she had sent letters to the entire senior faculty, Jonquil must have gotten their names from a listing on the college's website. A list which had brief bios but no pictures, if Maggie remembered correctly. The woman would not have known about the overlapping worlds of Merrion and Beaumatin.

The study door opened and Willis appeared.

"Did you find them? The papers?"

"Er, yes. Here they are."

Maggie handed him the documents but held back the anonymous letter.

To distract the detective, she pointed. "It's an updated membership list, a preliminary agenda for the meeting, and the names of people who want to sell their snowdrops at the event."

Willis frowned.

"I agreed to have the kick-off meeting here at Beaumatin. In February."

"I bet his lordship was pleased about that."

"He was less than enthusiastic," Maggie agreed.

The Greater Gloucestershire Galanthus Group

"Anyhow, that's why Jonquil came over. As for her reaction to Joshua, well, he's quite a celebrity. If you google him, you'll get some idea."

"And how do you know him?"

"We were colleagues at Harvard."

Maggie decided Willis did not need to know the entire history of her relationship with Paley. And that his goggle search, if he even did one, would not extend back far enough to uncover the "runaway fiancée" stories in the media.

"And as for Jonquil's body being in Joshua's trunk, er, boot. When did she die?"

"Sometime last night," Willis admitted grudgingly.

"Last night we had a small party. There were eighteen of us here. And Joshua... I doubt he had the opportunity to slip out, meet Jonquil, strangle her, dump her in his boot, and sneak back in. He was the centre of attention."

"I'll need the names..."

Yes, of course. Although you know most of them, too. Thomas' son William and his wife Gweneth. Gweneth's mother Muriel Stonor and Gweneth's uncle Clive Stonor. Anne and Laurence Brooks. Sir John and Lady Nesbitt. Giles Sumner and his wife Celia. And David and Chloe Osborne, the Ainswicks' daughter and son-in-law.

"And although I know you say that people don't always behave rationally after they've killed someone, even if Joshua had been so foolish as to leave a body in the boot of his car, he certainly had time this morning to find someplace better to hide it. Everyone slept in."

"Even his lordship?"

That gave Maggie pause.

"No. He was out on the estate, but doubtless with Ned. Ned Thatcher."

"And you're defending Paley because…"

"Because I know you well enough by this time to be aware of your tells. And I saw how you looked when you heard about Jonquil's reaction to meeting Joshua."

"Humpf."

"I admit I found the woman pushy. And not very likeable. So I would assume other people found her the same. Probably even more so, since she was murdered. But whoever put her in the boot of the Rolls was just taking advantage of an opportunity. There were half a dozen other cars in the drive last night. Joshua's was probably the only one that was unlocked."

"So you say."

"Yes, so I say. You have the papers Jonquil gave me yesterday. Now I need to warn Mrs Cook about having extra guests for lunch. And, since you and your team will most likely still be here, I will ask her to have some refreshments for you as well."

Maggie ushered the detective back into the hall and went to find the housekeeper. The anonymous letter remained unnoticed on her desk.

Chapter Twenty-One

Maggie found Mrs Cook peeling potatoes in the kitchen.

Before she could speak, the woman said, "It's all right, Lady Raynham. I figured there'd be four more for lunch. We're having leg of lamb so there's more than enough. And I have some lamb stew I'm thawing, which will do for the men."

Ned Thatcher, his son Jamie, and Wesley Harding, Thomas's groundsman, usually joined Mrs Cook for their Sunday lunch in the kitchen.

"I know it's a lot to ask, but if you could have something should the police get hungry…"

"The police!" Mrs Cook sniffed.

"DCI Willis is a big fan of your baking. And his new sergeant, Marcy Hickson, is very nice. I met her in Oxford last year."

"I hear it's that Mrs Pilkington who died. Who was always showing up here."

"Yes. But I don't know if she were killed at Beaumatin. It could be that someone also knew she had been coming here often."

"You mean like Mrs Murtaugh?"

Maggie was startled.

"Iris Murtaugh? Kill Jonquil? I really don't think she would. It seems so unlikely."

"Mrs Griggs' cousin Mildred works in the kitchen at Churn Valley College. And she says that it's Mrs Pilkington who wears the pants in that family."

"Really? I only met Mr Pilkington once, but he seemed perfectly nice."

If slightly exasperated, Maggie remembered. She gathered he had not been pleased to have to come all the way over to Beaumatin so that Jonquil could deliver another update on the progress of her snowdrop club which could just as easily have been done by email.

"Mildred says she's not very well liked."

"She was not an easy person," Maggie agreed. She took another mug of coffee and went to find her husband.

Thomas was in his study. He did not smile when she came in.

"Thomas? Willis says Stephen and Brooke and Jersey and Joshua can leave once they've given their statements. But the problem is... The police are keeping Joshua's car. For forensics. So I thought..."

"Yes?"

"I thought I would go back to Oxford after lunch rather than tomorrow morning. And take Stephen and Brooke and Joshua. But the Golf only holds four comfortably. So I wondered if you would drive Jersey to Kemble. She can get a train directly to Paddington from there."

Thomas said nothing but Maggie could tell what he was thinking. And she was out of patience.

"Really, Thomas! Is this going to turn into another case of Franz Bielke? With baseless suspicion and jealousy? It's not Joshua who's the problem, it's you. I've told you that you have absolutely no reason to feel threatened by him. He is a colleague. That's all. For you to act otherwise makes you look ridiculous. And you know what Oxford gossip is like. People will notice and think they're putting two and two together and..."

Thomas threw up his hands.

"All right. You may say your feelings for him are collegial but don't tell me he's not interested in you. Last night. That song. Yesterday? Bloody hell. Tell me that was collegial."

"So he flirted. It's his way. I expect he couldn't resist provoking you. You've made your feelings fairly obvious. And anyway, I think he's..."

Maggie was going to say she thought Joshua was becoming interested in Jersey but stopped herself.

"So will you please take Jersey to Kemble?"

"Yes."

"Thank you."

Maggie turned to go.

"Wait. What do you know about that Pilkington woman's being found in the boot of Paley's car?"

"Nothing. Except that she was found in the boot of Joshua's car. Strangled. Sometime last night."

"Humpf."

"It seems it was opportunistic. Joshua accidently left the car unlocked."

"But why was she at Beaumatin? Do they think it was someone here who…"

"No idea. You'll have to ask Willis."

"Willis."

Maggie decided it was a good moment to tell the others about the plan for lunch and transport.

Chapter twenty-two

Back at Merrion, Maggie said, "Joshua, do you have a moment?"

They went into her rooms.

"Drink?"

"Sure."

When she returned with some whisky for Joshua and white wine for herself, Maggie took the anonymous letter she had brought back from Beaumatin out of her briefcase and passed it over.

"This arrived at Merrion on Thursday."

Joshua read it.

"What the…"

"There have been three sets. The content is all pretty much the same. Stephen has gotten them too. And the rest of the senior faculty. Fortunately we have been able to intercept those."

"Why didn't anyone say anything?"

"Because we didn't believe they were true. I know you and I assured Stephen you were not a murderer and that your taste in females was for twenty-somethings, not undergrads."

"Thanks," Joshua said gruffly.

"But I do think I know who sent them."

"You do?"

"Yes. And that could be a problem."

Maggie had taken some of the papers from the Greater Gloucestershire Galanthus Group with her.

"Look at these."

Joshua scoffed.

"Your snowdrop club?"

"But look. It's the same paper. The same font."

Joshua compared the two pages.

"All right. So…"

"But don't you see? If they're the same, that means it's Jonquil Pilkington who sent the letters."

"Who?"

"The woman who was found murdered."

Joshua was flabbergasted.

"But why? I don't know her from Adam."

"Remember her strange reaction when you were introduced?"

"Oh. Yeah, I guess so. She wouldn't shake hands."

Joshua thought.

"Do you think she's a crank and just picks on someone at random?"

"That's possible, I suppose."

Maggie considered.

"One thing. I won't mention the letters to Willis if I can avoid it."

"Willis?"

"The policeman who's investigating the murder."

"Oh yeah. Him."

"Yes, him. And I'll ask Stephen not to mention them as well."

"Ok. Why?"

"Because Willis might think it gives you a motive."

"A motive?"

"You and I know they're not true. But Willis doesn't."

"But I never met the woman until yesterday. Or knew about the letters until you told me."

"I know."

"I don't like this, Elle. What should I do?"

Maggie thought.

"Do nothing. Act innocent."

"I am innocent!"

"Let me know if you hear from Willis. Meanwhile, I realise I don't know very much about Jonquil. Maybe writing anonymous letters was a hobby of hers. Or if she fixated on you for some specific reason."

"Like she's a celebrity troll?"

"It's possible. You're famous enough."

The thought made Joshua grin. His mobile sounded.

He looked at the screen.

"K. Er, thanks, Elle. Excuse me. I need to take this."

Joshua got up and moved towards the door, but not before Maggie had seen the screen. The caller ID read, "Jersey."

That was fast work, Maggie thought. She just hoped Stephen had meant what he said about deciding that Jersey should be "just a friend." And it would be great if Jersey were able to distract Joshua from herself.

Chapter Twenty-Three

Not putting off until tomorrow what she could do today, as her mother would recommend, Maggie switched on her laptop and went to work as soon as Joshua left.

She tried the obvious first, and googled Jonquil Pilkington.

There was not a lot about Jonquil. A mention that she was an alumna of her Cheltenham women's college. A couple of articles she had written for the Snowdrop Society newsletter. Maggie checked these out, but as they were technical discussions of the growing requirements of two of the woman's favourite Galanthus, they were not very useful.

Maggie went on Facebook and searched for Jonquil Pilkington. There was only one person with that name.

Jonquil had a page that was open for public perusal. Maggie checked the posts. Cutesy cat videos. Pictures of snowdrops. Photos of Churn Valley College in various seasons of the year. A Christmas tree. No shared memory of "A poison pen letter I wrote about the Churn Valley College's librarian two years ago." In fact, the entries only went back eighteen months.

Maggie thought, then googled Mark Pilkington and got a surprise. Mark had his own page in Wikipedia.

Mark was born in Winchester, where his father was a canon at the cathedral, and he had attended the famous public school there. He had graduated from Oxford with a first and become a junior research fellow at Merrion College but left after two years to take a position at the University of Bristol. That was short. The position at Merrion had not worked out.

Maggie did some quick calculations. Perhaps Andrew Kittredge might remember him. Mrs Steeples must have also known the junior fellow.

Most of the rest of the article focussed on Mark's bestselling book on English history. That was impressive. She considered downloading it onto her Kindle, then decided it could wait. She had more important things to do.

A daughter was mentioned. Rosamunde. Dead at twenty. There was no information given about the cause of her death.

Maggie googled Rosamunde Pilkington and was surprised and saddened by the result. Half a dozen newspaper articles reported on the suicide of the young woman who had been a sophomore at Simmons College in Boston. Was Rosamunde the girl mentioned in the anonymous letters who had been seduced and murdered? But the news articles seemed definite that her death was a suicide.

Before shutting down her computer and heading to the house on Hereford Crescent, Maggie did a final search for Iris Murtaugh. Nothing on Google. Nothing on Facebook. The woman was as much a cypher on the Internet as she was in person.

The Greater Gloucestershire Galanthus Group

Chapter twenty-four

The next morning, Maggie stopped by the Master's Lodge.

Mrs Steeples looked up.

"The Master is not here."

"That's all right. I wanted to talk to you."

"Yes?"

"Do you remember a Mark Pilkington? He was here…"

"Pilkington? Yes, indeed I do,"

Mrs Steeples tone expressed her distaste.

"He was here only two years as a junior fellow, then he left. I wondered what happened."

"Why?"

One of Mrs Steeples virtues was that she was not a gossip.

"His wife died yesterday. At Beaumatin. Perhaps Professor Draycott mentioned it? And I wanted to make sure I did the appropriate thing."

Maggie figured appealing to Mrs Steeples sense of propriety was the best way to get information.

"No, the Master hasn't said anything. But if the woman's dead, good riddance."

Maggie was shocked by the secretary's venom.

"Really?"

"The problem wasn't Pilkington. It was her!"

"Jonquil?"

"A stupid name for a stupid woman."

"What did she do?"

"She was a nightmare. Always complaining. Her husband's rooms weren't good enough. Another junior fellow's were better. The heat in their university housing—they were privileged to have gotten university housing!—was inadequate. The cooker wasn't new enough."

"Unpleasant."

"But the final straw was at a feast night. Jonquil bumped into Lady Crista and spilled sherry down her dress. Lady Crista had to go change—the dress was ruined—and the Pilkington never apologized. Claimed it was Lady Crista's fault and that she should have looked where she was going!"

Lady Crista was the wife of Alastair Carrington, the former Master, whose memory was scared to Mrs Steeples.

"She went on a campaign making disparaging remarks about both Lady Crista and the Master to anyone who would listen. Her husband was mortified but there was nothing he could do. Not surprisingly, his fellowship was not renewed."

Maggie shook her head. She liked Lady Crista and Carrington had been a most able Master.

"I don't suppose the Pilkington changed very much. Those sorts of women rarely do."

"No, she hadn't," Maggie confirmed. "Thank you."

Mrs Steeples returned to her work. Maggie wondered what the woman would say if she knew that it was Jonquil who had written the anonymous letters.

Maggie's next stop was Andrew Kittredge's rooms.

Overweight and balding, Andrew Kittredge was in his fifties and one of the worst dressed men in Oxford. He was also a leading expert on the often inaccurate economic figures of developing nations and was frequently asked to consult in Malawi, Tajikistan, and Papua New Guinea when they needed to calculate their inflation rate or GNP.

Kittredge was moody and one could never be certain if he would be grumpy or jovial. She knocked.

"Come."

Maggie was relieved to find that it was one of Andrew's cheerful days.

"Hi, Andrew."

"Maggie! What brings you here?" he asked in surprise.

While Maggie had great respect for Andrew's capabilities, they rarely interacted outside of faculty events.

"A question. Would you happen to remember a junior fellow from a quarter century back? A Mark Pilkington? You were here at the same time."

"Pilkington? Hmm…"

"Modern history," Maggie prompted.

"History. Oh. Yes. Pilkington. Yes. Quite brilliant. Should have gone far. Pity what happened."

"What did happen?"

"It was his wife. Some ridiculous name…"

"Jonquil."

"Something like that. Terrible wife for an academic. Not like my good lady. Anyhow she got into it with Lady Crista. The result? His fellowship wasn't renewed."

Andrew frowned.

"He did do something noteworthy later."

"He wrote a book on British history. A spoof. It was a best seller."

"Oh. Right. Too bad. He could have gone far," he repeated.

Maggie thought that writing a best seller was not negligible but reminded herself that this was Oxford.

"Thank you, Andrew."

"No problem."

Andrew turned back to the spreadsheets of figures that littered his desk.

CHAPTER TWENTY-FIVE

Maggie was back at Beaumatin. She came into the kitchen for her morning coffee, took a sip, and winced.

Mrs Cook noticed.

"A problem, Lady Raynham?"

"Yes. No. Well, a bit of a toothache. But I'm sure it will go away."

Mrs Cook frowned.

"You should see a dentist."

"A dentist?"

"Yes. It's whom people see when they have a toothache."

"I don't know any dentists. At least not around here. I usually go when I'm in Boston."

"Humpf."

Maggie took another cautious sip of coffee and winced again.

"There's a good man in Cheltenham. I'll call and make an appointment."

"Would you? Thank you."

Late that afternoon, Maggie walked into the practice of Doctors Woods and Perry. Even after having taken several Nurofen capsules, she was miserable.

A perky blonde who could not have been more than twenty greeted her.

"Lady Raynham? Dr Woods is out today. A family bereavement. So you'll be seeing Doctor Perry. Please have a seat and you'll be called."

"Thank you."

Twenty minutes later, the receptionist called out, "Lady Raynham, Room 4 please."

This caused curious looks from the others in the waiting room.

Doctor Perry turned out to be a cheerful brunette in her late thirties.

To make conversation while the woman arranged various instruments that reminded Maggie of the medieval implements that she had seen in Beaumatin's dungeon, she asked, "The receptionist said Dr Woods lost a family member?"

"Oh yes. It's terrible. His daughter. They're saying she was murdered."

This caught Maggie's attention.

"Really?"

"The poor man. Five years ago his wife died. Cancer. Then two years ago his granddaughter died. And now Jonquil..."

"Jonquil? Jonquil Pilkington?"

"Yes."

"I know her. Knew her."

"A friend?" Dr Woods asked cautiously.

"More an acquaintance."

Thus relieved, Dr Perry settled in for a good gossip while she pressed a peddle on the floor and Maggie's chair reclined.

"Say ah."

"Ah."

"After Dr Woods' wife died, Jonquil would come in here and find fault with everything. The magazines in the waiting room were not arranged attractively. The water in the cooler was not as good as the kind they got at the college. Our uniforms were not ironed properly. It got so everyone dreaded seeing her. One of the hygienists would hide in a closet to avoid her.

"It got worse after her daughter died. Poor girl. She was studying in America. Got depressed and jumped in a river. The police said they had no doubt it was suicide, but Jonquil refused to believe them. She insisted that some man had killed the girl because he had gotten her pregnant. She became obsessed."

Dr Perry poked and prodded and Maggie winced.

She poked some more, then said, "Rinse."

Maggie rinsed.

"I'm afraid you need a root canal. The lower first molar. I'll give you a prescription. Make an appointment and I want to see you back here as soon as possible."

Dr Perry raised the chair.

Back at reception, Maggie was surprised to see DCI Willis. He was talking to an attractive woman in her thirties wearing a blue tunic. A name tag said, "Debbie."

"DCI Willis. Hello."

Willis looked equally surprised. And slightly embarrassed.

"Hello, er, Lady Raynham. What are you doing here?"

"It seems I'm going to need a root canal."

"My sympathies. Er, Maggie, this is Debbie Mullins. She's a friend. And one of the hygienists here. Debbie, this is Lady Raynham."

"Maggie, please," said Maggie, shaking hands.

While Maggie made an appointment, she heard Willis say, "So Friday then," and Debbie reply, "Great. I'll cook."

Willis walked Maggie to her car.

"So, Maggie. Is it just a coincidence that you're here or are you sleuthing again?"

"Just a coincidence, I promise. Mrs Cook made the appointment. I had no idea Jonquil was Dr Woods' daughter."

"Humpf."

Maggie could tell Willis was sceptical.

"Really."

To divert Willis, she added, "Debbie seems very nice."

The detective flushed and mumbled something.

"I know you can't tell me any specifics, but are you getting any further on your investigation into Jonquil's death?"

Willis grunted.

"She was a very difficult woman, from what I hear. The kind that makes enemies."

"So you are sleuthing."

"No! But when there's been a murder… Well, people talk."

"People talk. So tell me what you've heard."

"She was intrusive. Bossy. At the college and at the dental office. You know of course she was Doctor Woods' daughter."

"Yes."

"And did you know that when her husband was a junior fellow at Merrion, she antagonized the Master's wife to the point that his fellowship was not renewed."

"At Merrion? That's your college. And Draycott's. And Paley's."

"Yes. But it was decades ago. The only people who are still around who were there at the time are Professor Kittredge and Mrs Steeples, the Master's secretary."

"Humpf."

"What about Jonquil's husband, Mark? Have you spoken with him?"

"Of course. He was working alone in his office during the crucial period. He has no alibi."

"He probably didn't know he would need an alibi," Maggie pointed out.

"That's exactly what he said. And he has no motive."

Maggie debated telling Willis about the anonymous letters, then decided against it. She was sure Joshua had had nothing to do with the murder and it was bad enough that Jonquil's body had been found in his car boot.

Her jaw throbbed. Maggie winced.

Willis noticed.

"Root canal, huh? Have fun with that."

Chapter twenty-six

Mrs Cook had the day off. Maggie decided she would cook Chinese but needed a ginger grater. There was a kitchenware shop in Stowe-on-the-Wold Anne had told her about. Thomas was out on the estate. She would go check it out.

Scotts did not have a ginger grater, but Maggie found some other small gadgets that looked useful. She was heading back to her car when she saw someone she knew.

"Iris!"

The woman's eyes were red. She slumped and her coat was misbuttoned. She looked like she had lost her best friend. Maggie reflected that in fact she had.

"Iris!" Maggie called again.

Iris jumped and looked around nervously.

"Iris. Hi. It's Maggie."

"Oh. Lady Raynham."

She sounded relieved.

"Please call me Maggie, Iris. How are you?"

"I'm... I'm..."

Iris' eyes filled with tears.

"You must miss Jonquil."

Maggie tried to sound sympathetic.

Iris nodded.

"How about having some tea?"

Maggie might not have been able to find a ginger grater in Stowe, but it seemed like every other storefront was a tea shop.

Maggie led Iris to one she thought looked promising and sat her down at a small table by the window. She ordered a cappuccino. Iris asked for English Breakfast and some chocolate cake. Iris had a sweet tooth.

The women were silent until their orders came.

Iris took a bite of cake, then asked, "Is it true what they're saying? That Jonquil was murdered? Strangled?"

"Yes."

"At Beaumatin?"

"Well, she was found at Beaumatin. We had a group of people to dinner that night. I think the killer decided to leave her body there to confuse things."

Iris flinched at the mention of Jonquil's body.

"She wasn't killed at Beaumatin?"

"I don't know. And the police aren't sure."

Iris looked unhappy and pushed the plate of cake away.

"Jonquil was my best friend. I would never have gotten through school without her. The girls could be so mean. She protected me."

Maggie nodded. She could see that, from Iris' perspective, Jonquil's more unpleasant traits were virtues.

"You mustn't think we won't go ahead with the snowdrop group. It will be Jonquil's legacy."

"Of course."

Iris poured the rest of the pot of tea into her cup.

"Iris, do you have any idea who might have killed Jonquil?"

Iris thought.

"I know she was difficult. People disliked her. But kill her? No. Except... She was killed on Saturday night?"

"Yes."

"Oh. Because... Because... That evening I went to see Jonquil and..."

A man suddenly appeared beside their table.

Iris gasped and shrank back.

But it was only Mark Pilkington.

"Hello, Iris. Lady Raynham," he said softly.

Maggie rose.

"Hello, Mark. I'm so sorry about Jonquil."

Mark's shoulders sagged and his face crumpled. He took a deep breath.

"Twenty-four years. We were married twenty-four years. I don't know what I'm going to do without her. Or how I'm going to tell the students and faculty."

He gave a shuddering sigh.

Maggie put her hand on his arm.

"Won't you join us? We're just having tea."

Mark took another deep breath and straightened.

"Thank you. But I just came in to get some carrot cake. They make wonderful carrot cake here. It was one of Jonquil's and my special treats…"

Mark was overcome again and blinked rapidly.

"Or perhaps some other time…"

He turned and quickly walked out.

Maggie realised that Iris had been sitting stiffly and had not said a word to her friend's husband.

"Iris?"

"He's very sad for someone who hated his wife."

"What?"

"I know people think I'm strange. They feel sorry for me. Because I'm not very outgoing. Or talkative. But that means I listen to people. I'm not just waiting for someone to finish speaking so I can say something myself. It gives me a lot of opportunities to observe. To learn things about people. And I've watched Mark and Jonquil. He didn't like her. And I know he blamed her for Rosamunde's death."

"Rosamunde? Their daughter?"

"Yes."

Maggie wondered. Could Mark have murdered his wife? He had seemed genuinely grief stricken.

Maggie put her thoughts into words.

"You don't think Mark might have…"

"I don't know. He wasn't… When I went…"

Iris stopped herself.

"I don't know."

Iris stood and put five pounds on the table.

"I need to go. My husband will be wondering what has happened to me."

Iris' husband. A farmer. Maggie couldn't imagine what he was like. Was he a cheerful extrovert? Or as laconic as his wife? Maggie pictured dinners eaten in silence in a dim farmhouse kitchen.

The woman had certainly given Maggie some things to think about.

Susan Alexander

Chapter twenty-seven

Maggie was about to shut down her laptop and set out for Hereford Crescent when Joshua appeared at her door. He was pale and breathing heavily.

"Maggie. My god. Maggie…"

"Joshua? What is it?"

"You have to come."

"Come? What's the matter" Come where?"

"My rooms."

Maggie fleetingly wondered if this were a ploy to get her into his rooms, which she had so far managed to avoid. But no. Joshua was genuinely upset.

She stood and followed him up the stairs.

At the door, he gestured for her to enter.

A woman's body lay prone on a sofa. Maggie's mind generated several explanations as to why a woman would be lying stretched out on Joshua's sofa until she saw who it was.

Iris. It was Iris Murtaugh.

A tie was wrapped tightly around her neck. Just like Jonquil Pilkington.

"Oh no. Iris."

"You know her?"

"Yes. She's a friend of the woman we found in your car boot."

"But what the hell... Why..."

Maggie sensed Joshua was about to break down.

"We should get out of here. Don't touch anything. Lock the door and come downstairs with me."

Back in her rooms, Maggie poured Joshua a generous glass of whisky.

"Tell me what happened."

"I was out to dinner with Roddy Hancock. He's a fellow at New College. I left here around six. When I came back, I found her. She was just... there."

Joshua downed half of his whisky.

"I'm going to call Stephen. And then I'm going to call DCI Willis," Maggie announced.

"Who?"

"The detective in charge of Jonquil Pilkington's murder."

"You think they're connected?"

"Of course they're connected."

Maggie called Stephen on his mobile.

"Stephen, we have an emergency. Can you come to my rooms right away, please?"

Stephen grumbled, but agreed to come over.

"What's so important?" he asked when he arrived.

"Come up to Joshua's rooms."

Stephen looked irritated.

"Please, Stephen."

They climbed the stairs. Joshua unlocked his door.

"Go on," Maggie urged, as Stephen hesitated.

"Good god."

Stephen peered at Iris.

"She looks just like… She looks like the woman in the car boot."

"It's Iris Murtaugh. She's the best friend of the woman in the boot."

"What's she doing here?"

"We have no idea."

"We have to call the police," Stephen reluctantly concluded.

"I'm going to call DCI Willis," Maggie announced. "But I wanted to let you know first."

"Willis? Not the local police?"

"I think this is connected to the other murder. It has to be."

Stephen looked down at the body. He noted the tie. Another Merrion repp.

"Stone, do you recognize this tie?" he asked.

Joshua took a step forward, squinted, and took a step back.

"No."

"It's not yours?"

"A striped tie? Me?"

Joshua smiled briefly.

"We should get out of here. And I need to call Willis," Maggie reminded the men.

"What? Oh. Yes. Of course."

Stephen had to force himself to stop staring at the corpse.

Back in her rooms, Maggie gave the men some whisky, then dialled the detective, who was in her contact list.

"Willis."

"Sorry to bother you at this hour. It's Maggie Eliot. Er, Raynham…"

"I know it's you. What is it? Find another body?"

"I'm afraid so."

There was dead silence, then, "And do you know whose body it is?"

"Yes. It's Iris Murtaugh."

"Iris… Who?"

"Iris Murtaugh. She was Jonquil Pilkington's best friend. Had you interviewed her?"

"No."

Another pause. Maggie could hear Willis moving around.

"Where is she?"

"That's the problem. She's in Oxford. In Joshua Paley's rooms. I know it's out of your jurisdiction, but she's been strangled. With a necktie. Just like Jonquil. The deaths have to be connected. So I thought I should call you and that you could contact the local police. Unless you want me to."

Willis grunted.

"Maybe DS Hickson knows who the best person would be to contact."

Willis grunted again.

"I'll be in my rooms. They're on the same staircase as Professor Paley's. He and Stephen Draycott are here with me too. The porter can direct you."

"Right. I'll need to make some calls, but I'll try to get there as soon as possible. And I'll alert the locals."

"Thank you."

"Make sure the room is..."

"It's locked," Maggie assured him and ended the call.

"Willis is taking care of things. I just hope we can avoid Inspector Moss."

"Morse?" asked Joshua.

"No. Moss. An unpleasant bungler."

"You wouldn't care for him, Stone," Stephen confirmed.

Maggie poured the men some more whisky and they settled in to wait.

Chapter twenty-eight

The pathologist and his crew were the first to arrive. Joshua showed them up to his rooms and unlocked the door, then returned. A police constable was stationed outside Maggie's door.

The detective inspector was a surprise. Brenda Bartlett was a short, dark, intense woman in her early forties. She peeked in Maggie's door, barked a brusque, "You all stay here. I'll be back," and disappeared.

When she returned fifteen minutes later, she was accompanied by a young man. In his twenties and conservatively dressed in a good navy suit, he had brown hair and intelligent hazel eyes. Maggie thought there was something familiar about him. Had he been a student? She knew the police recruited the occasional university graduate for fast tracking.

"Well, then," began the woman. "I'm Detective Inspector Bartlett and this is Detective Sergeant Dexter. We..."

"Dexter? Are you any relation to DCI Dexter of the Met?" interrupted Maggie, who realised why she thought she had recognised the sergeant.

Bartlett glared and the sergeant looked embarrassed.

"Yes, he's my uncle," Dexter admitted reluctantly.

"That's all very nice, but a woman's been murdered. How about we focus on that," Bartlett snapped. "Now, who are you people?"

"This is Professor Draycott, who is the Master of Merrion College, this is Professor Paley, in whose rooms the body was found, and I'm Professor Eliot," said Maggie.

"Right."

Bartlett turned to Paley.

"So who is the woman? Did you kill her?" she demanded.

Joshua raised his eyebrows and stretched out his long legs. He was wearing his signature cowboy boots, a good suit, and a shirt Maggie recognised as custom made by Charvet, another fact he avoided publicizing to his admirers.

"I have no idea who she is and no, I did not kill her. I was out to dinner and I found her in my rooms when I returned. Professor Eliot knows her, though."

"Professor Eliot?"

"Her name is Iris Murtaugh. She lives... somewhere in Gloucestershire. I'm not sure where, exactly. I can't imagine what she was doing in Oxford."

"Was Murtaugh a friend of yours?"

"More an acquaintance. She is a member of a group with which I am associated."

"What group?"

"A group of snowdrop enthusiasts."

"Are you having me on?"

"Snowdrops are very popular right now. It's a craze," Dexter explained.

Bartlett muttered something.

"So you don't know her?" she asked Joshua again.

"No."

"You never met? You're sure?"

"Yes. I am certain I never met the woman."

"Then what was she doing in your room?"

"I have no idea."

"Your room wasn't locked?"

"Er, no. I gather people rarely lock their doors at Merrion."

Bartlett scowled.

"And you? You've never met her? Or seen her?" she asked Stephen.

"N, never."

Bartlett turned to Maggie.

"So you're the only one who has any connection to Miss Murtaugh."

"Mrs. It's Mrs Murtaugh."

"Whatever. Answer the question."

"I'm sure Mrs Murtaugh has many friends and acquaintances. But none that I know who are at Merrion."

"And why is the Gloucestershire Constabulary interested in a corpse in Oxford?"

Maggie, Stephen, and Joshua exchanged glances. Bartlett noticed.

"What is it?"

"Last weekend a friend of Iris was murdered in Gloucestershire."

"Who was that?"

"Jonquil Pilkington."

Bartlett scoffed at the name.

At that moment, DCI Willis and DS Hickson came in.

"DI Bartlett? DCI Willis. And I assume you know DS Hickson."

The former colleagues greeted each other.

"Draycott, Paley," Willis acknowledged the men.

The DCI nodded at Maggie. He had visited her at the Hereford Crescent townhouse on a previous case but had never been in her rooms at Merrion. He looked around and thought the rooms suited her. Certainly more than the baronial grandeur of Beaumatin.

"Professor Eliot here was just going to explain what your interest was in all this. But perhaps you can enlighten me."

"It's related to a murder we're investigating. Jonquil Pilkington. Your corpse was Pilkington's best friend. I understand they were both strangled with a necktie. And they have another thing in common. You found the woman in the rooms of Paley here. We found our victim in the boot of Paley's car."

Everyone looked at Joshua.

"At Lady Raynham's stately home in the Cotswolds," Willis added.

"Lady Raynham?" Dexter asked.

Maggie had hoped that her title would not come up.

"My married name," she explained.

"So that's another commonality. You knew both women and one was killed at your home and one at your, er, workplace."

"We're not sure Pilkington was killed at Beaumatin. She could have just been dumped there," Hickson pointed out.

"Dumped in the boot of your car?" Bartlett asked Paley.

"Yes. I apparently left it unlocked."

"Yeah. He left a Rolls Phantom unlocked," Hickson informed her former colleagues.

Bartlett looked at Paley in disbelief.

"You have something against using keys?"

Joshua shrugged irritably.

"When can I get back in my rooms?" he asked.

"Your rooms where a murder was committed? And where we need to do a meticulous forensic analysis?"

"Yes."

"In a day or two. Or three."

"And what am I supposed to do?" Joshua demanded.

"It's all right, Stone. You can stay with me at the Master's Lodge. I'm sure we can find you some pyjamas and an extra toothbrush," Stephen assured him.

"And what about what I need for my work? My books. My papers…"

"Use the Internet," Bartlett said unsympathetically.

"And Professor Draycott, I assume you have CCTV. I'll need to see the tapes from today," she added.

"I'll speak to the porter. He can arrange that."

Dexter murmured to the DI.

"Right. Sergeant Dexter has reminded me. Where were you from mid-afternoon until you called DCI Willis."

"I was in the Master's Lodge. Except for an hour when I was in hall for dinner," Stephen said.

"And who can confirm that?"

"My secretary, Mrs Steeples, when I was in the Lodge, and the entire college during dinner."

"And you, Professor Paley?"

"I was in my rooms, then I had dinner at New College with Professor Hancock. On my return I found the woman, her body, and I immediately ran down and told Professor Eliot."

"Why Professor Eliot? Why not call the police?"

"She's my… a friend. And I'm still getting used to things here."

"And where were you before you were 'here'?"

Bartlett made quotation signs with her fingers.

"Harvard. That's in the U.S..."

"I know where Harvard is."

"And you?" Bartlett turned to Maggie.

"I was here. Working."

"Through dinner?"

"Yes."

"Can anyone confirm that?"

"No."

"Huh. Did you hear anyone on the stairs?"

"People go up and down the stairs all day. And night. I've learned to tune it out. Sorry."

Maggie knew this was not what the detective wanted to hear, but tough tuna. So she had no alibi. Surely no one could suspect she had any reason to kill either woman.

Susan Alexander

Chapter twenty-nine

Someone rapped on the door. Without waiting for a "Come," Thomas burst in.

He stopped abruptly and scowled as he surveyed the company. He found Maggie.

"We waited dinner for an hour," he began.

"Thomas..."

"And you are?" demanded Bartlett.

"This is Lord Raynham," explained Willis.

"Hi, Lord. Welcome to the party," said Joshua.

"We've had a bit of unpleasantness," put in Stephen.

Maggie regarded her husband. He was looking what she called very "twenty-eighth baron." He was also furious.

"Willis?"

"A woman's been murdered," the detective said.

"Iris. Iris Murtaugh. You remember. Jonquil Pilkington's quiet friend," Maggie reminded him.

"And so?"

"She was murdered here. At Merrion," Maggie explained.

"And your rooms have been commandeered by the police as their incident room?"

"Raynham, you can see we have the same group of... people," Willis just stopped himself from saying suspects,

"As were around when Jonquil Pilkington was murdered So naturally we need to talk to them."

"Did you know Murtaugh?" Bartlett demanded.

"Know? I had met the woman once. No, in fact, I saw her a second time. Briefly."

"Well, since you're here, would you tell us where you were from mid-afternoon until now?"

Maggie worried about how Thomas would respond. To her relief, he took a deep breath, then said coldly, "I was out on my estate. Ned Thatcher, my foreman, can confirm that. I went back to my home and changed. Mrs Cook, my housekeeper, can confirm that. I drove into Oxford to my house on Hereford Crescent, where I waited in vain for my wife. Mrs Royce, my housekeeper there, can confirm that. When Lady Raynham failed to appear for dinner, I came here to find her."

Maggie wondered if Thomas had come unannounced assuming he would find her with Joshua. Which he had. Although not in the way he had expected. She was thankful Stephen was there as well.

"My dear, get your things. We're going."

Maggie flushed with embarrassment.

Joshua gave her a look she interpreted as, "You prefer this jerk to me?"

She glanced at Willis in appeal.

"It's all right, Maggie. We know where to find you. And you gentlemen may leave as well. If it's all right with DI Bartlett."

The Greater Gloucestershire Galanthus Group

"Yes. Go. But I'll see you all again after we have the pathologist's report."

"And that will be? Stephen asked.

"Tomorrow, I hope."

Maggie quickly put her laptop in a briefcase, took a coat and hat, and followed Thomas out into the quad.

The rain, which had been torrential during the day, had slowed to a steady drizzle. As she trudged back to Hereford Crescent beside her husband, she thought about Iris. Quiet Iris. With her surprising revelations in the tea shop. Nervous. Cowering when Mark Pilkington suddenly materialised. Had she been afraid of the man or was she just startled by his unexpected appearance?

Why had Iris been murdered? Had she known something that made her a threat to the murderer? And why was the murderer trying to frame Joshua?

Did the murders have anything to do with the snowdrop group? Both chair and vice chair were dead. Did Colonel Aspinall have such a burning desire to head the group that he was prepared to murder two people?

No. Joshua had nothing to do with the snowdrop group. This had to do with Jonquil. The writer of the anonymous letters. Which had stopped when she died. The murderer was aware of a link between Jonquil and Joshua which would give him a motive for killing the woman. Did the murderer know Jonquil was writing the anonymous letters and about what was in them? Did Iris also know about the letters? Maggie regretted not having asked her.

They reached the Hereford Crescent townhouse. Thomas unlocked the door.

"Did you have dinner?" Maggie asked.

"No."

"Do you want…"

"I asked Mrs Royce to keep it warm."

Maggie followed Thomas down the back stairs into the kitchen, where a cottage pie was waiting in the Aga.

Thomas served and poured some Saint-Emilion.

He had finished half his portion when he pushed his plate away and said, "I thought we agreed you were going stay here and not in your rooms."

Maggie wondered briefly whether the adage "Never apologize, never explain," applied here. But this was probably not a good moment to test that.

"I had worked late and was just preparing to leave when Iris' body was discovered."

"Humpf."

"And I did not expect you until tomorrow.'

Thomas frowned and drank some wine.

"You have your study here if you need to work late."

Maggie had had it, as her mother would say.

"Thomas is this about Joshua? Or is it about my working at all?"

"You don't need to work, you know. I can only assume…"

"That you're not enough for me?"

Maggie was aghast at the turn the conversation had taken. She stifled the impulse to say, "You knew who I was when you married me," as being beyond cliché. She also was not going to mention how much the estate absorbed his attention. Or to remind him how badly he had reacted when he had been asked to consider the date at which he would turn over Beaumatin to William to avoid death duties. A date which had still not been decided, as far as she knew.

"You've made that obvious," Thomas said. He emptied his glass and stalked out of the room.

Maggie felt sick. Reluctant to leave the dishes for Mrs Royce, she washed up and put the remaining cottage pie in the refrigerator. She considered having more wine, but she was not fond of Saint-Emilion, so she recorked the bottle.

Upstairs she heard the drone of the TV behind the closed library door. She wondered how much Laphroaig Thomas was consuming. Well, it was his hangover.

She went to bed.

Susan Alexander

Chapter thirty

They drove back to Beaumatin separately, Maggie in her Golf and Thomas in the Land Rover.

Maggie had to stop for petrol, so Thomas got there first. By the time Maggie arrived, he had changed into his riding clothes and was out on the estate.

She went into the kitchen to say hello to Mrs Cook and get some coffee. Freya and Loki, Tibetan mastiffs that acted as Beaumatin's guard dogs, were there and indicated their pleasure at seeing her in their low-key way.

It was a sunny day and Maggie decided to take her coffee and the dogs into the gardens, which should be Thomas-free. Her husband would be with the sheep. And Ned.

"I'll be in the gardens, Mrs Cook. I have my mobile if you need me."

The gardens had mobile reception. Many parts of the estate did not.

Maggie wandered aimlessly, accompanied by the dogs, who stopped to sniff and mark. Some of the summer perennials were still flowering and birch leaves were turning yellow. She turned a corner and was surprised to see snowdrops. And pink and lavender cyclamen.

Maggie remembered that there were autumn flowering snowdrops. Reginae-olgae, after the Greek queen who was Prince Philip's grandmother. She bent over to read a label. "Pink Panther." A strange name for a snowdrop. She was sure there was some story behind it. She would have to check.

Or would she? She felt as though with Thomas, enough was never enough. She had resigned the Appleton fellowship and taken her current position so she could spend more time with her husband at Beaumatin. She had also rented out her comfortable flat and moved into the Hereford Crescent townhouse so Thomas could come to Oxford when the demands of the estate permitted. She had yet to find Beaumatin, which she referred to as "an ancestral museum" or the townhouse very congenial. She was a reluctant participant in the Church Ladies' Guild and had even opened a church fete. She had agreed to be involved in Jonquil's snowdrop group in the belief that Thomas wanted her to do that. And she went out of her way to be on good terms with Thomas' children and their families, with the exception of his daughter Constance. But there was nothing she could do about the woman's enmity.

Then there was Thomas' jealousy of Joshua. Who was not the first man of whom he had had groundless suspicions. And Joshua was not going away anytime soon. The Appleton fellowship was an open-ended appointment. Joshua could be at Merrion for decades. She just had to hope Thomas would get over it.

She was certainly not going to give up her career to be someone's wife, any more than she would ask Thomas to give up Beaumatin. At least until he had to for tax reasons. Was he that insecure? Perhaps he needed more attention, although she already felt that, except for when she needed to be at Oxford, he pretty much had things his own way. But if going the second mile, as Saint Matthew had it, would help, then she would do it. Anything to improve the situation.

Maggie heard footsteps on gravel and the dogs became alert. She saw DCI Willis coming towards her.

Willis pointed to the flowers.

"Snowdrops? I thought they came out in February."

"These are reginae-olgae. They flower in the autumn. And the cyclamen hederifolium as well," Maggie explained.

"Humpf."

He squatted down for a closer look.

"I see you've become an expert."

"Hard to avoid," Maggie gestured at the gardens.

Willis looked at Maggie. She looked tired. And sad. After the performance his lordship had given the night before, he thought he could guess why.

"I want to talk to you about the murders. I'm hoping you may have some insights."

"Insights?"

"You're the only person who knew—or claims they knew—our two victims. And you also know Paley. And the others. Jones. Draycott. Your niece."

"And you'd like to eliminate them from your inquiries?" Maggie smiled.

"I'd like to solve two brutal murders. Strangling's an ugly business. It takes time for the victim to die. They struggle."

Maggie winced.

"All right. You've made your point."

She led Willis to a pergola covered with wisteria vines. There was a bench underneath and she indicated that the detective should sit. She settled beside him.

"I met Jonquil Pilkington a few weeks ago. I can give you the exact date if that helps, but I'd have to check my agenda. She came to Beaumatin accompanied by Iris Murtaugh. Jonquil asked if I would be the patron of a snowdrop club she was forming. She called it the Greater Gloucestershire Galanthus Group. I agreed, under the impression that Thomas wanted me to accept. It turned out he didn't. I later learned that Jonquil had already asked Lady Ainswick, who declined. So they had to settle for a mere baroness.

"Jonquil tried to be ingratiating, but she was quick to take advantage and manoeuvred me into agreeing to have their first executive committee meeting at Beaumatin the following week. Iris, on the other hand, said almost nothing. Just smiled and nodded.

"The committee meeting. We met in the dining room. I can give you a list of names of the attendees. Again, Jonquil managed to get me to agree that they could have their first meeting at Beaumatin in February.

"I hope I don't seem too spineless. And Thomas is trying to commercialise Beaumatin's snowdrops. I did draw the line at their having a lunch here. They expect as many as one hundred galanthophiles. I can give you a list of the members... Oh, I already did. It was in the papers Jonquil gave me that Saturday."

Maggie paused. Did she want to tell Willis about the anonymous letters? Had Stephen already told him?

"Tom, may I trust you?" she asked.

At the use of his first name, Willis looked at her suspiciously.

"Are you going to tell me you know who did it?"

"No. But what I'm going to tell you might make you suspect someone whom I'm sure is innocent. Is being framed."

"Paley?"

Maggie nodded.

"So tell me."

"Did Stephen Draycott mention the anonymous letters?"

Willis scowled.

"No."

"Don't blame him. Stephen is someone who tries to avoid what he calls unpleasantness."

"Humpf."

"I got one on the day I returned to Oxford for Michaelmas term. So did Stephen and the rest of Merrion's senior faculty. Only Stephen intercepted those, as well as a second set. A third set came just before Jonquil was murdered. And there have been none since."

"What did they say, these anonymous letters?"

"That Paley is a murderer and seduces young girls."

Willis glared at Maggie.

"And you didn't think you should tell me this?"

"I am now."

The detective was about to threaten Maggie about the consequences of withholding evidence when he reflected that she was telling him now and sooner than she usually did in an investigation.

"I have one in my study I can give you. Stephen has the rest."

"And Draycott didn't do anything? He didn't report this?"

"No. As I said, trying to avoid unpleasantness."

"That's worked out well."

"But there's more. You see, I'm fairly sure the letters came from Jonquil Pilkington. They're on the same paper as the documents from the snowdrop group. It's this greyish, recycled stuff. It's very distinctive. And they use the same unusual font."

"So you're saying Pilkington wrote the anonymous letters?"

"It looks that way. To think two people might have used the same paper and same font would be too much of a coincidence. Unless, of course, it was someone else at Churn Valley College."

"Anonymous letters accusing him of murder and—what did you say—seducing young girls? Which could mean underage girls. That certainly gives Paley a motive."

"But Joshua didn't know about the letters."

"He could have received one."

"Stephen had the porter intercept all the letters. They were quite easy to identify. And none was addressed to Joshua. And how would he have known they were the work of Jonquil Pilkington? I only knew because of the

The Greater Gloucestershire Galanthus Group

similarities between the letters and the snowdrop group papers."

"And what about Iris?"

"Iris? Poor Iris. I had tea with her a few days ago in Stowe. For once she had something to say. But she was nervous. She kept looking over her shoulder and jumped when Mark Pilkington came up to us unexpectedly. But what she knew that got her killed... Always assuming her death was because she knew something about who murdered Jonquil..."

"CCTV shows a woman we believe to be Murtaugh entering Merrion with a man—at least we think it's a man—around seven o'clock last night. It was dark and pouring rain and the man was holding a very large umbrella over both of them that obscured their faces. Twenty minutes later, he comes back. Alone. Again with the umbrella, so we can't see his face."

"No details?"

"Medium height. Light raincoat. Dark pants and shoes."

"Not much like Joshua then."

"Assuming that was the murderer."

"DCI Willis, Joshua is not the murderer. Someone is obviously trying to frame him. He'd have to be an idiot to leave Jonquil in his car boot. And then Iris in his rooms."

"Or he's very smart."

Maggie shook her head.

"No. I know him."

"You know your colleague that well?" Willis scoffed.

Maggie's deep green eyes twinkled.

"I lived with Joshua for five years when we were at Harvard. We were engaged to be married. So yes, I do know him quite well. He's no murderer. And his tastes run to graduate students and the occasional faculty wife. Not young girls."

Willis looked as gobsmacked as Maggie had expected he would.

"You and Paley were engaged? And then you married Raynham?"

"It was eight years later. It wasn't on the rebound."

"You and Paley. No wonder his lordship…"

As if on cue, Thomas appeared. He stopped short when he saw Maggie and the detective. His expression did not change, but Maggie could feel the frost.

"Willis?"

Once again, Willis wondered what Maggie saw in this po-faced toff.

"Following up on our enquiries," he explained.

"Quite. If you've finished with your 'following up,' my dear, Mrs Cook has lunch waiting."

Thomas and Maggie walked the detective to his car in silence.

Chapter thirty-one

Maggie had returned to the dentist for her root canal. Dr Woods was still away so she was seeing Dr Perry again.

The dentist put the chair back, thoroughly numbed Maggie's jaw, and began to work. And gossip.

"It's too awful. Have you heard that a friend of Jonquil Pilkington's has been murdered as well?"

Maggie managed to nod.

"What can be going on? She was strangled too. Just like Jonquil."

Dr Perry picked up her drill and starting demolishing Maggie's tooth.

"You'd think there was a serial killer. Some psycho. Except one of our hygienists, she's dating the detective in charge of the investigation. And she says he thinks it's some Oxford professor. From America."

Maggie's grimace expressed both her discomfort and her concern. First, that Willis still suspected Joshua. And second, that Debbie—Maggie assumed the hygienist was Debbie—was telling her colleagues and who knew who else what Willis had told her. Which had surely been in confidence and was certainly against regulations.

"I asked her why the man hasn't been arrested before he murders some other poor woman and she said it's because the murderer has an alibi for both killings. But that the policeman is pressing the pathologist about whether the murders might have happened either earlier or later than what he said.

"Now open as wide as you can. This may be uncomfortable. I'm going to remove the nerve."

Dr Perry was right. It was uncomfortable and was made worse by the thought that Willis seriously suspected Joshua. Of course he had to consider her ex-fiancé, but surely he was looking at other possibilities too. Maggie hoped Perry's information had gotten distorted in the retelling, like in the old game of "telephone." As for Debbie's lack of discretion, well, that was Willis' problem.

Maggie returned to Beaumatin still numb and dispirited. She informed Mrs Cook she would not be having lunch, went to her room, and crawled into bed. She hoped she would feel better after a nap.

Chapter thirty-two

The next morning was Jonquil's funeral. Maggie felt obliged to attend. The service was held in the Churn Valley College chapel. Maggie found the campus easily enough. In the midst of a large park stood a massive Victorian mansion built by a well-to-do merchant. Childless, he had left the estate to be used as a school after his death. It originally catered to the male children of the prosperous and socially aspiring commercial and professional classes. Since the war it had embraced co-education and added a sports pavilion and a science centre.

The chapel was packed with faculty and students. Maggie spotted Colonel Aspinall, along with others from the Galanthus group committee, and squeezed in beside him. As she was sitting, she caught sight of Mark Pilkington in the front row. An older man sat beside him. Was it Jonquil's father, Dr Woods, the dentist?

"A sad occasion," the colonel murmured.

Maggie nodded.

The chaplain spoke movingly about Jonquil's contributions to the Churn Valley community, about her being a loving wife and daughter, and about the faith which supported her through the loss of her beloved Rosamunde.

After the service, Maggie decided to skip the actual burial, in the graveyard of a nearby church, and return to Beaumatin. Between murders, ex-fiancés, grumpy husbands, snowdrop societies, and weekend house parties, she was far behind in her work.

Sunday morning Maggie had just entered her study with a mug of coffee and was wondering whether she should organise herself by making a to-do list, when her mobile sounded.

It was Malcolm Fortescue-Smythe.

"Malcolm!"

"Maggie. I have some exciting news. How soon could you come down to London?"

Maggie thought. There was nothing to keep her at Beaumatin—except Thomas, an internal voice reminded her. Who was still communicating with her mostly by glares and grunts.

"Let me check my agenda."

She did.

"I could come down to town this evening."

"Perfect. The most fantastic thing. I was talking about your *PeopleFlows* project to a chap I know at the Arts Club who works for the BBC. He was impressed and... they want to turn the book into a documentary series! Kind of like David Attenborough, but with migrations of people instead of wildebeests."

"My goodness."

"You would appear and narrate some of the bits," Malcolm continued enthusiastically. "There will be a lot of contractual issues. And the book jacket will need to reference the BBC series. But it will certainly increase sales of the book."

They agreed to meet in the Global Press' Bloomsbury office at nine thirty on Monday morning and then go together to a meeting at Broadcasting House.

Maggie went to find Thomas to tell him her exciting news. As expected, he was in his study.

He was sitting at his laptop and looked up coldly.

"Thomas?"

"Not now."

"But..."

"Not now, I said."

He scowled and half stood. Maggie turned and quickly left.

He's making this easy, she thought to herself.

She went to her study and took out some heavy cream notecards embossed with the Raynham seal she used for thank-you notes and other social correspondence.

She uncapped her fountain pen and wrote, "Thomas, I'm off to London for some important meetings with Malcolm on the book. I'll be at the Belsize house. Back in a couple of days at most. Maggie."

Mrs Cook agreed to drive her to the Kemble train station. Maggie grabbed a change of clothes and the briefcase with her laptop and asked the housekeeper to give her note to Thomas.

All the way to London, Maggie wondered what she could do to repair her relationship with her husband. If only she didn't feel so guilty about the way she had broken off with Joshua. If only she were better at diffusing Thomas' jealousy. If only she could make it plain to Joshua that she didn't want his attentions, that it was over between them. If only. If only.

Maggie reached the house in Belsize and, as she put the key in the lock, her eyes smarted with tears.

"I am not going to cry. Only a lesser woman would cry because of some stupid marital difficulties," she told herself forcefully. She hoped she had left a bottle of white wine in the refrigerator.

Chapter thirty-three

Instead of his wife, Thomas found Maggie's note at his place at dinner, where Mrs Cook had left it. He was so angry the world turned red momentarily. He tore up the note into little pieces and paced. She had promised she would never go off without telling him. She had promised she would never leave him with just a note. She had promised... He wondered how many of the other things she had said were meaningless. Like her protestations that there was nothing between her and Paley. He conveniently forgot that he had refused to talk to her when she had come to see him.

He went to see Mrs Cook and told her he was not hungry. He took a bottle of Laphroaig and a tumbler and went up to the TV room. He drank and watched shows that he could not remember an hour later. He drank until he was numb and passed out on the sofa, the TV still turned on.

He awoke the next morning cold, stiff, hungover, and alone. He groaned and staggered down the hall and into his bathroom and was sick. He took some aspirin, drank some water to wash the tablets down, and was sick again. He managed to shower and shave and dress and hoped his stomach would accept some coffee.

He came downstairs and met Mrs Cook in the hall.

"Oh, Lord Raynham, I was looking for you. That policeman, Detective Chief Inspector Willis, is here. He asked to see you. I put him in the library."

She looked more closely at Thomas and shrewdly identified his condition. "Would you like some coffee? And some aspirin?"

"Yes. Thank you, Mrs. Cook. And I expect DCI Willis would like some tea."

"Yes, my lord."

Mrs Cook hurried away.

Thomas took a deep breath and immediately feared he was going to be sick again. He fought the nausea and went into the library. The detective was examining the books on one of the shelves.

"Willis?"

"Lord Raynham."

Willis looked at the baron and correctly assessed that the man had had a hard night. Why was that? he wondered. And where was Maggie? He had asked the housekeeper to speak to both Raynhams.

"What brings you to Beaumatin?"

"The Pilkington murder. We are trying to establish where the victim was murdered and need to search your grounds. Not the whole estate, but the area between the gates and the front of the house. I could apply for a search warrant, but I hoped you would give your permission."

Thomas' head throbbed.

"Yes. Very well."

"Is Lady Raynham here?"

Thomas became guarded. Willis noticed.

"No. Er, she's in London."

"London?"

"Yes. We have a place. In Belsize. She went down yesterday. Meetings with her publisher."

"I see. In that case… Lady Raynham has a document relevant to the case that she agreed to give to me. I wonder if we could look in her study?"

Thomas frowned. Normally he would have refused. But with his increasing suspicions of his wife, he was also curious about what might be in her desk.

"You may. But only if I am present."

Mrs Cook came in with a tray of tea and coffee and a plate piled with slices of banana bread.

"Mrs Cook, could you bring that into Lady Raynham's study please?"

They went into the room, bright with the morning sun.

"We'll serve ourselves, thank you, Mrs Cook," Thomas said.

Willis poured some tea and took a piece of banana bread.

"Just what is it that you're looking for?"

"Maggie and some of the other Merrion faculty received a series of anonymous letters making accusations against Paley. Maggie believes Jonquil Pilkington sent them."

Willis was watching him closely.

"Did Maggie mention them to you? Or show you one?"

"No."

Of course his wife would not mention them to a mere husband.

"She told me she had kept one. Draycott has the others."

Willis pulled on some surgical gloves and began methodically to go through the desk.

"Did you know Mrs Pilkington?" the detective inquired conversationally.

"No. I met her for the first time when she asked if I would be the patron of a snowdrop group she was forming. I begged off but she persuaded Lady Raynham to accept. Our only other contact was when I found her on my terrace with Lady Raynham and some members of her group."

"On your terrace?"

"I understand the group is having a meeting here in February and members want to set up tables and sell plants. The best place for that is on the terrace. Or they were going to. I don't know what will happen with Pilkington dead. And the other woman."

"Iris Murtaugh."

"Humpf."

"And that was all?"

"She was an extremely tiresome sort of woman and I tried to keep our contact to a minimum."

Thomas watched closely as Willis searched the desk. He opened a bottom drawer that had a rack for hanging files and flipped through the folders.

The Greater Gloucestershire Galanthus Group

"The Greater Gloucestershire Galanthus Group?"

Thomas shrugged.

Willis took out the file. He opened it and leafed through the contents. Lists of names. A board meeting agenda. Board meeting minutes. A proposal for an annual meeting. All printed on greyish recycled paper.

At the very end, he found it.

STONE PALEY SEDUCES INNOCENT YOUNG GIRLS

AND THEN MURDERS THEM

An envelope addressed to Professor Eliot at Merrion College, Oxford, was attached to the sheet by a paperclip.

Thomas made a noise of disgust. Willis grunted.

DS Hickson came in.

"Sir? They think they've found the murder site."

"Really? Good. Let's go."

"Is it on the estate?" Thomas asked.

"Yes."

"Then I'm coming too."

Susan Alexander

Chapter thirty-four

Police constables had already cordoned off an area about one hundred yards from the elaborate wrought iron gates that marked the entrance to Beaumatin. The discovery was at the foot of an oak where the earth had been disturbed. There were some distinctive footprints in the dirt and signs of scuffling.

DS Hickson took a small plastic bag from a police constable and passed it to Willis. Thomas, who had had to remain on the far side of the police tape, saw it contained some small, dark object.

Hickson and Willis were looking down at the ground. The sergeant shrugged. Willis called, "Raynham, could you come over here please? We need you to take a look at something."

Thomas ducked under the police tape and walked over.

Willis put out an arm to hold him back, then pointed down.

"See those footprints? What do you make of them?"

Thomas looked. Some of the shoeprints overlapped and the details were obscured, but one set was clear. There was a pointed toe, then a gap, then an angular heel that had sunk deep into the ground.

Thomas looked down at his own brogues.

"About a size eleven, I'd say. A tall man. Or a shorter one with big feet. And the pointed toe and the raised heel? To me they look like American cowboy boots. The pointed toe goes into the stirrup and the heel prevents the foot from sliding forward. Helps to control the horse."

"Cowboy boots?"

Thomas nodded.

"And while I don't want to make any accusations, Paley wears them."

Thomas felt ashamed of the pleasure he felt placing Paley at the murder scene. But he rationalised that he had only told the truth.

"And do you recognize this?"

Willis held up the plastic bag. It contained a brown button.

"A button."

He squinted.

"From a lady's coat? Or dress?"

"You don't remember seeing this before?"

"It's not very distinctive. And it's plastic. Not bone or mother-of-pearl."

Willis concluded such a button would not be found in his lordship's wardrobe.

"Thank you, Lord Raynham. You've been most helpful."

"I'll be in my study if you need me."

As he left, Thomas heard Willis telling his sergeant they needed to get a search warrant for Paley's rooms at

The Greater Gloucestershire Galanthus Group

Merrion and to check with the pathologist about whether the button matched what the victim had been wearing.

Susan Alexander

Chapter thirty-five

Maggie and Malcolm were taken to a conference room on an upper floor of Broadcasting House. There men in good city suits and others in more creative attire explored the possibilities for a series. Maggie let Malcolm do the talking. Business cards were exchanged. It was agreed the next meeting would be to discuss contracts. In the meantime, Maggie would prepare a proposal for the series and a sample chapter or two.

"That went well. I hope you're pleased," Malcolm said enthusiastically as they waited for a taxi.

"A bit overwhelmed, but yes," Maggie agreed.

Maggie's mobile sounded. She checked, both hoping and dreading that it was call from Thomas, but it was Tim.

"Tim?"

Lord Timothy Hillier—Tim—was the head of a secretive government agency that dealt with matters of national security in a very "hands on" fashion. Maggie had originally met Tim when he was in his previous position and she had consulted to the government on matters relating to immigration. More recently, he and his men had come to her rescue on several occasions.

Maggie was very fond of Tim.

"Maggie. You're in London?"

Maggie did not bother wondering how Tim was aware of this. She knew he had the capability to track her phone.

"Yes. At Broadcasting House."

"I'll have a car pick you up in front in ten minutes."

Tim sounded very subdued. Maggie wanted to ask why he wanted to see her but knew better than to ask. He would tell her when she saw him.

Malcolm was proposing a celebratory lunch.

"I'm sorry, Malcolm, but something's come up."

"Is everything all right?" he asked in concern when he saw her expression.

"Yes. No. I don't know. I'm being picked up."

"I'll wait with you, then."

"You really don't need to, Malcolm."

"You're sure you'll be all right?"

"Yes. And we'll formulate an action plan later today or, worst case, tomorrow."

Malcolm flagged down a taxi.

"You're sure?"

"Yes."

Malcolm gave Maggie a quick kiss and a hug, then gave the cabbie the Global Press' address and was driven off.

Not long after, a black BMW with darkened windows arrived. The driver got out, opened the rear door, and said, "Get in, please, Professor Eliot."

Paul Simmonds was blond and slim and looked like the computer geek that he was. Less obviously, he was

The Greater Gloucestershire Galanthus Group

expert in several schools of martial arts. Maggie had met him the previous spring.

"Hello, Paul. How have you been?"

But Paul was not in the mood for pleasantries. In fact, he looked grim. He nodded and mumbled something unintelligible.

Maggie began to worry.

Paul drove them expertly through the London traffic to Westminster. He turned into a ramp leading down between two anonymous government buildings. At the bottom was a solid steel door and a keypad. Paul entered a number and the door rose slowly to reveal a small underground parking area.

In the far wall was another door. Since she had last been to Tim's office, the keypad had been replaced with a retinal scanner. Paul leaned in, the scanner made a low humming noise, and the door opened.

Before them was a short corridor. Maggie was nervous. She noted security cameras and supressed an impulse to wave. At the end was another blank door with another retinal scanner. The door slid open to reveal a small elevator.

The elevator rose to a single floor of an unspecified number.

The elevator stopped and the door opened. Maggie and Paul walked down a long, featureless hall that was utterly silent. At the end was another door with a retinal scanner and another security camera.

Maggie walked into a setting that might have been lifted from an exclusive London gentlemen's club, with fine oak panelling, oriental carpets, leather club chairs, a fireplace, and a large antique desk.

Tim was standing in the middle of the room as though he had expected her to appear at just that moment. He was Maggie's height, had well cut, medium brown hair, a tidy moustache, and unremarkable features. She noticed he looked tired.

"Maggie. Thank you for coming at such short notice."

"Of course. What…"

"Sit down, Maggie."

Tim indicated one of the chairs.

Now she was alarmed but did as Tim requested. He sat in the other chair, leaned forward, and took her hands.

"I'm afraid I have some bad news," he began.

Thomas? Was it Thomas?

"Lennox Archibald-Atherton is dead. He was killed in the service of his country."

Maggie stared at Tim numbly as she took in what he had said. Crispin—Lennox liked her to call him Crispin—was dead?

The room dimmed.

"Maggie, drink this."

Tim handed her a glass of brandy he had already poured.

Maggie took a gulp and nearly choked on the burning liquid.

She had a thousand questions. How had he died? Had he suffered? Who had killed him? But she knew any answers Tim might be able to give her would not change the basic fact. Crispin was dead.

Lennox Archibald-Atherton had been about to graduate from Magdalene when his fiancée had run off with his best friend. In response, he had taken his first and joined the SAS. A drawer-full of medals attested to his outstanding service. Back in civilian life, he had been introduced to Tim, who had an opening for an Oxbridge grad with special forces skills.

Maggie had met Crispin when she needed some help to catch a murderer. The relationship had not remained professional, although Maggie refused to consider it an affair. She could count on the fingers of one hand the number of times they had made love, and each had been in the heat of the moment. There had been no clandestine meetings at country inns or secret texts on burner phones.

Still, the last time Maggie had seen Crispin, the previous spring, he had promised he would come back for her when he had finished his new assignment. He was turning fifty. He was going to retire. He wanted her to leave Thomas and be with him. Not knowing whether he had been serious or if it were simply another example of Crispin's impetuousness, she had not thought much about it. And now it was no longer an issue.

Tim pressed her to finish the brandy.

"Sarah Cartwright was also killed."

"Oh no."

Maggie knew Sarah, a cheerful blonde who had acted as both nurse and bodyguard to Maggie.

Tim watched Maggie. She had taken his news better than he had feared she would. He knew there had been some sort of relationship between Maggie and Lennox beyond the strictly work-related.

"Before he left on his assignment, Lennox gave me this to give to you in case… in case things went badly."

Tim reached in his pocket, pulled out an envelope, and handed it to Maggie.

On it was written in Crispin's bold handwriting, "Maggie Eliot."

Maggie opened the envelope, removed a sheet of paper, and read:

My dearest Moppet,

If you are reading this, things have gone pear-shaped and I will not be returning to you as I had promised. Don't blame Tim. I knew there were dangers when I accepted the assignment and believed the mission was important and worth the risk.

I am the last of the Archibald-Athertons. Aunt Sarah died shortly after you last saw her and I was her heir. She has a lovely place in Dorset called Longview. Along with my other assets, I am leaving it to you, as I trust you not to turn it into a home for stray cats. And since you seem to enjoy life in the provinces, it will give you an alternative should you decide to ditch his lordship. Go see old Barnaby, my solicitor. He knows all the details and has the paperwork.

What can I say except life does not always turn out as we hope. Mourn me, but not for too long.

You have all my love,

Crispin

Maggie blinked back tears. She handed Tim the letter and walked over to the windows while he read it.

After a minute she heard Tim clear his throat. She turned.

"I was aware of Lennox's testamentary dispositions and made an appointment for us to go see Mr Barnaby this afternoon, if that suits you."

Maggie nodded.

"Is there… Has there been a funeral?"

"Tomorrow late morning. We can go together. It's in Dorset. You can see the estate while we're there."

Maggie nodded numbly, glad that Tim was taking charge.

Susan Alexander

Chapter Thirty-Six

Mr Josiah Barnaby had his practice in Lincoln's Inn Fields. Maggie suspected the offices of Barnaby, Barnaby, and Perkins had not changed since Queen Victoria's Diamond Jubilee. And had not been properly dusted since Queen Elizabeth's.

A young male secretary showed them into Barnaby's office. The man himself was in his early seventies, Short and round and jowly, he wore a well-worn suit with a vest and a pocket watch and went with his surroundings.

"Lord Timothy. And, er," he consulted a paper on his desk. "Professor Eliot. Please sit down."

He gestured to a pair of chairs that were placed in front of a desk piled high with papers.

Barnaby rummaged around and, with a grunt of satisfaction, produced a document.

"Here we are."

He smoothed it out on the desk.

"This is the last will and testament of Lennox Herbert Montagu Archibald-Atherton."

Like a scene out of Agatha Christie, he proceeded to read the will. The executors were Josiah Barnaby, Esq, and Lord Timothy Hillier. Fred Pilchard—The Fish—was to get Crispin's Porsche and a fund for the education of his two children was to be established. Maggie inherited everything else, which included an apartment in Chelsea and Lennox's financial assets. She was also the sole beneficiary of the Archibald-Atherton Family Trust.

The solicitor produced a second document. This was for the trust, which had been set up to protect the family estate in Dorset from the depredations of the tax authorities. The trust paid for the maintenance of its Grade 2 listed residence, two hundred acres of park, and a staff of five including a butler, housekeeper, and gardener. There were four hundred additional acres that were leased to a local farmer. There was an allowance for Maggie equivalent to the salary of a professional worker that would be increased if she took up residence at Longview.

Maggie was feeling overwhelmed and imagined Crispin's spirit looking down from heaven and laughing as she wondered how she could ever explain this to Thomas.

She decided her husband did not need to know.

"This is… I don't need the income. Well, I don't need any of this, really. But is there any way the income could just stay in the trust? Accumulate?"

"I'm sure something can be arranged," Tim assured her.

"And what about taxes?"

"If you sell the Chelsea flat—I assume you have no use for it—it should cover any tax obligations."

Crispin's flat. She had had no idea that Crispin had a flat or even where he lived. She had never really thought about it. Maggie was flooded with a wave of loss.

Barnaby misinterpreted Maggie's expression.

"Don't worry, Professor Eliot. Hillier and I will take care of things for you," he said avuncularly.

Tim expected Maggie to react to the idea that she needed to be taken care of and worried when she said, simply, "Thank you."

Tim's car and driver were waiting.

"We've both missed lunch. Let's get something to eat. And drink."

Maggie had no appetite but agreed.

Tim had the driver take them to a trendy Italian place on Archer Street in Soho.

"It specialises in small plates, good wines by the glass, and gelato," said Tim, believing that all women had a fondness for ice cream.

Tim was obviously known at the restaurant. They were shown to a table in a corner.

Maggie assumed this was not a place to discuss Tim's work. Or Crispin.

"How are you?"

"A bit in shock. Sad. And this comes in the midst of..."

Maggie was not going to mention her problems with Thomas. So she told Tim about the *PeopleFlows* project and the BBC's interest in making it into a series.

"Congratulations. You know how much I admire your work."

They chatted about neutral topics while they ate. After three glasses of white wine, Maggie declined the gelato and had a double espresso. Tim ordered them grappa.

"To Lennox," he said.

"To Lennox," Maggie barely managed.

Tim's car was waiting outside.

"I'm going to walk back to the office. Are you going back to the Belsize house? Give George the address. I'll pick you up there at eight tomorrow."

Maggie had a moment's confusion, then remembered. The funeral. In Dorset.

"All right. And thank you, Tim."

She gave him a quick kiss on the cheek. They hugged. Then Tim opened the door of the waiting car. Maggie got in and the car drove off.

Chapter thirty-seven

Maggie had bought the Belsize house the year before, ostensibly as a surprise for her husband but, in reality, because she wanted her own space, someplace not part of the Raynham holdings. An investment had paid off at the same time Clive Stonor was selling the house where he and his partner had lived when they had their antiques business in London and Maggie had jumped on the opportunity.

The gracious terraced house was too big for just Maggie and Thomas, and Maggie knew that Thomas' second son James, who was a Commodore in the Royal Navy and had a third child on the way, was looking for a larger home. So Maggie had had the house divided in two. She and Thomas had the lower two floors and James and his family the upper floors and attic. There was also a pleasant garden where the children could play.

At the moment the house was empty, as James had been sent on assignment to Brussels for a year as a British representative to NATO and taken Victoria and the children with him.

Back at the Belsize house, Maggie rushed into the bathroom and vomited violently. Afterwards she felt better physically, but that left her alone with her feelings.

"Oh Crispin," she murmured.

While she still had the presence of mind, she texted Malcolm that a friend had died and she was attending his funeral the next day. She trusted him to reach the most beneficial agreement he could for the documentary series and she would have some material to send to the BBC as soon as possible.

She had to contact Thomas as well. What could she say? He disliked Crispin. In the end she texted, Ongoing meetings with the BBC. M.

There. Now she could focus on her friend. Comrade. Lover.

While with Joshua she had let her head rule her heart and with Thomas her heart rule her head, with Crispin both head and heart had shrieked alarms from the first time they had met. The man was decidedly mad, bad, and dangerous to know, and Maggie was not one of those women who was attracted to bad guys, at least not emotionally. She could not deny the sexual chemistry.

While she felt guilty about, well, call it what it was, the adultery, and knew that Thomas must never, ever know, she rationalized that one could hardly call her relationship with Crispin an affair. They had never spent a night together. Never organised an illicit assignation. Never had a stolen weekend at a country inn.

Months would pass when she would barely think of the man. Yes, she was fond of him. Very fond. She could even say she loved him, but she was not "in love." He had saved her life. More than once. At the same time, he often terrified her. And she had lacked the courage to ask too closely about some of the things he did for Tim.

But, oh, Crispin. With his curly dark hair, hard blue eyes, and muscular body.

And now his legacy. What was she going to do about that? While she would do her duty, she had no use for some Dorset estate. And she was quite sure Crispin's intent was to cause her problems with Thomas, assuming he ever found out. Which she would make sure he never did. Another secret.

Maggie cried for a long time. Then she took one of the sleeping pills Anne had given her, turned off her phone, and crawled into bed.

Susan Alexander

Chapter thirty-eight

The funeral was held in a small village church and was attended by Fred Pilchard ("The Fish"), Paul Simmonds, and Martin Hewitt, in addition to herself and Tim. The vicar was a kindly, white-haired man in his early seventies. He had not known Lennox but had known his aunt well. Lady Sarah Archibald-Atherton had been a pillar of the community and a benefactor of St Cuthbert's. Now Lennox was being laid to rest beside his aunt and generations of other Archibald-Athertons.

The day was cool and grey. Afterwards, they went to lunch at the local pub. Fred, Martin, and Paul entertained the table with stories about Lennox's various exploits—at least those that were not classified.

Maggie had not seen Fred since the previous spring when he had been severely burned in the stable fire at Beaumatin. Maggie was relieved that he seemed to be all right. Of course, she could not see what was under his grey suit.

After the meal, the men headed back to London.

"Time to visit Longview," Tim said.

Longview was in West Dorset, in an area designated AONB, or Area of Outstanding Natural Beauty, like the Cotswolds. The estate was aptly named. On top of a rise, it was possible to see a thin blue strip in the distance that was the sea. The house itself turned out to be a gracious, three-storied Queen Anne mansion of red brick set in the middle of a well-maintained park, with an extensive garden in the back.

Maggie was greeted by the Trevelyans, a couple who served as Longview's butler and housekeeper.

A butler? Good grief, Maggie thought.

While Tim conferred with Trevelyan, Mrs Trevelyan gave Maggie a tour of the house which, even on a grey day, was light and lovely. Rooms were in pastel shades and family portraits were interspersed with rural landscapes and still lives.

Maggie also met Milly, a young English springer spaniel. The dog greeted Maggie enthusiastically and made herself one of the tour party.

"There's a cook, Mrs Quincy, and a woman who comes in from the village to help with the cleaning. There's Roberts the gardener, who lives over the garage, and a gardener's boy. Mrs Quincy is away visiting her mother in Norfolk," Mrs Trevelyan explained.

The Longview staff was bigger than Beaumatin's, Maggie realised. She thought it a pity to have the house sitting empty, but she could certainly not live there. She would have to consider an alternative solution. One that did not involve cats.

On the ride back to London, Maggie said, "Tim, Longview is wonderful. It seems terrible to have the house empty. Someone should be there. I just can't imagine how to find such a person. Or whether that would violate the terms of the trust."

"You and his lordship wouldn't like a weekend place? A holiday house?" Tim teased.

"I can't tell Thomas about this! He would never understand. And he's so bound to the estate. It's a big deal for him to get away to Oxford for a day or two."

The Greater Gloucestershire Galanthus Group

"Poor Maggie."

"I am not poor Maggie. It's just that I feel some responsibility…"

"Yes. Lennox thought you would."

That stopped Maggie. That Crispin thought she was the person he knew who would be most responsible.

"Well, if you really don't want to throw it all in and move to West Dorset, let me think about a workable solution."

"Thank you, Tim. I'm sorry. I know you have much more important things…"

"It's all right, my dear. I also feel some responsibility where Lennox is concerned."

Susan Alexander

Chapter thirty-nine

Thomas was in his study trying to catch up on paperwork but having trouble concentrating.

Someone knocked on the door.

"Come."

It was Willis.

"I'm sorry to disturb you, Lord Raynham," said Willis in a tone which indicated he was not sorry at all. "But I have been trying to reach Lady Raynham on her mobile and it seems the phone is turned off. Have you spoken with her? Since she arrived in London?"

"No." Thomas was terse.

"No," Willis repeated. "Is there a landline perhaps? In this, er, place of yours? In Belsize?"

"No."

Willis regarded the baron. Something was wrong here, although whether it had anything to do with the murders, he was not sure. He knew from experience Raynham's relationship with his wife was often difficult. And his own feelings for the man ranged from dislike to contempt. Feelings which were mainly related to how he treated Maggie.

"I see. Well, Lord Raynham, if you do speak with your wife, would you please let her know I need to talk to her and would appreciate a call."

Thomas nodded. Curt.

"Thank you." Willis left.

Thomas sat. His mind raced. Why had Maggie turned off her mobile? There was only one reason he could think of and the more he thought about it, the more he became convinced. She was with Paley. That had to be it.

He got up and paced. Glanced at the portrait of Maggie that hung over his study fireplace. Scowled. He had keys to the Belsize house. But was she really in London? Perhaps she was in Oxford. Well, he had keys to her rooms there as well. Oxford was more or less on the way to London. He would check. Although if they were holed up in a hotel together… She had not taken a car so he could not check the LoJack. Had that been on purpose?

He went and told Mrs Cook he was going to be away for the rest of the day. Possibly the next as well. He wanted to catch his wife and Paley in flagrante delecto. Then he would know the truth and he could end it. He had a sudden image of Maggie and Paley in bed together and had to swerve suddenly to avoid hitting a horse and its rider.

Thomas took a deep breath. He needed to calm down.

He reached Oxford and parked illegally near the entrance to Merrion.

"Hello, Roger," he nodded to the porter, who knew him by now, and went to Maggie's staircase. Outside her door, he paused. He could not hear any noise from inside. He knocked softly. No response. He quietly inserted his key in the lock and opened the door. The room was dim. Empty. He crept across to the bedroom door. There was no indication of any living presence, but he still turned the handle as quietly as possible and then burst into the room.

Empty. The brass bed was covered with Maggie's antique quilt and clean sheets were folded at the foot. He

THE GREATER GLOUCESTERSHIRE GALANTHUS GROUP

went into the bathroom. The sink was dry and the porcelain sparkled.

She was not here then. Perhaps she was in London after all.

As he was leaving, he stopped at the porter's lodge.

"By the way, Roger, have you seen Professor Paley?"

"No, my lord. I believe he is away for the day."

Thomas tried hard not to show what he was feeling.

"Thank you, Roger."

He went back to the Land Rover, which had been fortunate to avoid a ticket, and got in. He needed to get a grip, as Maggie would say. He started the car and headed to the M40 and London.

Susan Alexander

Chapter forty

Thomas reached the Belsize house but did not immediately look for a parking space. Instead he cruised the surrounding streets to see if Paley's Rolls were parked nearby. He didn't see it but decided Paley could have easily taken a train. Paddington was only a short taxi ride away.

He finally parked not too far from the house. He went up the front steps and paused. There was no sign the house was occupied. No lights. A commercial flyer stuck out of the mailbox labelled Raynham. He scowled and opened the front door with as little noise as possible.

He stood in the hall. It was silent. No music. No cooking smells. No aroma of coffee either, which he would have expected if Maggie had been in residence. Perhaps she and Paley had gone to some chic urban boutique hotel. Or one of those country house places with a spa. And a hot tub.

Now glowering, he unlocked the apartment door. Still quiet and, although the day was overcast and dim, no lights. He peeked into the study. It was tidy and the desktop devoid of Maggie's laptop, which he would have expected to see. Maggie was never without her computer.

The bedroom was also neat, the bed unslept in, with no clothing lying on its surface or on one of the chairs. The bathroom was also unused, the sink and shower dry.

He stood at the top of the stairs and heard a low murmuring. Ha! He slipped off his shoes and crept down.

The sitting room was unoccupied, but he discovered the source of the noise. The TV was on, tuned to the BBC News, the volume low. He looked around. On the coffee table in front of the sofa was a half-empty bottle of white wine and a wine glass. But the wine glass was half obscured by crumpled tissues. A mound of them. Others had fallen off onto the floor.

Thomas went into the kitchen. A clean coffee mug stood in front of the coffee machine, which was also empty. He looked in the sink. Paley enjoyed his whisky. But there was no tumbler, and an unopened bottle of Laphroaig was standing in a cabinet.

He opened the refrigerator. Empty.

Thomas returned to the living room, hesitated, then opened the door to the guest bedroom. This bed had been slept in. He peeked in the adjacent bathroom. There was a toothbrush and toothpaste on the shelf over the sink. A towel showed signs of use.

Going back to the sitting room, he noticed Maggie's briefcase resting on one of the chairs. He crossed and opened it. Her laptop. A journal. A book. Some papers. To support her story that she had been in Belsize? When actually she and Paley had been...

Again he banished with difficulty the image of Maggie and Paley together and decided he would wait. She would have to come back eventually. Perhaps she would even return with Paley. The Land Rover was parked far enough away so that it would not be obvious that he was there.

He poured himself a Laphroaig, changed the TV to the History channel, and settled on the sofa to wait.

Chapter forty-one

Half an hour later Thomas heard a noise. He quickly turned off the TV. A key turned in a lock. Footsteps. It sounded like only one pair.

Maggie stood at the top of the stairs. She was wearing the same creamy fisherman's sweater and jeans she had been wearing the last time he had seen her. She had on sunglasses and was carrying a bulging plastic bag. She started down, then, where the stairs turned, peered. In the dim light it was hard to see, but it looked like…

"Hello? Is someone there?" she called.

When there was no response, she called again, sounding alarmed, "Hello? Who's there?"

She took a step, misjudged, and stumbled down the remaining stairs. She landed in a heap at the bottom. The contents of the bag she was carrying spilled out.

"Oh!"

"Maggie!"

Thomas came over and unceremoniously hauled her to her feet.

"Are you all right?" he asked brusquely.

"Ow. Yes. I think so. You surprised me. I didn't expect you."

"No? Whom did you expect?"

"Whom? Why, no one. No one. That's why…"

She looked down at the scattered groceries. A container of cottage cheese had opened and was oozing onto the floor.

"Oh dear."

She bent to retrieve the container, overbalanced, and sat down hard.

"Here. Let me."

Thomas sounded exasperated. He helped her up again.

"Sorry."

"Humpf."

She removed her sunglasses and Thomas saw that her eyes were red and puffy, her nose was red, and her upper lip was chapped. The way she looked when she had been crying. For an extended period of time.

"Go sit. I'll clean this up."

He took the bag into the kitchen, returned with some paper towels, and mopped up the mess.

"I'm happy to see you of course," Maggie said while wondering if she were in fact happy to see him. "But it is a surprise."

"Your mobile is turned off."

"No, it's not. But I forgot the charger and the battery ran out."

Thomas' scepticism was obvious.

"We had a visit from your friend Inspector Willis."

"Willis? Why?"

Thomas shrugged.

"He wants to talk to you. As you couldn't be reached, I came to let you know."

Maggie doubted that this was true. She looked at Thomas. He was as hostile as he had been when she had left Beaumatin.

It was too much.

"I'm tired. I'll use the guest room. I hope some of the food survived if you're hungry and, if it's not what you want, you know what the resources are in the neighbourhood. The sheets on the bed upstairs are clean.

"Or now that you've conveyed your message, you can drive back. It's not late. I'll take the train in the morning."

"What about Willis?"

"Willis can wait."

Maggie stalked off.

Thomas fumed. He poured some more whisky. Where was Paley? Already on his way back to Oxford? Had he come too late?

He emptied his glass and poured another. Went into the kitchen and looked at what Maggie had bought. Some organic yogurt. A loaf of artisanal bread studded with seeds. A cantaloupe. A plastic container of curried carrot soup. Good thing that hadn't opened when Maggie had fallen. But nothing he wanted to eat.

He went back to the sitting room. Turned on the TV. Turned it off. Paced. Finished his whisky. Poured some more.

He had to know, he decided.

Thomas opened the door to the guest suite and entered the bedroom. The bed was empty.

Where was the woman?

He heard a sniff and saw Maggie sitting in a corner on the floor, legs pulled up, arms wrapped around them, head on her knees. More used tissues were piled beside her.

"Maggie."

He crossed to her and pulled her to her feet.

"What?"

She swiped at a runny nose with a tissue.

"Where's Paley? He's not at Oxford," Thomas demanded.

"How do you… Oh, good grief, Thomas. Please don't tell me you went looking for him. If anyone found out…"

Thomas was silent. They glared at each other.

Finally Maggie said, "I got the impression that he and Jersey are spending a few days together."

"Paley and Jersey?"

"Yes."

"Then that's what all this is about? Paley break your heart?" he picked up a handful of crumpled tissues and tossed them into the air.

Maggie looked incredulous.

"Thomas Raynham, for someone who is quite intelligent, you can really be just so incredibly stupid!"

Maggie was suddenly furious. Her hand shot out and the whisky left in Thomas' glass splashed up in his face. He gasped and grabbed for her. Maggie tried to avoid him, but he pinned her against the wall.

"Now you're going to tell me. About you and Paley."

"About Joshua and me? There's nothing to tell!"

"I don't believe you."

"Is that why you came? Because you thought you'd find me with Joshua? My god, Thomas."

"I have to know."

"There isn't anything to know."

"No?"

Maggie briefly considered trying to talk her husband down but was too tired and fed up.

"This is crazy, Thomas."

She pushed him away and he staggered back.

"Crazy," she repeated and retreated to the sitting room.

Thomas hesitated. Was he wrong? Had she told the truth? Was there really nothing between her and Paley?

Maggie was standing at the French windows that opened out to the garden and starring out into darkness.

Thomas came up behind her.

"Maggie?"

He put out his hand, but she stepped away.

"No! Don't touch me."

"Maggie. Please. Listen to me..."

"If you dare try to tell me you've been an idiot and that you're sorry, I'll... I'll..."

"Then I won't," he interrupted. And he pulled her to him and kissed her.

"Oh no..."

"Shh."

Maggie began to cry again. She was exhausted, both physically and emotionally. She just wanted... She didn't know what she wanted.

She sniffed. Thomas handed her a tissue.

"Sorry. My handkerchief's upstairs."

Maggie woke up back in Thomas' arms. Felt an initial rush of contentment, then an equal flood of ambivalence.

She began to draw away but Thomas tightened his hold.

The Greater Gloucestershire Galanthus Group

"Inspector Willis..." she began.

"Inspector Willis can wait."

Susan Alexander

Chapter forty-two

Maggie needed to get back to Oxford.

"I can take a train. Or you can drop me off," she told Thomas.

Thomas, who had hoped she would return to Beaumatin with him, grudgingly agreed.

"Thomas, I have work. My students. And the BBC…"

"The BBC?"

"I've been trying to tell you, but you wouldn't listen. The BBC wants to make *PeopleFlows* into a documentary series. It's a big deal. Malcolm is ecstatic. It's the reason I had to go to London."

"Really?"

"What do you mean, really? Of course really."

"Congratulations," Thomas finally offered.

Maggie decided Thomas was containing his transports of delight at her news because it was one more thing that would keep her away from Beaumatin.

The ride up to Oxford took place in silence. Fortunately traffic flowed.

"Just drop me at Merrion, please."

Thomas looked grumpy.

"You're going back to Beaumatin?"

"Yes."

"I'll try to have things under control by Wednesday afternoon. But you have the car…"

"I'll come and pick you up."

"Thank you."

Maggie leaned over, gave Thomas a light kiss on the cheek, got her bags from the backseat, and went into the college. She did not look back.

Thomas slammed the car into gear and drove off.

The drive back to Beaumatin gave Thomas plenty of time for reflection.

If he accepted what Maggie said about her relationship with Paley, that there was nothing going on between them, then he had acted like an ass. It would not have been for the first time.

But if she were lying and she were having an affair… Well, in that case, he knew what he would do.

Chapter Forty-Three

Maggie found her stairway busy with police going up and down. She saw DS Dexter and stopped him.

"What's going on?"

Dexter paused. His inclination was to say he could not comment on an ongoing investigation, but he had checked Maggie out with his uncle and thought it wise to treat her with some respect.

"We're executing a search warrant," he admitted.

"Oh dear."

Maggie did not need to ask whose rooms they were searching.

A white-suited forensic technician rushed by carrying a large plastic evidence bag. Inside Maggie saw a pair of cowboy boots.

That wasn't good.

Back in her rooms, Maggie removed her mobile from her purse and plugged it into the charger. The screen indicated she had missed a dozen calls. Half were from Thomas. The other half were from DCI Willis.

Willis. She remembered Thomas had told her she needed to contact Willis.

Well, the last call from Willis was nearly a day ago. If he still wanted her, he would call again. It wasn't as though she were a suspect or had anything else she could tell him.

As though summoned by her thoughts, Willis came in.

"So there you are," he said grumpily.

Maggie decided she had had enough of sullen men.

"Yes. Here I am."

"You didn't return my calls. In fact, your phone's been turned off," he continued accusingly.

"The battery died. I'm charging it now. And I only knew about your calls last night when Thomas told me."

"Really."

"Yes. Really. Do I need an alibi? All right. You can check with the BBC. My publisher, Malcolm Fortescue-Smythe, can give you the names of the executives with whom we met. And otherwise I was with Tim. You know Tim. I'm sure he'd be happy to vouch for me if you asked."

Willis knew Tim. And pigs would fly before he'd ask the man anything. Especially if Maggie was concerned. He figured Maggie also knew that was a call he would never make. Not that he even knew Tim's phone number.

"So, Tom, what's going on? Why are you searching Joshua's rooms?" asked Maggie, using his first name.

"There's new evidence…" Willis began, when he was interrupted by DS Dexter.

"DCI Willis, the guv would like a word."

"Humpf. You'll be here?"

It was more of an order than a question.

"Yes. Or at Hereford Crescent. I'm returning to Beaumatin Wednesday evening."

Willis left with Dexter. A moment later, Joshua burst in. His dreadlocks were in disarray and he looked distraught.

"Elle! Thank god you're back. The police. They're searching my rooms. And treating me like I'm a suspect. I told them I'm being framed. I don't think they believe me."

He threw himself down in a chair and pulled at a strand of hair.

"I need your help. You have to help me. I'm afraid I'm going to be arrested. Me! Stone Paley! Arrested! And for murder! Two murders! And I didn't even know these women!"

Stone was getting hysterical.

Maggie got up and put her hand on his shoulder.

"You're upset."

"Of course I'm upset..."

"Let me get you a drink."

Maggie went and poured out several fingers of whisky. She handed the tumbler to Joshua, who swallowed half.

He coughed.

"I don't know what to do. Do I need a lawyer? Do you know any lawyers? What a nightmare!"

He took another large sip.

"Yes, I do know someone," she began.

"Not someone Lord Fubsy face Hayseed uses."

"No, he's... This man helped me last spring when... Anyhow his name is Luke Fitzroy. I'll get you his number and I'll alert him that he may be hearing from you. And Joshua, if the police caution you, or inform you that you're a suspect, say nothing, really, absolutely nothing, until you have a solicitor with you. It's like the U.S. You're allowed to have a lawyer. And you mustn't say anything unless he's there with you."

"Right." Joshua finished the whisky.

"Do you know what the police are looking for? They went over your room after Iris' murder. There must be something new."

"No idea. They don't tell you anything. Or they don't tell me."

"That's normal, Joshua."

"If the media get ahold of this..."

Joshua lifted his glass and looked surprised to find it was empty. He extended the tumbler to Maggie, who took it and poured in a smaller amount. An inebriated Joshua was the last thing she needed.

"Look, Joshua. Trust me for now. Let me see what I can discover. I believe that someone is trying to implicate you. I have some ideas, but I need to find out more."

"You believe I didn't do it?"

"Of course you didn't," Maggie stated emphatically.

Joshua got up and pulled Maggie towards him in a crushing hug.

The Greater Gloucestershire Galanthus Group

"Oh god. You believe me. I'm so glad someone believes me."

There was a knock on the door. It was Stephen. Maggie pushed Joshua away but not before Stephen saw them.

"Am I interrupting?" he asked.

"No. Joshua was just relieved when I told him I believe he is innocent."

"Is there any doubt?"

"I think the police have their issues."

Stephen looked grim.

"I told Joshua I will do what I can to help."

"Quite."

Stephen turned to Joshua.

"Maggie saved me when my wife was murdered. She also helped Jersey. And Gordon Ross, a former Merrion fellow whose rooms you have."

"Former?"

"He was trading recommendations for sex."

Joshua grimaced. For all his faults, Maggie knew he would never do something like that. Just like she knew he would never kill anyone.

"Have you had lunch? Come over to the lodge. Since your rooms are out of bounds," Stephen proposed.

Joshua accepted, but Maggie declined. She had too much work to do.

The men left.

Maggie had just sat back down at her desk when Willis returned.

He looked around.

"Paley not here? I thought I saw him…"

"He just left for the Master's Lodge for lunch. With the Master."

"Humpf."

"Won't you sit down? Would you like some tea? Coffee? I'm afraid I can't offer any lemon drizzle cake, but I have some biscuits…"

Willis hesitated, then sat.

"Tea, then. Thank you."

Maggie returned with tea and a plate of ginger biscuits for Willis and a mug of coffee for herself. She sat in the other chair.

"Well, DCI Willis, I assume something new has turned up for you to be searching Paley's rooms."

Willis regarded Maggie. He knew he should say he could not discuss an ongoing investigation. On the other hand, she was the only one he knew who could bridge the gap between Oxford and the victims.

"We found the place where Jonquil Pilkington was murdered," he began.

"Really? Where?"

"At Beaumatin."

"Beaumatin?"

"Yes. About one hundred yards from the main gate. Among some trees beside the drive."

"Oh."

"And we found some footprints."

"Yes?"

"Your husband identified them as being made by, er, cowboy boots."

"Cowboy boots," Maggie echoed, while her mind raced.

"And he mentioned that Professor Paley is known for wearing them.

Thomas would enjoy ratting out Joshua, Maggie thought bitterly.

"So we searched Paley's rooms and found half a dozen pairs. One of which was an exact match for the boot prints at the murder scene."

Maggie was stunned. Was it possible that Joshua… But no. No, Joshua was not a murderer. There must be another explanation.

"Very well. I accept that the boot matches the print. But can you prove that it was Joshua who was wearing it when the murder was committed?"

"We are comparing soil residue on the boot with the soil at the scene."

"Anything else?"

Willis scowled.

"One thing. There were no fingerprints on the boots. They had been wiped."

There was silence while Maggie thought about this.

Finally she said, "But what reason would Joshua have to wipe his fingerprints off of his boots? That makes sense only if someone else... It supports my assumption that someone is trying to frame him for the murders."

"Perhaps."

"Perhaps?"

"If Paley is trying to make us think he is being framed, he might have wiped his prints off the boots himself. The man is no dummy, I'll give him that."

"Or the real killer is no dummy," she countered.

Which reminded her of... something.

Willis saw her expression change.

"What?"

"Nothing. It's just... No, I can't..."

"Maggie, if you're holding out on me..."

"No, I'm not. It was just an impression. Not even. I promise if I remember what it was, I'll tell you."

"You'd better. And you should tell your friend Paley he might consider getting a solicitor."

"I know."

Willis took another ginger biscuit.

"Did you know DS Dexter is DCI Paul Dexter's nephew?" Maggie asked conversationally.

"No, I didn't," said Willis in a tone indicating that nor did he care. "But he's all right. So is DI Bartlett. So if you're here, and not in Gloucestershire, and something comes up, you should tell them."

Willis stood.

"Thank you for the tea. And I should warn you, it's not looking too good for your pal Paley."

He grabbed the last biscuit and left.

Susan Alexander

The Greater Gloucestershire Galanthus Group

Chapter forty-four

Maggie had gotten a text from Colonel Aspinall that Iris' funeral would be held at St Andrew's Church in Cold Aston on Saturday morning and she felt an obligation to attend.

Maggie had never visited the small Cotswold village, which she got to by turning off from the main road to Stowe. Its location explained why she had met Iris in the nearby town.

She had left Beaumatin early in case she got lost and now sat waiting in the near-empty church. She passed the time reading a flyer describing the church's history.

> St Andrews church building dates from the twelfth century. It is almost certain that the first church on this site was built around 904 AD when Werfith, the Bishop of Worcester, gave land to a thegn named Wulfsig…

What in the world is a thegn, Maggie wondered.

Her thoughts were interrupted by Colonel Aspimall's sitting down beside her.

"Such a sad occasion," he murmured.

"The group sent a wreath. Lilies," he added.

Maggie nodded. She had also sent flowers. Spider mums in whites and creams and pale yellows.

They were soon joined by the other members of the committee. Norm Weaver and Irma Swinford and Marjory Eaton.

The church was filling up. A man walked by, escorting an older couple, followed by two teenage boys. All looked devastated and unable to comprehend that this could be happening.

Maggie assumed these were Iris' husband and parents and sons. She had not known that Iris had children. The younger boy was trying not to cry but failing.

There were a dozen people from the church present. Trying to turn around discretely, Maggie saw Mark Pilkington and, in the back, Willis and Marcy and Bartlett and Dexter, who were not hiding their interest in the funeral attendees.

The service started and Maggie realised she was coming to know the words by heart. It was her third funeral in as many weeks.

Iris was being buried in the church graveyard. Maggie stood at the edge of the crowd and was joined by Willis.

"I see you got your friend that fancy solicitor you used for the Linley case," Willis said softly. "He's going to need him."

"Oh?"

"We're just waiting confirmation on the results of the soil sample from the boots," he continued.

"You're going to charge him?"

"You didn't hear it from me," Willis cautioned.

"I won't say a word to Joshua. Or anyone," Maggie assured him. "I do appreciate your telling me."

Willis grunted.

Maggie thought. Surely there must be some way to prove Joshua was innocent or find evidence that would point to the real killer.

She watched impatiently as the coffin was lowered into the grave. She had to get busy. The best thing she could do for Iris—and Jonquil—was to discover the murderer and achieve justice for his victims.

Susan Alexander

Chapter Forty-Five

Maggie arrived back at Beaumatin in time for a late lunch. She found Thomas already seated at the table, aggressively spooning his soup. He did not get up when she entered and pull out her chair, which was his custom.

What now, Maggie wondered. Or was this just part of his prolonged snit?

"Thomas?"

"You're late. I wasn't even sure you were coming."

"I was attending Iris Murtaugh's funeral. My presence was expected. You were out on the estate, so I sent you a text," explained Maggie, while berating herself for sounding apologetic.

"You did?"

Thomas got up and left the room. He returned with his mobile. He swiped, found Maggie's message, and read it.

"Humpf."

He glanced at his watch, pushed his soup bowl away, and stood.

"I'm going to watch the cricket," he announced.

Maggie looked stricken. He ignored her and left.

Well, be that way, she thought angrily as she pushed her own plate away.

Her mobile sounded to indicate she had a message.

It was from Alice Hawkins. Alice and her spouse, Patty Rizzoli, shared the flat on the garden level of Maggie's Boston townhouse.

She read, "Hey Maggie. The boiler's broken. No heat. No hot water. Had the emergency services guy in. He says it's kaput and you need a new one. Please advise."

Oh dear. Life's just one thing after another, Maggie thought.

A second text came in.

"At least the stove uses gas and Patty and I are showering at our respective universities."

Their universities. Maggie remembered. Alice was a professor of sociology at Boston University, while Patty was a sports coach at Simmons.

Simmons. The women's college Rosamunde Pilkington had been attending when she had committed suicide.

Maggie wanted to find out more about Rosamunde's death. And boilers were expensive. Maggie decided she needed to go to Boston to deal with the heating repair and, while she was there, see what she could find out about Rosamunde Pilkington.

She replied to Alice that she would fly over the next day and hoped they would not be too cold. She would confirm the time once she had booked her flight.

Alice immediately replied that they would be delighted to see her and, in the meantime, she and Patty would try to keep each other warm.

The Greater Gloucestershire Galanthus Group

Maggie went off to break the news to Thomas.

Susan Alexander

Chapter forty-six

As she had expected, there was cricket playing on the television, but her husband was napping.

In fact, he seemed to be dreaming. Thomas' eyes were moving back and forth behind closed lids. His hands opened and closed, and Maggie was surprised to hear him mutter, "No. Not here. No. No."

This was unusual Thomas behaviour. She decided the dream was not pleasant and perhaps she should wake up her husband.

She laid a hand on his shoulder.

"Thomas?"

She shook hm gently.

"Thomas?"

He started awake, squinted at her, then exclaimed, "Maggie!" and pulled her to him.

"I couldn't find you. I was afraid you had gone," he murmured into her hair.

His dream, Maggie thought. Which was not going to make her announcement about the Boston trip easier.

"I'm here. It was just a dream, Thomas."

He grunted and shifted his position so Maggie nestled in the crook of his arm. He played with her curls.

Maggie let a few minutes pass. Then she ventured, "Thomas?"

"Yes, my dear?"

"I've had some news. From Boston."

"Your mother?"

"No. No, mother's fine as far as I know. It's the house. The boiler. It's broken and needs to be replaced. Poor Patty and Alice have no heat or hot water. Neither would we if we were there."

"Yes?"

"Replacing a boiler. It's expensive. Alice is reluctant to take responsibility for the decisions needed. About boiler options. She asked me to come over."

"To go to Boston?"

"Yes."

Thomas disengaged himself.

"When?"

"If I left tomorrow, I could deal with the problem on Monday and take a plane back on Tuesday."

Maggie knew Thomas was unhappy about this, even though she was making a perfectly reasonable request. And why did she even feel she had to frame this as a request? Did she really need to ask his permission? Did he expect her to?

Finally Thomas said, "Very well. I'll drive you to Heathrow. Let me know your flight time."

"Oh Thomas, you don't need to. I won't be gone that long. I can leave the car in a parking and then drive back."

"No, I want to."

"And my return?"

"I'll meet you."

Maggie reflected ruefully that Thomas did not believe her about the boiler and the necessity for the Boston trip. Maybe he thought Paley was joining her. Or, even worse, maybe he thought she was lying altogether and that she and Joshua were going to sneak off somewhere.

Instead of protesting, she said, "Thank you," leaned over, and gave Thomas a kiss. Then she stood.

"I'd better go see if I can book a flight. I'll text you the details."

She left and Thomas fumed. Oxford. London. And now, Boston. He had thought when she had resigned the Appleton fellowship and accepted the Weingarten chair that it would free her to spend more time at Beaumatin. With her husband. But it seemed that she was busier than ever. And then there was Paley…

Thomas glanced out the window and noticed that the sun was shining. Maybe a ride would put him in a better humour.

Susan Alexander

Chapter forty-seven

Maggie allowed the steward to wrap her in a cashmere throw and the stewardess to refill her glass with the Meursault Premier Cru that were perquisites of a British Airways first class transatlantic flight.

She had rationalised the extravagant ticket price by reminding herself that, at such short notice, there were no business class seats available on the flight that would get in late afternoon on Sunday so commercial travellers would be back in their offices or ready for an early meeting on Monday morning.

She sipped her Meursault—it really was very pleasant—and tried to formulate a plan. She had so little time before her return flight on Tuesday evening.

She had dutifully called her mother, apologized for the lack of warning, explained the boiler situation, and asked if she were free for dinner that evening. Her mother had grudgingly agreed and said she would see if her brother Samuel and his family were free.

Before her family dinner, Maggie figured she could talk to Patty and Alice and ask Patty if she remembered Rosamunde's death. It had been only two years before and Maggie assumed suicides were not common at Simmons. It must have had an impact on the college community. Perhaps there were school records that might be accessed.

First thing Monday morning the boiler man was coming. That was convenient. With jet lag, Maggie knew she would be awake early and would be free to investigate the rest of Monday and all of Tuesday before her evening flight. Perhaps she could find a reporter who had covered the story. Or, even better, a police officer. Best of all would be seeing the police records. She had no contacts in the Boston police force, but perhaps someone she knew would know someone. It was the way the world worked.

Maggie realised she was exhausted. From the BBC meeting. From Crispin's death and his outrageous legacy. From Joshua's peril. From Thomas' suspicions. After a delicious meal, accompanied by some more of the Meursault, she succumbed to the warmth of the cashmere throw and slept until a solicitous flight attendant woke her so she could prepare for landing.

Maggie had taken only a carry-on suitcase and her laptop bag, so she did not need to wait for baggage. She was quickly through passport control and customs and found the driver from the car service used by the Eliots at the arrivals exit. It was late afternoon but before the worst of rush hour traffic and Maggie was soon at the Marlboro Street townhouse.

She let herself in. It was cool, but not uncomfortably so. The temperature was in the sixties. She texted Alice, "I'm here. Do you want to come up or should I come down?"

"Come down," was the immediate response.

Alice and Patty greeted Maggie with hugs and kisses. They sat her down in a comfortable chair beside a gas-heated fireplace and offered her coffee or something stronger.

Maggie opted for coffee. While Patty bustled about, Maggie looked around at the cosy flat, decorated in shades of blue and peach and yellow.

"I'm sorry about the boiler," she began.

The Greater Gloucestershire Galanthus Group

"Not as sorry as we are that you had to drag yourself across an ocean to take care of it," Alice countered. "How was the flight?"

"Pleasant. No complaints. They took good care of me."

Patty returned bearing a tray with mugs of coffee and a plate of homemade peanut butter cookies.

Maggie took one.

"Yum. Now I know I'm back in the U.S."

The women chatted. Maggie told them the boiler guy was coming at eight the next morning. She invited the pair out for dinner Monday evening. They should pick a place and let her know where and when.

After a lull while mugs were refilled, Maggie began, "Patty, I have what you might find a strange request. Two years ago, there was a suicide at Simmons. A girl named Rosamunde Pilkington. I wondered if you remembered…"

"The Pilkington suicide? Of course I remember. There was a memorial service. Grief counselling. Suicide prevention seminars. The whole circus. I don't think there'd ever been a suicide at Simmons before. Or at least not that anyone remembered. Why are you asking?"

"It's complicated, but Rosamunde's mother, Jonquil, was murdered a couple of weeks ago. Her body was found on our property. A friend of mine is under suspicion. I'm sure he didn't do it and I have this feeling there is a connection between the suicide and the murder. And since I'm here, I want to find out as much as I can."

"Rosamunde's mother was murdered? Wow," said Patty.

"The poor family. So much loss," sympathized Alice.

"Rosamunde was an only child. Jonquil's father is still alive. He's a dentist. Her husband Mark is the headmaster of a school called Churn Valley College. It's not a college like in the U.S. It's more of a private boarding school. They have students from age six to eighteen or nineteen."

Patty looked thoughtful.

"I didn't know Rosamunde myself. She wasn't into sports. And it turned out she was pretty much of a loner. She wasn't a bad student. Solid Bs, I seem to remember. She hadn't gone to classes the week before she killed herself."

"How did she die?"

"Jumped off a bridge into the Charles. It was February. If she hadn't drowned, the hypothermia would have finished her."

"How sad," said Alice.

They sat in silence for a minute. Finally Maggie asked, "Patty, do you think the school has records of this that I might be able to see? I really need to learn as much as I can."

Patty thought.

"I can ask Kevin. He works in the Provost's office. He might know about any records. Let me give him a call."

"I don't want to impose or get anyone to get into trouble."

"Nah. Kev and I are tight. We work with the LGBTQ group on campus. Let me give him a call."

Patty left. Maggie heard a low-voiced conversation and a couple of barks of laughter. She returned smiling.

"Kev is on the case. He'll go in early tomorrow and, if there are any records, he'll find them."

"That's really nice of him..." Maggie began.

"It's your title, dearie. Not the academic one. He's psyched about meeting a baroness. He wants to call you 'your ladyship' and was disappointed he wasn't supposed to curtsy. He may anyway. He proposed lunch at noon tomorrow. A Thai place near campus. Is that all right with you?"

"Yes. I'm sure I'll be done with the boiler guy by then."

"Wear your tiara. Or at least have a lorgnette."

"I'm afraid I left the tiara at home," Maggie laughed.

"There's really a tiara?" Alice asked.

"Yes, I'm afraid so. Edwardian. Diamonds. I have no occasion to wear it, so it stays in the safe, with the rest of the family jewels. I did bring the pearls, though."

"Pearls?"

"Long, luscious strands. You'll see."

Maggie had packed the pearls to wear to dinner with her mother, with whom she had a difficult relationship. They were a confidence booster.

"Then I guess they'll have to do," Patty grinned.

Susan Alexander

Chapter forty-eight

Maggie's family dinner went as expected. She had brought her mother the traditional bottle of Bombay Sapphire from duty free. Her oldest brother Samuel and his wife Ariadne had been able to come, but both of her nephews sent their regrets. It had been too short notice and they had already made plans.

Tall and thin like her daughter, with softly curling white hair, Frances Eliot greeted Maggie tepidly and allowed her to kiss her cheek. Ariadne was more welcoming, while Samuel gave her arm a squeeze and a quick peck on the forehead.

For dinner, Frances served a hearty New England beef stew with dumplings. It was a dish Thomas would have enjoyed, Maggie decided.

Ariadne, an athletic blonde who played tennis and golf and had little in common with her sister-in-law, asked Maggie about her work, more out of politeness and to make conversation than any real interest.

Maggie began to tell her about *PeopleFlows* and the possibility of a BBC series.

"The BBC?" her mother asked disdainfully. "Not HBO or Netflix or one of the major networks?"

"Perhaps PBS will air it," said Maggie with an edge to her voice. "But I have to write it first."

"Ah yes. 'There's many a slip twixt the cup and the lip,'" Francis quoted smugly and turned to her son to ask him about his day at work.

Ariadne looked embarrassed and Maggie reflected that having a mother like Frances was what had forced her to be strong and independent and indifferent to others' opinions. Was this one of her problems with Thomas? Who seemed to expect her to seek his approval and even, at times, his permission?

She missed her father, who had been supportive of his only daughter. It would be three years since his death this coming December. She also missed her Great Aunt Margaret, after whom she had been named. A professor of Greek at Maggie's alma mater, she had set the bars high for her grandniece, but expressed her confidence that Maggie would be able to clear the hurdle if she made the effort.

So tough tuna, she thought, as Samuel entranced his mother with his latest neurosurgical triumph.

When offered coffee, Maggie apologized.

"I'm sorry. It's after two o'clock in the morning in England. And the boiler man is arriving at dawn tomorrow. I asked the car service to come…"

At that moment, the doorbell chimed.

"Ah. This must be the driver."

Maggie received perfunctory hugs from Samuel and her mother, and a genuine one from Ariadne.

"Give us more warning next time. The boys were disappointed not to see their favourite aunt."

Maggie was their only aunt, but she decided Ariadne was sincere and hugged her sister-in-law back with equal affection.

The Greater Gloucestershire Galanthus Group

She dozed on the ride back to Marlboro Street. Without heat, the house was chilly. She quickly pulled on her nightgown, put an additional blanket on the bed, and got under the covers. She was asleep in moments.

Susan Alexander

Chapter forty-nine

Maggie had been up for several hours and had consumed three mugs of coffee by the time the boiler guy arrived. He was a cheerful man in his fifties, bald, and paunchy. An embroidered patch on his green work shirt read "Al."

Al looked at the boiler, shook his head, and confirmed that a new one was needed. He estimated that a decent boiler would run around eight thousand dollars plus the labour costs to install it. If Mrs Eliot wanted it installed that week, another thousand would jump her to the front of the queue.

Al, a shrewd judge of human nature, was not surprised when his client agreed to pay for priority.

After Al left, promising to be back Wednesday at the latest, and getting contact information for Alice and Patty, Maggie had nothing left to do except get herself up to look like "Lady Raynham" for her lunch with Kevin.

She had a dark brown wool knit dress that set off the pearls. She lacked a hat, but this was an off-campus Thai restaurant and she didn't want to look ridiculous. Her hair, though, could use some attention.

Maggie called a nearby beauty salon and was lucky that they had an opening for a shampoo and styling.

Back at the house, Maggie checked herself out in a mirror. In her eyes, she looked like an ordinary, middle-aged woman who somehow had acquired an impressive necklace of pearls. She hoped Kevin would not be too disappointed when he met his baroness.

Susan Alexander

Chapter Fifty

The Thai place was on Huntington Avenue, a few blocks from the Simmons campus. Maggie took a taxi and found Patty already seated at a table with a second person who had to be Kevin.

Kevin Hegarty could best be described as willowy. In his late twenties, he had chocolate brown eyes and carrot coloured hair that was short on the sides and styled into an impressive quiff on the top. He wore a burnt orange suit with a nipped-in waist and tight pants, a brown shirt, and a deep yellow tie. Autumnal colours.

Patty was more casually dressed in jeans and a Simmons sweatshirt, blue with a blue and yellow "Sharks" mascot on the front. She made introductions.

"Maggie, this is Kevin Hegarty. Kevin, this is Lady Raynham."

Kevin studied her for a moment. Then he gave a small bow and said, "Pleased to meet you, your ladyship," in a well-modulated tenor.

Thankful that she had passed muster, Maggie extended her hand, which he took.

"How do you do, Kevin," she smiled.

Patty nudged him in the ribs with her elbow.

"Don't be a doofus, Kev."

Kevin glared.

"If I'm a doofus, then you're…"

"Why don't we sit down," Maggie intervened.

"Yeah. And order. I'm starving," said Patty.

They studied the menu, which had the usual Thai favourites.

"Wine?" Maggie asked.

"Sure," said Kevin.

"I'd better not," said Patty ruefully. "I've got to coach all afternoon."

Maggie ordered a bottle of Chardonnay and a stir fry with Thai basil that would not be too challenging to eat while they talked. Kevin had green chicken curry and Patty, Pad Thai.

While they waited, Kevin said, "Patty told me you're interested in the Pilkington suicide."

"I am. Do you know anything about it?"

"Oh yes. I was there at the time. It created quite an uproar. Fingers were pointed. Blame needed to be assigned. Then her parents flew over. Daddy was all right. A bit of a Casper Milquetoast. But Mommy Dearest... Well, they had a right to be upset, but she was a harridan. You could hear her screeching all over the academic campus. She got so hysterical they had to send for a doctor to sedate her.

"For sure they dropped the ball with the girl. She was depressed. Hadn't gone to classes for a couple of weeks. Had few if any friends. Her roommate had a boyfriend at Boston College with an off-campus apartment and she was spending most of her time there. So she hadn't noticed the state our Rosamunde was in. And, oh yeah, Rosamunde was pregnant. Oops."

"Rosamunde was pregnant?"

The Greater Gloucestershire Galanthus Group

"Yes. About three months, according to the coroner."

"Do they know who the father was?"

"No. But it seems he left her holding the bag. Or, I should say, the baby."

"Bastard," said Patty.

"There's no evidence that he—whoever he was—even knew Rosamunde was preggers," said Kevin, in defence of his sex.

"Anyhow, I managed to copy Rosamunde's files."

Kevin reached down beside his chair and brought up an elegant attaché case. He looked around to make sure there was no one he knew to observe him, took out an envelope, and handed it to Maggie.

"Here you are, my lady."

Maggie had to try not to smile.

"Thank you, Kevin. And please, call me Maggie."

Kevin blushed.

Maggie poured Kevin and herself some more Chardonnay.

"Do you mind if I take a look?" she asked.

"No, of course not. Please go ahead."

The contents included a picture of Rosamunde, her transcripts—solid B's with some A's in history, her dormitory assignments and roommates. A Candace Frisch her freshman year and a Melody Jackson her sophomore. It seemed Rosamunde and Melody had been assigned to share a room when neither indicated a roommate preference.

"Melody Jackson. Is she still a student?" Maggie asked.

"I checked and yes. She's a senior."

"I don't suppose it would be possible..."

"To speak to Melody? Hmm. Tricky. I could find out her schedule and let you know where her classes are. Then it would be up to you to accost her. And see if she'd want to talk."

"All right."

"Tell me, though. Why are you so interested in Rosamunde? Did you know her?"

"Didn't Patty tell you?"

"No. Just that you wanted to know about the suicide."

"I didn't know if you wanted me to say anything. Not that I know much," explained Patty.

"Oh. Well, Rosamunde's mother Jonquil. The harridan. She was murdered a couple of weeks ago. Her body was found on our land. I wondered if there might be some connection with Rosamunde's death. A friend of mine is a suspect, so I wanted to find out more about her suicide to see... Well, to see if it would indicate who else might have done it. Jonquil's murder."

"Someone murdered that terrible woman? How very Agatha Christie!"

"And you're sure Rosamunde wasn't murdered?"

"The police said it was definitely suicide. Why?"

"Because before she died, Jonquil was writing anonymous letters accusing my friend of seducing Rosamunde. And being her killer."

"Whoa," said Patty.

"Oh my. Poison pen letters. I feel just like Miss Marple. And you're Lady Bantry. Or, no, maybe you're… Doesn't matter," Kevin finished.

"Thank you so much for your help, Kevin. I really appreciate it," Maggie said.

"A pleasure," Kevin assured her.

"Now if only I could see the police report," she mused.

"The police report?" Kevin asked.

"Yes. It will have a different perspective from the college's," Maggie explained.

"Hmm. Maybe my cousin Eamonn. He's a detective in the BPD. Would you like me to ask him?"

"Could you? That would be great. I hate to be a bother. Or seem like some sort of crank. Or voyeur. I'm just worried about my friend's being wrongly accused."

"This friend. It's not you, is it?" Kevin asked.

"No. No, he was a colleague at Harvard. And he's now at my college in Oxford. I think someone's trying to frame him."

Maggie explained about the weekend at Beaumatin, the body in the boot, and the corpse in Joshua's room.

Patty and Kevin were fascinated. Then Kevin checked his watch.

"I need to get back to work. But I'll check with my cousin."

"Thank you."

Maggie rummaged in her purse.

"Here's my card."

She handed Kevin one of her Lady Raynham visiting cards, thinking he would prefer that to her Merrion one.

"Ooh la la," he said, and reverently pocketed the engraved piece of paper.

Chapter Fifty-One

Maggie returned to Marlboro Street and changed into more casual clothing. Then she took the MBTA over to Harvard Square. She browsed through the Coop and found a couple of history books she thought Thomas would enjoy, then explored the shops on Brattle Street. There was still time to get back to the house before dinner, so she walked through the Harvard campus. She saw no one she knew. Ten years was a long time in the life of a university. She still knew many on the faculty, of course, but had decided not to contact her old friends during her brief visit. She had too much on her plate.

Back at the house, she got a text from Alice.

"Meet us at Legal Seafood at seven. Reservation's in the name of Eliot."

Maggie considered her limited wardrobe options. In the end, she chose a black gaberdine pants suit, a cream silk blouse, and the pearls, which blended with the blouse and were mostly obscured by the jacket.

She was the first to arrive and was surprised to be escorted to a large table.

"This is for Eliot?" she asked.

The maître d, or host, or whatever his title was, nodded and left. Another staff member approached and asked if she'd like a drink while she waited for her party.

"An Absolut Bloody Mary, not too spicy, please," she said and hoped it would be a good one, with lime, horseradish, celery salt, a celery stick, and a not-too-heavy hand with the Tabasco sauce. A proper Bloody was hard to find in England for some reason. Unless one made it oneself.

Alice arrived.

"Are you sure this is the right table?" Maggie asked.

Alice nodded.

"Be surprised. Patty sounded very pleased with herself."

Maggie decided it must be something to do with Rosamunde's suicide.

"We had a nice lunch with a colleague of hers. Kevin."

"So I gathered."

The waiter reappeared with Maggie's Bloody Mary and took Alice's order for a gin and tonic.

"And nothing fancy. Just Gordon's and Schweppes and lime," Alice insisted.

"G&T with a stick of cucumber? Or a desiccated orange slice for a garnish? Can you imagine?" she asked Maggie in disgust.

Maggie was telling Alice about progress with the boiler when Patty arrived. She was accompanied by Kevin and two men who were strangers.

"Hi, Maggie. I hope it's all right I invited some people who can help you. This is my cousin, Eamonn Dolan. And this is Nick Holmes. Both are detectives in the Boston PD. Nick is Eamonn's partner," explained Kevin proudly. "Nick, Eamonn, this is Lady Raynham."

The Greater Gloucestershire Galanthus Group

"Call me Maggie, please," she said as she shook hands.

Tall and muscled, Eamonn was in his early thirties and had dark hair, blue eyes, and rugged features. Nick was a few years younger. He was a handsome Black man, as tall and as well built as his partner, with close-cropped hair.

A waiter appeared. The policemen ordered Sam Adams, while Kevin wanted a Hendricks G&T. Alice nudged Maggie.

Conversation turned on the prospects for the Celtics, Red Socks, and Patriots. Maggie was surprised to find that Kevin was a passionate Red Socks fan and even had season tickets. She had little to contribute, not having much interest in sports and being out-of-touch with the Boston teams in the years she had been away.

Once main courses were served, Kevin said, "So Maggie, I told Eamonn about your interest in poor Rosamunde's suicide. He looked into it and found out that Nick was the detective on the case."

"Yeah, it was my first case after I'd joined the criminal investigation unit. You don't forget that one."

"So what can you tell me?"

"I've found out since then it's not even that unusual. Depressed college student jumps in the river."

Maggie nodded. Oxford also had students. And rivers.

"You're certain it was suicide."

"Oh yeah."

"Her mother insisted she was murdered."

Nick scoffed.

"There were half a dozen witnesses. They all swore no one was anywhere near the girl when she jumped. If there had been, someone might have stopped her."

"Well, that seems to be conclusive."

Maggie thought.

"Do you know why Rosamunde killed herself? Was there anything in particular?"

Nick shrugged. "Who knows? She was pregnant. And she had this obsession with this guy. A local celebrity."

"Do you know who?"

"Hang on. I brought my notes."

Nick reached in a pocket and brought out a small, battered notebook.

"I've kept all my notebooks. Souvenirs," he grinned.

He leafed through.

"Okay. Here it is. When we searched her room, instead of posters of Justin Bieber or Tom Brady, what you'd expect from a college kid, we found a whole wall covered with pictures of this dude that she had cut out and taped up. Newspaper clippings. Magazine photos. Whatever she could find about him."

Maggie suddenly thought she knew who "this dude" was.

"Stone Paley," she said.

Nick looked surprised.

"Yeah, that's him. How'd you guess?"

"Because Rosamunde's mother was convinced that Paley had murdered her daughter. And that he was the baby's father."

"Couldn't have murdered her. Like I said, there were witnesses. And just to be sure, we checked. Paley was giving a class in front of forty students when she jumped."

"And the baby?"

"You mean do a DNA test? No law against getting someone pregnant if they're willing and of age. And Paley had serious juice. We weren't even allowed to question him."

"Was there a note?"

Rick flipped back a page.

"Yeah. She left it on the desk in her room. But all it said was, 'I can't go on. Sorry.'"

Poor Rosamunde, Maggie thought. From her picture, Joshua would have never looked twice at her.

"If you don't mind my asking, why are you so interested?" Nick asked.

"There've been two murders. In England. Rosamunde's mother Jonquil and a woman friend of hers. Paley's now in England and the police learned about Jonquil's fixation on him, about believing he seduced and then murdered Rosamunde, so he's a suspect. He's also a friend of mine."

Alice suddenly remembered Maggie's 'friendship.'

"Paley? Wasn't he your…"

"Yes," Maggie interrupted repressively. "I know Paley's not a murderer. As I had to come over because our boiler died, I thought I'd take the opportunity to find out about the suicide."

Nick nodded. "If your local police have any questions, they can contact me," he said and passed her his card.

"I remember the mother. She was a real ballbuster, if you'll excuse me."

"I didn't know her very well, but she had that reputation," Maggie agreed.

Conversation dwindled while the group enjoyed their food. Maggie was relishing her fried clams when Eamonn suddenly asked, "Kev said you're some sort of British aristocrat. But I got the impression you're from Boston."

"I am from Boston. Born and bred. But two years ago I married a British man who happened to be a baron, which made me a baroness," Maggie explained.

She hoped that Eamonn, like some Bostonians of Irish descent, would not hold Thomas' Englishness against him.

"We met him last summer. Lord Raynham could be one of the cast from Downton Abbey. Except he's better looking," Patty added.

"And you should see the stately home where they live. You can google it," Kevin added.

Now Maggie was embarrassed.

"But really, I'm still just a college professor."

"Don't worry. We won't hold that against you. Your title or your being a professor," Nick reassured her.

"Thank you," said Maggie sincerely and went back to enjoying her fried clams.

Susan Alexander

Chapter Fifty-Two

Thomas was waiting for Maggie at Heathrow. She thought he seemed to be in a better mood than when she had left, not knowing that he had checked and ascertained that Paley was, in fact, in Oxford.

Back at Beaumatin, Maggie presented Thomas with the books she had gotten him plus a long woollen muffler in Harvard's colours of crimson and white.

"How was the trip?"

Maggie decided Thomas did not need to know about her efforts on Joshua's behalf.

"You won't believe how much it costs to replace a boiler. And I had to pay a hefty premium to have it installed this week. Fortunately the weather has been mild, but that could change.

"I had dinner with Mother. Along with Samuel and Ariadne. The nephews were busy. She served a New England beef stew you would have liked. With dumplings. I'll make it for you the next time Mrs Cook's away.

"Otherwise I spent an afternoon in Cambridge and took Patty and Alice out to dinner. That's about it."

"I missed you."

"And I missed you."

Maggie yawned.

"I'm going to unpack, wash, and take a nap."

"It's a pleasant day. Let's go riding this afternoon."

"That would be nice."

Maggie decided not to kill Thomas' mood by pointing out she needed to go back to Oxford the next day. That could wait until after dinner when her husband would be mellow with Bordeaux, pie, and the History channel.

Chapter Fifty-Three

Maggie was back at Oxford and explaining to Joshua what she had discovered.

"So I found out what I could about Rosamunde's death."

"Rosamunde?"

"Jonquil Pilkington's daughter. Whom Jonquil was accusing you of murdering."

"Oh yeah. Her."

"I spoke to someone in the Provost's office at Simmons, where she was a student, and saw her file. She was depressed and had been missing classes. I got a picture of her. Does she look at all familiar?"

Maggie showed Joshua the picture of Rosamunde that Kevin had provided.

Joshua studied it, then handed it back.

"Familiar? Not offhand. She could be anyone. Well, not anyone. But she's not very attractive, is she?"

Maggie wasn't sure how to respond to this, so she moved on.

"I was also fortunate to talk to the police detective who investigated Rosamunde's death. And who assures me there was no way it could have been a murder, as Jonquil implied in her anonymous letters. It was definitely suicide. But the thing is, Rosamunde had a crush on you. More than a crush. A wall of her dorm room was covered with pictures of you. News stories. Magazine articles."

"She was stalking me?"

"No, not exactly stalking. Everything she had was publicly available. But she was definitely obsessed."

Joshua took the photo back from Maggie, looked at it again, and shook his head.

"Of course it was pretty common to have some fan or other stopping me when I was walking from my place to the campus. Or between buildings. Wanting an autograph. Or to ask a question about my work as an excuse to make contact. But those girls. They all looked pretty much the same. I wouldn't have necessarily noticed one in particular."

Paley shrugged.

"And then... Rosamunde was three months pregnant when she died. Are you certain you..."

"It wasn't me who got her pregnant. Couldn't have been."

Joshua was definite.

"You're sure you didn't sleep with her?"

"Doubt it. She's not my type. Much too young. But even supposing I had, I couldn't have gotten her pregnant."

"Why not?"

"Because..." Joshua looked uncomfortable.

"Yes?"

"I'd had the snip."

"The snip?"

"Yeah, the snip. I'd had a vasectomy."

"You did?"

Maggie was astonished.

"Er, yes. Precisely to avoid just this. The Rosamundes. Who'd tell you they were on the pill but thought it would be cool to get knocked up by a celeb. So I had the snip. Had myself tested afterwards to make sure. Sperm free."

Maggie frowned.

"Just when did you have this done?"

"Um, when I was at Berkeley."

Maggie was speechless.

Joshua was avoiding her eyes.

"And you didn't tell me? Had I said I didn't want children?"

"Well, no. But I had a lot of sperm frozen before. A whole bunch. So if you did want... You could have... Although I'd hoped you wouldn't want any. You were already forty and..."

Maggie fumed, then decided to move on.

"Still, Rosamunde was pregnant."

"Like I said, it wasn't me. Even assuming I had slept with the girl. Which I'm pretty positive I hadn't. Seems like she was a wacko."

Joshua paused and thought.

"But if that woman who was murdered…"

"Jonquil Pilkington…"

"Yeah. Her. If she believed that I'd done that. Gotten her daughter pregnant and, er, refused to accept responsibility. If she believed that the girl committed suicide because of me. Well, that might give her a reason to want to kill me. But why would I want to kill her?"

"I don't know. Maybe to avoid a scandal?"

Joshua scoffed.

"This is 2014. Not 1914. The girl was old enough. And she could have gotten an abortion."

That was true. The days when Joshua would have had to resign his position because of such a scandal were over. Even if he had had sex with Rosamunde, which seemed unlikely, they would both have been single, consenting adults.

"Anyhow I have the contact info for the detective who was on the case. I'll pass it on to Willis and tell him what I know. I hope it will make him consider who else might have killed Jonquil. And Iris."

"Thank you, Elle."

Joshua crossed to Maggie, who was perched on the edge of her desk, and pulled her into his arms.

"I wasn't sure you still cared."

"Of course I care, Joshua," said Maggie, trying disentangle herself.

"You mean there's a chance…" he began when Maggie's door opened with a bang.

The Greater Gloucestershire Galanthus Group

It was DI Bartlett and DS Dexter.

"There you are. Paley, you're coming with us to assist us in our inquiries," Bartlett said.

"What?"

"Come with us, Professor," repeated Dexter.

"Maggie! Do I have to?" Joshua pleaded.

"Yes, you have to go with them, Joshua. But don't worry. I'll call Luke Fitzroy. And talk to Willis. Just don't say anything, anything at all, until Fitzroy gets here. And if you have to wait, drink tea. Police station coffee is awful."

"Professor?" Dexter repeated.

Joshua gestured helplessly, gave Maggie a hurried embrace, and left with the detectives. Maggie picked up her mobile and began to call.

SUSAN ALEXANDER

Chapter fifty-four

A few hours later, there was a knock on her door and DCI Willis came in.

He was reverting to his usual style in sartorial terms. His suit needed pressing and his necktie was askew. Maggie wondered if Debbie's indiscretions had ended her relationship with the detective.

"So, Maggie, you said you had some important information. I'm surprised."

"I told you I'd let you know if I learned anything."

"So you did," Willis conceded.

"I had to make a quick trip to Boston. I have a house there and the boiler had died. As long as I was there, I decided to look into the death of Rosamunde, Jonquil's daughter. I have tenants and one of them works at the college Rosamunde was attending when she died."

"Of course he does," Willis said ruefully.

"Not he. She."

"Okay. She. So what did you find out?"

"Patty, Patty Rizzoli, my tenant, introduced me to a man who works in the Provost's office. He let me see Rosamunde's file. She was a loner. Severely depressed. Jonquil did not take her death well. While that's completely understandable, Jonquil made scenes. There was a lot of drama. She refused to believe Rosamunde had killed herself."

Willis grunted.

"And I managed to meet the detective who investigated Rosamunde's death. He was the partner of a cousin of the man who worked in the Provost's office."

"Of course he was."

"And Nick—Nick Holmes is his name—said it was definitely suicide. He interviewed half a dozen witnesses who saw her jump and they all swore there was no one near her at the time. He gave me his card if you want to contact him."

Maggie rummaged in her purse and handed Willis Nick's card.

"But there's something else. Rosamunde was three months pregnant when she died. I think that's what the bit about the vile seducer in the anonymous letters refers to."

"Oh?"

Willis looked interested.

"Well, she may have been pregnant, but it wasn't Joshua."

"And you know this how?"

"Joshua's had a vasectomy. Years ago. He couldn't have been the father."

"Humpf."

"I'm sure he'd agree to be tested if it would exonerate him."

Willis looked unhappy.

"So the letters accusing Joshua of murder and seduction, they're not true. I think blaming Joshua was

Jonquil's way of dealing with her guilt about her daughter's suicide."

"Why fix on Paley?"

"There is that. Apparently Rosamunde had a crush on Joshua. A wall in her dorm room was covered with newspaper and magazine photos and articles about Joshua. But nothing to indicate she was stalking him. She wasn't like Linley. Just where other college students might have posters of movie stars or pop singers, Rosamunde had pictures of Joshua."

"Paley's like a rock star?"

"You've seen him. He's quite a celebrity in the U.S."

"Right."

"All of which supports my theory that Joshua's being framed by someone who knew about Jonquil's vendetta against him. And realised that Joshua's coming to Oxford would be like waving a red flag at a bull."

"Like who?"

"I would think that is something the police should investigate," Maggie responded primly.

Before Willis could come back with something snarky, someone knocked on Maggie's door. This time, the person waited for Maggie's "Come in."

It was Luke Fitzroy, followed by Joshua.

Luke Fitzroy was a tall, distinguished-looking man in his forties. He had sandy hair and grey eyes and wore a superbly tailored, navy chalk stripe suit. Maggie reflected that Thomas would be able to identify the stripes in his silk tie.

His appearance formed a contrast to Joshua, who was definitely bedraggled.

"Hello, Maggie," Luke beamed.

He noticed Willis.

"And you're... Wilson? Wilcox?"

"Willis," the detective offered grudgingly.

"Willis. Of course. And you seem to be recovered. Splendid."

The last time Fitzroy had seen Willis, the detective had been recuperating from a knife wound that had nearly killed him.

"You're not arrested? They let you go?" Maggie asked Joshua anxiously.

"Yes. Thanks to Luke here. It seems that all the evidence against me is circumstantial."

"I'm so glad," Maggie said while Willis scowled.

"And Stone tells me you found out some interesting information while you were in Boston," Luke continued.

"Yes. I..."

"You've been lucky, Paley," Willis interrupted. "Just don't leave town, all right?"

The detective left.

The three looked at each other.

"Tea? Coffee? A celebratory whisky?" Maggie asked.

"Whisky for me," said Joshua.

"I'll join you, as I'm not driving," Luke concurred.

After she had served the men tumblers of their preferred tiple, Maggie told Luke about what she had learned in Boston and her conclusions.

The solicitor looked thoughtful.

"You told all this to the police?"

"I told Willis. And gave him the contact info for the detective who investigated."

At that moment the door opened and Thomas entered.

"Hi there, Lord," drawled Joshua.

"Raynham," said Fitzroy, recognizing his lordship.

"Fitzroy?" Thomas frowned.

Maggie was glad the solicitor was there acting as a duena.

"Thomas. You're early."

"Traffic was light."

Maggie was sure Thomas' unexpected appearance was to check that she was not with Joshua, but she let his prevarication pass.

"The police took Joshua in to 'assist them in their inquiries,' so I called Luke and told Joshua not to say anything until he arrived," Maggie explained.

"And a good thing you did," Fitzroy agreed. "Everything the police have is circumstantial or can be explained. And you have a solid alibi for the second murder."

"Yeah, but I still think they would have charged me if you hadn't been there."

"But I was there," said Luke reassuringly. "And I'll be there whenever the police come within a hundred yards of you."

He turned to Maggie.

"And with what you found out in Boston…"

"What's this about Boston?" Thomas demanded.

Rats. Rats and phooey. Maggie was about say something evasive, then remembered. The best defence is a good offense.

"You know my tenant Patty. She works at Simmons, the college Rosamunde Pilkington attended. I asked her to find out what she could about Rosamunde's death, as it seems to be related to the murders."

"And just who is Rosamunde Pilkington?"

"She was Jonquil Pilkington's daughter."

Maggie could tell Thomas was angry, but tough tuna.

"Humpf."

He noticed the men's tumblers of whisky, went, and poured himself a glass.

"So if you're here, Fitzroy, I assume the police consider Paley to be their prime suspect?" he asked, trying to keep a note of satisfaction from his voice.

"They took him in so he could assist them in their inquiries, yes," Luke confirmed.

"Elle warned me not to say anything without a solicitor and connected me with Luke," Joshua added, then turned to Maggie. "I haven't really thanked you. Without Luke, I'd probably be sitting in a cell right now."

Maggie suspected that Thomas would be quite pleased to have Joshua sitting in a cell but kept that thought to herself.

Luke finished his whisky and stood.

"I'll be in Oxford for a few days. I'm staying with the Master of my old college. So I'll be on the scene in case the police give you any more trouble," he told Joshua.

"Thank you. I'm finding all this rather unnerving," Joshua admitted.

Luke left. Joshua drained his glass.

"Thanks again, Elle. I don't know what I'd do without you."

He glanced slyly at Thomas as he stood.

"Well, all this is not getting my work done. I'll see you, Elle. Lord."

He ambled out.

Maggie reflected that "all this" was not getting her work done either.

Thomas was not finished.

"I thought you went to Boston because the boiler needed replacing. Not that you were going to help out Paley."

Maggie "had had it," as her father used to say.

"Do you want me to show you Alice's texts about the boiler problem? Or give you the name of the boiler guy? Or show you the large sum of money I had to transfer for the repairs? Well, I won't. Good grief, Thomas. Don't you trust me at all?"

Thomas' stony expression answered Maggie's question.

Finally he said, "These murders have nothing to do with us. Neither does what happens to Paley."

"Nothing to do with us? Jonquil was murdered at Beaumatin. Poor Iris was killed just a few yards from where we're standing. And, although I hesitate to mention this, given how you feel, Joshua is someone with whom I have a significant bit of personal history as well as a colleague."

Thomas glared, then muttered, "Pig-headed."

"Perhaps."

Maggie checked the time. She was exhausted. She began to pack up her laptop.

"Hereford Crescent?"

"Yes."

"Good."

Chapter fifty-five

Maggie was walking across the Merrion quad when she was hailed by Andrew Kittredge.

"Maggie!"

"Hello, Andrew."

"Remember you were asking me about Mark Pilkington? Well, the strangest thing. I saw him. Here. At Merrion."

"You did?"

"Yes. He was wearing a gown and coming from your staircase. I knew he looked familiar, but I thought it was someone from the faculty of another college. Then, just last night, it popped into my mind who he was."

"You're certain he was coming from my staircase?"

"Yes."

"When was this?"

"That's what I'm not sure about. But it was definitely since you asked me about him."

Maggie was trying to think about what Pilkington's presence at Merrion might mean.

"Quite a coincidence. A fellow I hadn't seen for a couple of decades. Then you ask about him. And he turns up here."

"Yes, quite," Maggie agreed, while a voice in her head reminded her, "There are no coincidences."

Andrew hurried off and Maggie continued to her rooms. She tapped to wake up her laptop but did not sit down at her desk.

What had Pilkington been doing at Merrion? In her staircase?

He hadn't come to see her. Or if he had, he had not left a note. That left... Joshua.

Someone had been trying to frame Joshua for two murders. Was it Pilkington? Who hated his wife, according to poor Iris. His wife who had cost him his Oxford career. And Paley, whom Jonquil blamed for the death of their only child.

And Iris? Had she known something that would have made the man a suspect?

The police had been so focussed on Joshua, they had not really considered the headmaster, even though he had no alibi for the night of Jonquil's murder. And Iris? Was Pilkington the man with the umbrella? Had he been unable to resist killing Iris in Joshua's rooms? Driving what he saw as another nail into the man's coffin?

And why Joshua? Well, that was easy. Mark must have known about Jonquil's conviction that Paley was behind Rosamunde's death. Might even have found one of the anonymous letters—they had been printed at the school, after all. He would not have been happy about that. What would be the consequences if it were discovered that the headmaster's wife was sending anonymous letters? Even at the new, more tolerant Oxford, there would be career consequences. She doubted Stephen would have been elected Master had his flagrantly unfaithful wife Kitty still been alive.

The Greater Gloucestershire Galanthus Group

Maggie was standing at a window, musing, when she noticed a figure crossing the quad. A man wearing a gown. As he got closer, she recognised him.

It was Mark Pilkington.

Susan Alexander

The Greater Gloucestershire Galanthus Group

Chapter Fifty-Six

Maggie stepped back so she was out of sight as Pilkington headed straight to her staircase.

It was dinner time and Joshua, whose rooms she assumed were Pilkington's destination, would be dining in hall.

Maggie rushed to her door and listened. Through the sturdy oak she could just about make out someone mounting the stairs.

What should she do?

She would wait a moment, and then go find out what Pilkington was up to.

Quietly opening her door, she heard soft footsteps stop, then silence.

Had Joshua begun locking his door?

Moments passed. Pilkington did not come back down, so Maggie assumed he had gotten into Joshua's rooms.

At least he had been alone. He was not murdering anyone. Like poor Iris. So what was he doing?

Maggie crept up the stairs.

Joshua's door was closed.

She grasped the doorknob, slowly turned it, and opened the door a crack.

The room was dim. And empty.

Was Pilkington in Joshua's bedroom?

Maggie opened the door wider and stepped inside.

"Mark?" she called softly.

There was no response.

Maggie took another step into the room. The door banged shut behind her and, before she could turn around, she was knocked to her knees. Something wrapped around her throat and was pulled tight.

Maggie struggled and tried to reach back and wrench the hands away that were yanking on the garrot. When that failed, she dug her fingernails into flesh. At least there would be DNA...

At that moment, the door suddenly opened and someone yelled, "What the..."

Mark Pilkington pushed Maggie to the floor and stood upright, panting.

"Pilkington?"

It was DCI Willis, along with Joshua, Stephen, and Luke Fitzroy. Behind them were DI Bartlett, DS Dexter, and DS Hickson.

"Elle!" Joshua cried out and began to move towards her.

"Paley!" Pilkington howled and leapt on him. He wrapped his hands around Paley's throat and squeezed.

"Hey!" Willis yelled.

The Greater Gloucestershire Galanthus Group

The detective tried to grab Pilkington, but the room was overcrowded, as Dexter and Barlett also tried to intervene.

"Do something!" Stephen cried.

DS Hickson pushed past her colleagues who were struggling with Pilkington and went to help Maggie get up.

"Are you all right?" she asked anxiously.

Hand to her throat, Maggie nodded.

The group trying to subdue Pilkington reminded Maggie of Laocoön and his sons fighting the serpent. Torsos writhed, arms flailed, legs strained. The outcome was inevitable. With cries and groans, they crashed to the floor.

Marcy calmly put handcuffs on Pilkington while her colleagues disentangled themselves and scrambled to their feet. DI Barlett had a cut lip while DS Dexter had what promised to be a black eye, sustained when he had been elbowed by a colleague.

Maggie pulled Joshua to his feet.

"Are you hurt?" she asked.

Joshua grimaced while he rubbed his neck.

"Yes. No. I don't know," he managed.

Luke Fitzroy stepped over Pilkington who was struggling on the floor and cursing.

"How are you, Maggie? Stone?" he asked.

Joshua shook his head.

"Better than I might have been." Maggie managed.

Willis and Dexter hauled Pilkington to his feet, who tried to shrug off their hands.

"You know, I could have been the Appleton Fellow. Or even the Master. Except for that bitch. She ruined my career. And she was going to do it again. Anonymous letters? Did she think no one would find out who was sending them? I'd have had to resign in disgrace. I wasn't going to go through that a second time."

"And you, Paley! Who the hell do you think you are? With your cowboy boots and your stupid hair! You were the perfect patsy. I'd have enjoyed watching you get sent away. Too bad they don't hang people anymore."

Stephen came over. He noticed the tie that was still draped around Maggie's neck.

"That's our college crest. Another Merrion tie!" he said in disgust.

"Give me that. It's evidence," Willis demanded.

The detective extended an open evidence bag and Stephen dropped the tie into it.

"What is it with all these ties? Does Merrion have an online shop?" Joshua asked.

"No. You buy them at local men's outfitters. Although… May I take a look again?" Stephen asked Willis.

Willis extended the bag and Stephen turned it.

"Hm. This is an old tie. The shop's gone out of business."

Maggie cautiously cleared her throat.

The Greater Gloucestershire Galanthus Group

"You know, Pilkington was a junior fellow here. Decades ago."

"Really? Before my time," said Stephen.

"Andrew Kittredge remembers him. So does your Mrs Steeples. It explains the neckties. And their age," Maggie pointed out.

A couple of PCs had appeared to escort Pilkington to a waiting car. Dexter recited the caution.

"No, just a moment. I have a question," Maggie said.

The PCs looked at Bartlett, who indicated they could wait.

"Mark, I understand about Jonquil. But why Iris?"

"That stupid woman. Jonquil and she were like Tweedledee and Tweedledum, dumb being particularly apropos for Iris. She came to see Jonquil at Churn Valley the night I... Anyhow she knew I wasn't there working in my office like I said I was. I managed to convince her that I had been in the loo and that it was Paley who had killed Jonquil and that we should go confront him. She agreed and..." he shrugged.

"And what were you doing here tonight?"

"The police weren't moving fast enough. Paley hadn't been arrested. So I figured I'd help things along by planting some more evidence. And then you barged in," he indicated Maggie.

"If I'd had just a couple of minutes more, there's no way Paley wouldn't have gone down. For three murders," he added callously.

DI Bartlett jerked her head at the constables, who led Pilkington away.

Maggie felt chilled. She had been fortunate.

Willis echoed her thoughts.

"You were lucky we showed up when we did."

"Yes."

Maggie looked at all the people who were still in Joshua's rooms.

"And just how was it that my good fortune happened to occur?"

"I was at dinner when the Gestapo showed up to arrest me 'on suspicion of murder,'" Joshua answered.

"It was quite a scene. I hope someone got it on video. I'd win an Oscar for best performance of righteous indignation. Fortunately for me, I had invited Luke to join me for dinner. Stephen was also unhappy about the bad timing. He and Luke convinced the fuzz to let me come back to my room to ditch my gown and get a coat. And it seems we were just in the nick of time," he scowled at Willis.

Willis shrugged.

"Paley, everyone I arrest claims they're innocent and expresses their righteous indignation. And, in your case, the evidence was certainly there."

"False evidence."

"Yeah. Pilkington was smart, I'll give him that."

The detective turned to Maggie.

"And just what were you doing here? Were you trying to get yourself killed?"

"I happened to be looking out my window and saw Pilkington crossing the quad. In his academic gown he looked just like any other don. I realised he'd gone up to Joshua's rooms and I'd already concluded he had to be the murderer..."

"A conclusion you didn't think to share with the police?"

It was Willis' turn for righteous indignation.

"It was a very recent conclusion. Anyhow, I wanted to see what he was up to and he surprised me. And then you all came in."

Maggie's adrenaline was wearing off. She thought briefly about what would have happened if her rescuers hadn't come in when they did. And what Thomas would have said. He would never believe her presence in Joshua's rooms had been innocent.

Luke noticed and put his arm around Maggie.

"DCI Willis, is it all right if I take Lady Raynham back to her rooms?"

"Er, yes. Fine. In fact, you should all get out of here—we'll need to do a search."

"Again?" Joshua fumed.

"To see if Pilkington left anything else to try to incriminate you, Paley. And someone will be along to take your statements, so stay put until then."

Willis rubbed his jaw, where a bruise was developing.

"You know, if only Pilkington had left well enough alone, he might have gotten away with it. He's an unlucky sod, isn't he?"

Chapter Fifty-Seven

Back downstairs, Luke solicitously sat Maggie down in one of her chairs.

"Would you like a drink?" he asked.

"There's a drinks cabinet in the bedroom. And there should be an open bottle of white wine in the small refrigerator."

"Whisky, gentlemen?" he asked Joshua and Stephen.

The men nodded.

When everyone had a drink, Luke settled himself in the other wingback chair, while Joshua and Stephen drew wooden seminar chairs closer.

"You certainly had a close call, Maggie. But it's had a happy ending. For you and for my client here."

"Yes. I couldn't believe they were really going to arrest me," Joshua marvelled.

"Believe it," Luke commented dryly.

The solicitor took a sip of whisky, then asked, "So tell me, Maggie. I'm still not sure I understand how you figured out that it was Pilkington who was behind the murders. And why he was targeting Joshua."

Maggie drank some wine. Her throat was not too sore. That was good. She gathered her thoughts.

"Mark Pilkington was a junior research fellow at Merrion a couple of decades ago. Everyone thought he would have a brilliant future. A distinguished career. Mrs

Steeple remembers him. So does Andrew Kittredge. Then he married Jonquil.

"There was an incident at a feast night. Jonquil spilled some sherry on Lady Crista Carrington, the Master's wife, and failed to apologise. Jonquil blamed Lady Crista for the accident and, I guess you could say, went on a campaign against the Master and his wife.

"There was only one way that was going to end. Mark's research fellowship was not renewed. He was fortunate to find a position at the University of Bristol. A daughter, Rosamunde, was born there.

"Mark wanted a more idyllic setting to raise his child, so he applied for the position of headmaster of Churn Valley College, a Gloucestershire boarding school. His being offered the position was helped by his having written a best seller—a spoof on British history.

"All went reasonably well for years until Rosamunde announced she wanted to attend university in the United States. Her choice was Simmons, a women's school in Boston. Rosamunde was an adequate student but made few friends. She developed a crush on a local celebrity. That would be you," Maggie indicated Joshua. "She wasn't a stalker, but her dorm room wall was plastered with clippings from magazines and newspaper articles about you.

"Rosamunde became severely depressed. One February day she jumped off a bridge into the Charles River. There were witnesses who swore that there was no one else near her at the time. The autopsy found she was three months' pregnant, the father unknown.

"It wasn't me," Joshua was quick to say.

"No. She left a note saying she was sorry but that she couldn't go on.

"Mark and Jonquil Pilkington flew over to Boston. Based on the evidence of Rosamunde's room, Jonquil insisted her daughter was murdered by the father of her unborn child and blamed you, Joshua, although you were giving a lecture at the time."

"The police were satisfied it was suicide, but Jonquil nursed her belief that Joshua had seduced her daughter and then murdered her. That was two years ago.

"Then you were awarded the Appleton Fellowship. Jonquil began to write poison pen letters about Joshua and send them to Merrion's senior faculty. Oh, I guess I should say that around this time Jonquil started a group for local snowdrop enthusiasts and asked me to participate. It's how I met her. And her closest friend, Irish Murtaugh.

"Jonquil knew me as Lady Raynham and had no idea I was a Merrion professor, so I also received the anonymous letters. I realised the paper and font she used for the letters were the same as the material she had been giving me for the snowdrop group and that Jonquil was the author.

"Jonquil came over to Beaumatin to deliver some paperwork relating to the group when Joshua was there. Mark was driving her. He had found out about the anonymous letters and decided he wasn't going to let Jonquil ruin his career a second time. So that night he somehow got Jonquil over to the estate, strangled her, and left her body in the boot of Joshua's car, which had been conveniently left unlocked.

"And it seemed he had managed to get ahold of a pair of your cowboy boots and left boot prints at the place he had strangled Jonquil. Might you have left a pair in the trunk of the Rolls?" Maggie asked Joshua.

"Could have, I guess," he shrugged.

"The police, of course, questioned Mark, who said he had been working in his office but had no one to verify that. The problem was that Iris had come by to see Jonquil and knew Mark was not where he said he was. So Iris had to go.

"Mark convinced Iris that it was Joshua who had murdered Jonquil and that they should go to Merrion to confront him. And perhaps Mark also believed you were behind Rosamunde's pregnancy and were the reason she killed herself. So he had no compunction about trying to frame you. It was justice, in a way.

"Today Andrew Kittredge told me he remembered having seen Pilkington coming out of the stairway here. Pilkington had been wearing an academic gown and Andrew thought he was just another don. He couldn't pinpoint when the sighting took place, though. I was standing at my window thinking about this when I saw Mark crossing the quad, again dressed like a don. He went up to Joshua's rooms. I followed him to find out what he was doing and... well, you know he rest."

There was silence while the men thought about this.

"I'm just glad it's been cleared up. No more anonymous letters or dead bodies or police interrupting dinner," Stephen said thankfully.

Maggie nodded. Now if only her problems with Thomas could be resolved. And she could catch up on her work.

Chapter fifty-eight

Maggie was peer reviewing an article for an academic journal and finding it tough going. While there was nothing wrong with the man's research, his prose was something else. Pretentious and turgid, it always used a four-syllable word when a two-syllable one would have done.

Maggie yawned. She had stood up to refill her coffee mug when there was an energetic rapping on her door.

"Come in."

The door opened and a radiant vision paused on the threshold.

"Jersey!"

"Hiya, Maggie."

Jersey gave Maggie a hearty embrace. She was wearing grey flannel pants and a blue cashmere sweater that matched her eyes.

"What brings you to Merrion?" asked Maggie, while assuming it was Joshua.

"Ah, I have news. And wanted you to be the first to know."

"All right. Would you like some coffee? I was just getting some."

Maggie indicated her empty mug.

"Sure."

She returned with two steaming mugs to find Jersey examining a forest of papers taped to the wall by her desk.

"Is this for your BBC series?" Jersey asked.

"Yes."

"That is so dope. You having your own TV series."

"Yes. But, er, how did you know?"

"Small world, broadcasting. Word gets around. Stone is so jealous."

"Really?"

"Nah. Well, maybe a little."

"I'm sure any of the networks would jump on Joshua for a programme. Well, not Fox. But all the other broadcasters."

"Hm. I'll have to suggest that."

Jersey shifted in her chair.

"But about Stone. It's why I came to see you."

"Yes?"

"You have to promise not to say a word to anyone. Or let Stone know I told you."

"Cross my heart," said Maggie, making the sign and preparing to listen to a confidence.

"Stone. He's just so hot. And I'm pretty sure he thinks I am too. So... He's decided Oxford isn't turning out the way he'd hoped. After the murders. And his almost getting arrested. And I talked to my network and... We've decided we're going to New York. Together. I'll do my show from there and he has an offer from New York University…"

"He's going to resign his fellowship?"

Maggie was surprised. The Appleton people would be unhappy. Stephen would be exasperated. Merrion would be short faculty. Of course, Thomas would be pleased.

"I guess so. Is that a big deal?"

"Well, yes. It's quite an honour to be chosen."

A slight frown creased the space between Jersey's eyes, then cleared.

"I guess it's just tough tuna, as you'd say."

"I was afraid when he came that he'd feel like a fish out of water."

"A fish… that's funny. Tuna. And a fish."

Jersey finished her coffee.

"You don't mind? That he's leaving? With me?"

"Mind? No. No, of course not. I hope you'll both be happy. And successful. You'll be quite the celebrity couple, you know."

"Yeah. I thought of that," Jersey grinned.

Maggie was sure that Joshua had also thought of that. She was also certain that the relationship was based more on its being mutually beneficial than its being a grand romantic passion.

"When do you leave?"

"Monday."

Monday? But it was Thursday. Stephen would have a fit. And she was sure her and Chitta's workloads would need to be increased to make up for the gap Joshua would leave.

"And Joshua's mother is letting us have her place to live in. It's a whole floor in some swanky Park Avenue apartment building. It even has a maid's quarters and a nursery…"

Maggie was surprised that Jersey was sounding wistful at the mention of a nursery. She wondered if Joshua had told her about his vasectomy. Well, it was none of her business.

"So if you're ever in New York, you'll have to come see us."

"I will."

"Stone promised me lunch on the river. Gotta do the Oxford thing as long as I'm here. So toodle pip."

Jersey gave Maggie a kiss and left.

Maggie sighed and returned to the journal article.

Late that afternoon someone else knocked on Maggie's door.

It was Stephen. He looked unhappy and Maggie thought she could guess the reason.

"Drink?"

He nodded.

"Did you know?" he asked, after Maggie handed him a glass and he took a large swallow.

"Only this morning. Jersey came and told me."

"Stone saw me after lunch. He's not even going to finish out the term. Apparently he has a standing offer from NYU that he can take up at any time he feels like it. He didn't care about the impact it would have on the college."

Stephen sounded bitter.

"The Appleton people are going to be furious. And now we'll have two senior faculty spots unfilled."

"Gordon Ross' as well as the Appleton chair."

Stephen nodded.

"You and Chitta and Andrew will have to take up the slack."

"I know."

Which will mean spending more time at Merrion. Another source of tension with Thomas, Maggie thought unhappily.

Stephen stared into his whisky.

"Do you mind? Not about the administrative hassle. But about Jersey and Joshua?" Maggie asked.

"No, I don't. Well, maybe just a little. A bit of wounded pride. But it's mainly the impact on the college. He could have at least finished out the term," Stephen repeated.

"I'm afraid Joshua isn't known for his consideration of others."

"Of course, this murder business didn't help."

"No."

"Getting escorted out of hall in front of the entire college."

"Upsetting."

"I'm trying to look on the bright side. At least he wasn't actually arrested."

The whisky was restoring Stephen's mood. He drained the glass.

"Some more?"

He checked his watch.

"No. Thank you. Almost time for cocktails anyway. Coming?"

"No. I've got to finish this article. Peer review."

"Any good?"

"The writing is so bad it's hard to tell."

Stephen laughed.

Chapter Fifty-Nine

Maggie had been out riding. When she returned to the house, she saw a silver Aston Martin parked in front. As she got closer, Joshua got out.

"Another rental? Joshua Bond?"

Maggie pointed at the car.

Joshua smiled sheepishly.

"I came by because I wanted to say... I wanted to tell you... To let you know in person..."

"You've resigned the Appleton fellowship."

"You know?"

He was startled.

"Oxford's like Harvard. Perhaps worse. Did you really think you could keep it a secret?"

Joshua shook his head.

"Yes. Well. I had the Appleton people put a clause in my contract that I could have a two-month trial period. And... Well... New York University had made me an open offer. That I could come and take up a position there whenever I wanted. And my mother's now dividing her time between Hilton Head and East Hampton and offered me her apartment, so I thought I'd take NYU up on their proposition. As Merrion had not turned out to be exactly as I had hoped," he added pointedly.

"I see."

"And I wanted to thank you before I left. That I'm not sitting in one of your good Inspector Willis' cells."

They stood awkwardly.

"There's something else."

Maggie waited.

"It's about Jersey. We've... anyway, she's coming with me. She negotiated with her network in London and they have an affiliate in New York and she'll be able to do her show from there."

Maggie realised Joshua was waiting for her reaction.

"It seems like it will be a good move for both of you, then."

Joshua looked relieved.

"Yes. Well, I wanted to tell you myself. And not have you hear... I didn't want you to think..."

"Thank you, Joshua. That's very kind."

"But Elle..."

"Yes?"

"I'm still... I still... I know you. And this..." he gestured at the house. "This isn't really you. You and Lord Fubsy-Face Umptieth Baron Hayseed."

Joshua's composure slipped.

"So I wanted to tell you... To let you know... That I still..."

He grabbed her and pulled her to him.

"You only have to say the word, Elle. Just one word. And I'm... I'll..."

He wrapped his hands in her hair and kissed her.

*Oh hell, Elle."

He released her, got in the car, and drove off.

Maggie watched him until he was out of sight.

She sighed and turned to go back into the house.

Thomas was standing in the doorway. Maggie wasn't sure how long he had been there, but it must have been at least long enough for him to have seen Joshua kiss her. And now he wasn't Sub Zero or even Absolute Zero. This was Nuclear Winter.

Maggie stared at him and saw a stranger. An inimical, judgemental stranger standing in the doorway of this great house that she would never really feel was her home. And which was probably just as well, as it looked like he was going to throw her out of it. Again. And she felt like something was breaking inside.

He turned to go back in, but she rushed up and entered before he could close the door in her face.

"No. Oh no. You come with me," she said in a determined tone. She took Thomas' arm and propelled him forward to her study. Her turn for home court advantage.

She thrust him inside, closed the door and ordered, "Sit."

Thomas didn't move.

"All right. Fine. Stand. Whatever."

She perched on the edge of her desk.

"That was Joshua. Well, you know that. And I assume you saw…"

She stopped as she saw the look on Thomas' face. She took a deep breath and continued.

"He came to thank me for my efforts on his behalf. That he wasn't sitting in some gaol. And also to tell me… to tell me that he was leaving Oxford. That he had resigned his position and was going back to the U.S. To NYU. Um, New York University. Apparently they made him an offer.

"And he's not going alone. Jersey is going with him. Her network has an affiliate in the city and she can do her show from there.

"I imagine they will be quite well suited to each other. They both know how to work the media. I give them a month before they make the cover of *People*. That's a magazine, in case you didn't know," she added.

She waited for Thomas to react. Nothing. She reached a decision.

"And also so you know, I'm going back to Oxford. I just need to gather some things. I'll leave the car for you at Hereford Crescent."

She unplugged her laptop and began to put it in her bag.

"What is it that you like to say? That we're finished? Well, at the moment, I'm finished. Finished with your jealousy and your suspicion and your lack of trust."

There was a pause.

"That's all, Thomas," she said dismissively.

When he didn't move, she turned and walked out. She heard him say, "Maggie..." but she kept going.

Twenty minutes later she was driving out through the elaborate wrought iron gates that marked the entrance to Beaumatin. She remembered the first time she had seen them and blinked back tears.

"You are not going to cry," she admonished herself.

Susan Alexander

Chapter sixty

There was a knock on her door. Maggie tensed.

"Come in."

It was Chitta. Maggie relaxed.

"Hi."

"Hi."

Chitta looked at her friend.

Maggie was haggard. She had circles under her eyes. Her hair had escaped its clip, which was dangling from a single lock.

"Maggie? Are you all right?"

"Of course. I'm fine."

Maggie paused and her eyes filled with tears.

"No. I'm not fine. Not at all," she sniffed.

"What…"

"I've left Thomas."

"What?" Chitta was shocked.

"Joshua came to say good-bye. To tell me he was leaving. With Jersey Jones. Which I already knew, but… Anyway, it was nice of him. And he kissed me. And Thomas saw and got all… he thought he had caught us… The look on his face…

"And it was not the first time. Or even the second. That he assumed I was… With Joshua. And I just kind of felt like I'd had it. So I told him I was leaving. And coming here. And I did. That was Sunday. There's been no contact since, so I suppose... Maybe he's just relieved to be rid of me."

Maggie's voice broke and a tear ran down one cheek.

"But how could he think you and Paley..."

"I know. There's no reason for him to think. But he gets so jealous. I don't know why he finds it so difficult to trust me."

"What do you want?"

"I don't know. I left the ball in his court. It's not like I can go back, drive up, and say 'Honey, I'm home.' I'm too afraid I'd find the door was locked."

"Or that your key wouldn't work."

"Ha. The lock in that door must be three hundred years old. It's not like he can change it. And I don't even have a key."

Maggie paused to wipe her eyes.

"But I'll tell you what I don't want. I don't want to go on with his jumping to wrong conclusions. And his rages. And his telling me..." Maggie stopped and groped for a tissue.

"And every time there's a knock on my door, I think it's someone coming to serve me with divorce papers."

She ran her hands through her hair and the hair clip slipped off onto the floor.

"And living in that house. You don't know what it's like. It's so... alien. The only place I'm comfortable is when I'm working in my study. Or asleep.

"And I certainly don't make Thomas happy. It seems like he's always angry at me about something. Well, not always, but often enough.

"I feel like such a failure. I tried so hard to make this work. Being married. But I also feel so guilty. And that this is some sort of karmic payback for how I treated Joshua."

"What do you mean?"

Maggie explained about her relationship with Joshua and its ending.

"It's the worst thing I've ever done. The absolute worst. And when I told Thomas about it—well, I thought he had a right to know about our relationship—he immediately started to worry that I'd do the same thing to him. Just leave like that."

Maggie reached for another tissue.

"And then Joshua shows up here wanting to pick up where we left off."

"Even though you were married?"

"He called Thomas 'Lord Fubsy Face Umptieth Baron Hayseed.'"

Chitta laughed.

"Yes, I know. Rather too close for comfort. I don't think Joshua saw Thomas as an impediment. And Thomas became convinced we were having an affair and nothing I said made any difference. Even when Joshua and Jersey started seeing each other."

Maggie sighed.

Chitta looked thoughtful. She crossed to Maggie and gave her a hug.

"I'm sorry," she said simply.

"I know. Me too."

THE GREATER GLOUCESTERSHIRE GALANTHUS GROUP

CHAPTER SIXTY-ONE

"It's Mr Einhorn to see you, my lord," said Mrs Cook from the doorway of Thomas' study.

"Stanley? Humpf. Show him in then, please, Mrs Cook."

"Hi, Thomas."

Stanley bounded in holding a folder stuffed with papers.

"I came to drop these off for Maggie, but apparently she's in Oxford. So I thought I'd..."

Stanley looked at Thomas more closely. The man looked ravaged, with circles under his eyes and sunken cheeks. He exuded a faint odour of whisky.

"Actually, that's not true. I know she's in Oxford. It's why I came."

"Oh?" Thomas' tone was not encouraging.

"Yes. I don't need my foundation's programme director, not to mention the holder of a very costly chair I'm funding, moping around with a broken heart. It has a seriously negative impact on a person's productivity."

Thomas stiffened.

"And I also don't need gossip circulating that the reason she's looking so forlorn and bereft is that Stone Paley took off back to the U.S. with Jersey Jones. Now there's a match made in media heaven. And that she's back living in her rooms because you threw her out in a jealous rage."

"What? But I didn't…"

Stanley shrugged. "You think people didn't notice how you felt about Paley? And that you'd show up at Merrion unexpectedly hoping to catch him and Maggie in the act? Doing the deed?"

Thomas looked even more wretched, if that were possible.

"I told you not to worry, that Maggie was true blue. But did you listen?"

Stanley was irate. He noticed Thomas' expression.

"And don't say it's none of my business. Maggie's miserable, which makes Chitta unhappy, which makes it my business. And you don't look so well yourself. In fact, Raynham, you look like hell, so I assume you're not happy about this either."

"Maggie's miserable?"

Stanley glared.

"I never took you for an example of inbreeding among the British aristocracy, Raynham. Of course she's miserable. Did you think she was out partying?"

Thomas shrugged.

"You know what I think? Well I'm going to tell you. I think, when you're not in some sort of jealous funk, you take Maggie for granted. Do you ever bring her flowers? Yes, I know you have a garden full of them, but do you know which are her favourites? Do you know the name of that wonderful scent she always wears? Do you know what films she likes? Do you ever even go with her to see a movie? Or a play? Or a concert?

The Greater Gloucestershire Galanthus Group

"You're married to this extraordinary woman and you offer her a life of shepherd's pie and the History channel and then you wonder why you're worried she may be susceptible to other men."

Thomas squirmed,

"Now I'm going to tell you what I think your problem is. And then I'm going to tell you what you're going to do about it."

Susan Alexander

Chapter sixty-two

Maggie got a message from Malcolm Fortescue-Smythe. The BBC proposed a meeting on Thursday morning. Could she attend?

Maggie hesitated. Normally she would leave for Beaumatin on Thursday evenings. Then she remembered. She would not be going to Beaumatin.

She replied that Thursday morning was fine, and she would meet him at Broadcasting House. He should let her know the time.

A refrain from a Janis Joplin song echoed. "Freedom's just another word for nothing left to lose."

Had she nothing left to lose? Perhaps in terms of her relationships. But she was still Professor Margaret Spence Eliot. That had been enough for her for years. It would have to be enough again.

Thinking of her relationships reminded her of Crispin. She called Tim.

"Tim? Maggie. I have another meeting with the BBC on Thursday morning and wondered if I could go see Lennox's flat afterwards. Is there a way to get a key?"

Tim checked and said he was free. Why didn't they have lunch and then they could go over afterwards. He had keys. And it was, after all, her flat now, he finished gently.

They agreed to meet at a gastropub near the King's Road at one.

Having no desire to stay in the Belsize house, Maggie took an early train and arrived at Portland Place five minutes early. Malcolm was already waiting in the lobby.

Maggie had dressed carefully for the meeting in her good navy suit and a pale peach silk blouse. Her curls were gelled and would, she hoped, stay under control.

"Hello, Malcolm. Do you know if there's any specific reason why they want to meet?"

"I got the impression that they want to present their concept for the series."

"Do we have a contract yet?"

"Nearly there."

"So no signing ceremony."

"No. And I would want you to review any contract with a solicitor before you signed."

Maggie nodded.

A young woman walked across the lobby and greeted them.

"Professor Eliot, Mr Fortescue-Smythe, would you come with me please?"

She led them to the conference room where they had met before. Six men were there in the middle of a discussion. A laptop was set up on the table and a screen had been lowered on one wall.

Maggie supposed she had met some of the men on her previous visit. It was hard to tell, they all seemed so very much alike.

The Greater Gloucestershire Galanthus Group

One of them, who had hair shaved to a stubble that matched his beard and was wearing a suit that was nipped in at the waist, seemed to be in charge. He addressed Malcolm.

"We've spent some time throwing ideas around since your visit and thought you should see what we've come up with, based on the content you sent us."

Maggie had worked hard to produce an outline and a couple of provisional chapters.

"Hit the lights, won't you, Ced," he ordered.

Ced crossed to the wall and flipped a switch. An overhead projector lit the screen.

PeopleFlows read the title slide.

"For a narrator, I'm thinking Joanna Lumley," said the man in the too-tight suit.

"Or Alan Rickman. He'd be perfect, don't you think, Colby?" Ced offered.

Even with the lights dimmed, Maggie could see Colby's dismissing the idea.

To a background of a neutral female voice explaining how many species migrated, there was a video showing wildebeests moving across an African plain. Then it showed lions hunting one poor beast down and killing it.

The narrator discussed the migrations of Arctic terns and Monarch butterflies, then moved to salmon. Here there was footage of the fish fighting their way upstream, only to be snared by grizzly bears and consumed.

Maggie shifted restlessly as she watched a closeup of a hapless salmon being ripped apart.

The presentation moved on to Native Americans crossing the Bering Strait. Animated diagrams showed their dispersal throughout North and South America.

"That's one theory. But there are others," Maggie murmured to Malcolm.

A second animated diagram showed colonisers from Europe travelling to the New World. The next minutes highlighted conflicts between the new settlers and the Native Americans and the toll it took on the latter.

The following segment showed the routes of the slave trade from Africa and the suffering of its victims.

"But slavery isn't a migration," Maggie commented to the publisher.

After five more minutes of violence and misery, Maggie had had enough. All the anger and grief she felt about Thomas' irrational jealousy and Crispin's untimely death coalesced and found a target.

She slammed her hands down on the table and stood. This got the men's attention.

"You, Colby. And Ced. And the rest of you... people. This horror show of atrocities is a complete travesty of my work. Malcolm, you said there has been no contract signed?" she demanded.

Malcolm shook his head no.

"And I assume the Global Press has secured all the intellectual property rights to my work."

The Greater Gloucestershire Galanthus Group

Malcolm nodded in the affirmative.

"Good. Then we're leaving."

The men were exchanging glances messaging "What's her problem?" and "Isn't she old for PMT?"

Maggie and Malcolm were nearly at the conference room door when it opened and another man entered. He was in his fifties, with thinning blond hair and shrewd grey eyes, and wearing a suit of which Thomas would approve.

The men snapped to attention and Colby stood.

"Sir David!"

Sir David noted the men's discomfort, Maggie's stony face, and Malcolm's grim expression.

"Is there a problem, Colby?" he asked.

"Er, no, of course not, Sir David."

"On the contrary, there certainly is," Maggie insisted.

Sir David raised his eyebrows while Colby tried to regain control of the situation.

"Sir David, this is Malcolm Fortescue-Smythe, the head of Global Publishing, and Maggie... Maggie..."

He groped for Maggie's name.

"Lady Raynham," supplied Maggie and extended her hand. If her assessment of Sir David were correct, a baroness would carry more weight than a mere professor.

"Raynham? You're Baroness Raynham?"

"Yes."

"Hello, David," put in Malcolm.

"Hello, Malcolm."

"David and I were up at Magdalene together," Malcolm explained. "He's the person I told about *PeopleFlows*."

"A worthy project. It should make a riveting series."

Sir David regarded his minions.

"So I repeat. Is there a problem?"

"Yes, Sir David, there is," Maggie persisted.

Sir David glared at the table.

"Perhaps you can explain it to me over lunch, Lady Raynham. And Malcolm, of course."

"Thank you, Sir David. But I already have a lunch commitment. With Lord Timothy Hillier. However, I'm sure Malcolm can explain my issues. Or we can make another appointment."

"Hillier? Greystock's son?"

"Yes."

Sir David regarded Maggie respectfully.

"I hope you're free, then, Malcolm?"

Malcolm nodded.

Sir David glared at his subordinates again and Colby and his mates squirmed.

"Let me arrange a car for you," he smiled at Maggie.

"And Colby, be in my office at three o'clock."

If Maggie had not been so angry, she would have felt sorry for Colby.

Susan Alexander

Chapter sixty-three

Sir David escorted Maggie down to a waiting car. She gave the driver the address of Tim's pub and left Malcolm and his college chum to their reminiscences and, she hoped, to a productive discussion of the *PeopleFlows* problems.

Tim's gastropub turned out to be a just that and doubtless served pie and fish and chips. Maggie was early so she window-shopped the trendy boutiques on nearby King's Road for half an hour while she calmed down.

She met Tim just as he was getting out of his car.

"Maggie!"

They hugged, she gave Tim a kiss on the cheek, and they went inside.

They were seated and given menus. Maggie had been right about the pie and fish and chips, but the place also offered more sophisticated fare.

Still feeling agitated after her experience at the BBC, Maggie ordered a Bombay Sapphire gin and tonic.

"That sounds good," Tim commented and did the same.

"How was your meeting? Making progress?" Tim asked conversationally.

"No!"

Tim raised his eyebrows.

"Sorry, I guess I'm still upset. But you can't imagine. These... men. They're all men. Smug. Condescending. They completely distorted my work. The points I am trying to make. They had done some sort of preliminary demo. It started with videos of lions eating wildebeests and bears ripping apart salmon. Nature red in tooth and claw. Literally. And it just got worse.

"Fortunately their boss appeared. Sir David... I was too angry to catch his last name. Assuming I was even introduced. They use my first name. Only my first name. So I introduced myself using my title."

"Professor?"

"No. My other title. Which I hate to do, but he recognized the name and... Respect!" she used the football slogan.

"I don't mean to be boring on. But you'd have thought we were back in the 1950's. And then to have to sit there and watch how they were mutilating my work..."

They ordered. Maggie was amused when Tim ordered the steak and ale pie, while Maggie skipped the beet risotto which would have been her usual choice and had duck. Rage had given her an appetite.

After coffee, they stood outside.

"Where is the flat from here?" Maggie asked.

"You don't know?" Tim was surprised.

"No. No, I don't," said Maggie, equally surprised that Tim would have thought she had been a visitor.

"Just around the corner on Ifield Road."

Ifield Road was lined with what had originally been modest Victorian terraced houses with white stone fronts that gave way to brick on the upper two stories. About fifty

The Greater Gloucestershire Galanthus Group

yards up, Tim paused, then went down some steps behind an ornamental iron railing. At the bottom there was a shiny, black-enamelled door with a knocker in the shape of the head of Aeolus, the god of wind.

"This is it."

Tim removed a key from a jacket pocket and opened the door.

"It's not very big. Two bedrooms, one of which Lennox used as a study. A small patio. The original flat was expanded to enlarge the kitchen and add the second bedroom. Lennox was not a gardener."

Maggie was curious. She knew next to nothing about Crispin's daily life. What was she about to discover?

They came into a combination sitting and dining room. It had a dark brown leather chesterfield sofa and some matching chairs. Good oriental carpets in shades of blue and brown. Some watercolour landscapes on the walls. A sleek modern table. No clutter. But it was not the stark minimalism of Joshua's Cambridge flat. This was masculine. Strong. No nonsense. Like Crispin himself.

"A char comes in every two weeks to keep things clean," Tim said.

They went through to a kitchen, with white enamel cabinets and stainless-steel appliances. A microwave. No Aga.

A door opened to a small, slate-paved patio that had a round wooden table and four matching chairs.

Beyond the kitchen was Crispin's study. A wall of bookcases. A comfortable chair for reading with a lamp. A massive wooden desk. On the desk, a photo in a silver frame. It was Maggie. She was standing on a hilltop, cheeks flushed, hair windblown, laughing. She assumed she was at Beaumatin, but when the picture had been taken or how Crispin had gotten a copy, she had no idea.

She blushed and realised that Tim was watching her. Time to address the elephant in the room, she decided.

"Tim, you should know. Lennox and I were... we were not having an affair. I had not seen or heard from him since last spring. Before that, it was when there was the problem with the Niqabi. And the Sun Lee Won. And before that when I was hunting those stolen snowdrops. When you introduced us. That was the extent of our relationship. It was all very heat of the moment. I won't deny I cared for him. But there were no clandestine meetings or stolen weekends or..."

Maggie paused, embarrassed.

"And I have no idea why he made this extraordinary bequest."

"Because he was the last of his family. And he trusted you."

"Perhaps, but..."

"And I think it amused him. To imagine what you would do."

"Amused..."

She changed the subject.

"I wonder if there's any coffee. I noticed a coffee maker in the kitchen."

The Greater Gloucestershire Galanthus Group

In a cupboard Maggie found some coffee capsules as well as some tea bags.

They took their cups and sat down in the sitting room.

"You know, Maggie, in my... business, it is a requirement not to have too much empathy. It's not like policework, where the detective hands the perpetrator over to the Crown Prosecution Service, or the military, where mostly targets are anonymous. We usually know the people we pursue and, if we had too much fellow feeling, too much compassion, it would be difficult to do our job. I need to send my people into harm's way and still sleep at night. Well, most nights. It's why the majority of my team are young. And single."

"There's The Fish. Er, Fred Pilchard. He has a wife. And children."

"Fred is the exception. His background is very different than Lennox's and he is able to compartmentalize. Plus he has a wife in a million."

"Yes, Crispin said the job was hard on relationships."

"He was right. Er, if you don't mind my asking, why do you keep referring to Lennox as Crispin?"

Maggie laughed.

"The first time we met, he told me his name was Crispin. I think it, well, you would say that it amused him. Shortly afterwards, I met him at a dance. He was escorting his aunt, Lady Sarah, and of course his real name came out. But he asked me to keep calling him Crispin anyhow. So I did."

Tim shook his head and checked his watch.

"My driver will be here soon. Do you want me to talk to Barnaby about putting the flat on the market? It will need to be cleared out."

Maggie thought.

"Tim? Can that wait? It might suit me to have a small flat in London."

Tim nodded.

"Before he left on his last mission, Lennox asked me to keep an eye on you. Which is not difficult, given the agency's resources. And I noticed... You have hardly left your rooms in Merrion for the past two weeks."

Maggie looked sad.

"The new Appleton fellow? Joshua Paley? I knew him at Harvard. In fact, we were engaged to be married. I broke it off when I came to Oxford. But a certain amount of collegial interaction was inevitable and Thomas... He became irrationally jealous. He had already indicated he would prefer me to be at Beaumatin full time, give up being an academic, and be a wife. Which I'm not about to do. So I decided we would benefit from some space. Thomas needs to decide what he wants. And I... I also have some decisions to make."

Tim nodded noncommittally.

"Then when you've had a chance to think, let me know what you want to do. With the flat and its contents. I've removed all of Lennox's legal papers. Bank statements. Tax declarations. But there's still... all this," he gestured.

He took a set of keys from his pocket.

"Here are the keys. The alarm code is 0614."

Her birthday. What had the man been thinking?

Tim kissed her gently on the forehead and left.

Maggie sat, mind blank. Then she realised there was a room she had not seen. Crispin's bedroom.

She set her mug down, walked the few steps, and opened the door.

Simple. White-walled like the rest of the flat. A large bed with a crisp linen navy duvet and matching pillow covers. A built-in closet. A chest of drawers. A comfortable chair. Two bed tables with lamps.

Uncluttered. Maggie remembered there was a cleaning lady. Was it this neat when Crispin had been in residence? Or had the SAS taught habits of tidiness?

She hesitated, then approached the closet and opened the doors.

Suits. Crispin's suits. Wherever he had been, the mission had not required him to dress. Or perhaps he had to take clothes that did not reveal their origins. These suits would have identifying tailor's labels.

She picked up the sleeve of a suit jacket she remembered Crispin had worn the first time they had met. Sniffed it. It still had a faint aroma of the man.

She opened drawers. Shirts. Socks. Underwear. Casual sports tops. Jeans. All carefully folded.

Her mobile sounded. It was Malcolm.

"I had a productive lunch with David. The contract will include clauses giving you power of approval over everything in the series, to the last detail. I hope with that you'll be willing to go forward."

"My goodness. In that case, yes."

"I'm sorry I did not specify that as a requirement from the beginning. I had no idea they would take your concept and come up with what we saw. Which you rightly called a travesty.

"And David is going to put someone new in charge of the project whom you may find more congenial. A woman named Andrea... Andrea someone. I forget. And David would like to take us to dinner when the contract is signed."

"Fine. Send me a copy of the contract and I'll have my solicitor look at it."

Her solicitor. Not old Barnaby. But a woman in the law firm used by the Raynhams who specialised in contracts.

"So all's well that ends well," Malcolm finished and terminated the call.

All's well that ends well, Maggie echoed. Was that true? Perhaps for *PeopleFlows*. Certainly not for Crispin. And as for her and Thomas?

Despite the coffee, Maggie felt exhausted. She had no idea what she wanted to do. She was certainly not going to keep Crispin's flat intact, like some sort of shrine, as though he were going to come walking through the door at any moment, as she had read mothers who lost children sometimes did.

It was rush hour. The idea of finding a taxi and fighting through the traffic to Paddington and taking a train back to Oxford was overwhelming. She had no reason to be

The Greater Gloucestershire Galanthus Group

in Oxford that evening anyway. And she was not keen to go to Belsize and its memories. She would stay at Crispin's. Which was now, apparently, hers.

She slipped out of her clothes and pulled back the duvet. White linen sheets were perfectly pressed and felt cool and silky to the touch.

On impulse she pulled open the drawer of the bedside table. Inside she found a favourite scarf she thought she had lost and one of her hairclips.

Maggie cried herself to sleep.

Susan Alexander

The Greater Gloucestershire Galanthus Group

Chapter sixty-four

Maggie arrived back in Oxford late the next morning. She had just changed out of her suit and into her work uniform of tailored pants and a cashmere top when her mobile sounded. It was Stephen Draycott.

"Maggie? Could you come over to my office? It's, er, important."

Oh dear. Important wasn't good. For something minor Stephen would have just dropped by her rooms. But at least it would not be more anonymous letters.

Maggie made sure her hair was fastened properly and that her trousers and top were not too casual. She reapplied some lip gloss, took a deep breath, and set off for the Master's Lodge.

Mrs Steeples indicated she should go through to the Master's study. Maggie looked inquiringly, but the woman just shrugged and returned to her word processing.

Maggie went in and found Stephen sitting with two distinguished-looking men in their sixties. They were drinking whisky but put down their glasses and stood when she entered. Maggie thought the men seemed vaguely familiar.

"There you are, Maggie."

Stephen was smiling warmly, so perhaps whatever he wanted her for was not a problem after all.

"This is Lord Holloway and Mr Jessop, who are here representing the Appleton Trust. Lord Holloway, Mr Jessop, this is, er, Lady Raynham. Or would you prefer Professor Eliot?"

"As we are at Merrion, Professor Eliot please," she smiled and shook hands.

Lord Holloway was tall and hearty, with a ruddy complexion and a full mane of white hair. Jessop was smaller, grey, balding, and somewhat desiccated looking.

"Is it possible we met before, when I was interviewed for the Appleton fellowship? I'm sorry. I was so nervous, the event is rather blurred."

Lord Holloway nodded. "Yes, we did indeed meet. And I certainly noticed no nervousness. You gave an impressive presentation and your work as the Appleton fellow was also outstanding."

"And I'm sorry I had to resign but..."

"We understand. You had conflicting demands on your time. And we appreciate that you were honest about that and did not simply give the fellowship the short end of the stick. Which others might have done," said Jessop.

Maggie produced a self-deprecating smile while she wondered why she was there.

"Maggie, take a seat. And may I get you a drink? These gentlemen have a proposition you may find interesting."

"Thank you, Stephen."

Stephen went to get her some wine and the group sat.

"So, Professor Eliot. As you are doubtless aware, since your tenure we have lost two Appleton fellows soon after their appointments. As you can imagine, the Trustees are not pleased about having to undertake a third search,

The Greater Gloucestershire Galanthus Group

given the time and expense involved in awarding the fellowship. So we met and voted to change the nature of the grant. We presented our idea to Professor Draycott and he thinks it is a good one," Lord Holloway said.

Maggie took a sip of her wine, a pleasant Viognier, and waited.

Jessop continued, "We intend to turn the fellowship into an, um, stipend. To fund work that might be outside the scope of the person's normal, um, area of specialisation."

"For instance, if Eunice Enderby, whose field is colonialism and post-colonialism, wanted to study the forms of government of the new republics created after the fall of the Soviet Union, Appleton might fund the work," Stephen explained. "Not that she has expressed any such interest," he added.

"And given your achievements while you were the Appleton fellow, and the success of your most recent work, we wanted to ask if you would be interested in the award. To fund work outside the scope of your duties as the Weingarten Fellow, which I understand mainly focusses on the third world." Holloway continued.

"The stipend could be used to fund such things as a project you once mentioned to your publisher. I believe you called it, *The Valuation of Things*, if I remember what Fortescue-Smythe told us correctly. Good title, by the way," said Lord Holloway.

"The award is...." He named a substantial figure.

"And it can be renewed annually for as long as you would be interested. And your work continues to be of the same high quality," Jessop added.

"We ran this past Stanley Einhorn and he has no problem with your accepting the funding. In fact, he said he would be eager to read your work," Stephen said encouragingly.

Oh my. She would have to talk to Thomas, Maggie thought, then reminded herself that talking to Thomas about her life decisions might no longer be necessary.

"My goodness, Lord Holloway. And Mr Jessop. I'm most honoured. And quite interested. May I give you my answer on Tuesday? As I should also talk to Mr Einhorn. And to Malcolm Fortescue-Smythe."

"And Lord Raynham as well, I'm sure," said Lord Holloway.

"Yes, of course." Maggie's smile was non-committal.

"We will hope to have a positive answer from you in a few days, then," said Mr Jessop.

Maggie nodded. She stood. The men stood. Everyone shook hands. She left.

Chapter sixty-five

Friday afternoon Maggie was working in her rooms when she got an SMS.

It was from Thomas.

"Dinner tonight?"

Maggie sighed. She had not heard from Thomas for more than two weeks. While she had been licking her wounds. In turmoil about what she should do. Unless, of course, he was just relieved to be rid of her.

Well, she could not avoid the man forever. He was still her husband.

"All right," she texted back. "Time? Place?"

"Outside the Merrion gate at 4:00."

That was early, Maggie thought. Did he plan to take her back to have dinner at Beaumatin? She really wasn't ready to go back to Beaumatin. But she had said yes, so...

"OK."

Send.

That gave her a bit more than an hour. She would shower. Put on makeup and a dress. A dress might boost her morale. Stiffen her spine. Especially if Thomas had decided that it was over, that the marriage hadn't worked out, and that he wanted a divorce.

It was an unseasonably warm day. She decided on a dress in a fine silky knit in an eggplant shade that had long sleeves and a high neck and that was gathered diagonally across the bodice into a rosette of fabric at the waist. She had splurged and gotten stockings in the same shade and a pair of matching suede shoes with low heels. She debated a long time about wearing her wedding ring, then decided against it.

She was expecting the Land Rover and so was not paying attention when a Mercedes limousine with darkened windows drew up. A driver got out, opened the rear passenger door, and said, "Lady Raynham?"

Maggie was startled and drew back, then saw that Thomas was seated in the back.

"Oh."

She got in. The driver closed the door and drove off.

Maggie risked a glance at her husband. He was wearing one of his best suits. Shirt cuffs showed a perfect half inch below his jacket sleeves and were closed with cufflinks engraved with the Raynham seal. He also had on a Hermes tie Maggie had given him patterned with fluffy white sheep—and an occasional black one.

She noticed he looked tired and that there were fine lines around his eyes and mouth that were not there the last time she had seen him. How many days ago had that been? She felt sick to her stomach from nervousness and had to remind herself to breathe.

She looked out the window and was relieved to see they were not going in the direction of the A40 and Beaumatin. What was their destination, then? A country gastropub? But if that were the case, Thomas would be wearing tweeds, and he was dressed for a night out on the town, although they were not heading towards London, either.

Maggie risked a glance at the man again. He had on his unreadable face that made it impossible to tell what he was thinking. Or feeling. He had not said a word, and Maggie did not want to be the one to break the ice. What could she say?

The car pulled up at a sturdy fence topped with barbed wire. A guard opened a gate and the car pulled through onto tarmac. The driver got out and opened Thomas' door, then went around and opened hers. Thomas helped her out.

Maggie found herself standing by a sleek private jet. The steps were down and an official of some sort was waiting at the bottom, while a flight attendant stood at the top.

"Thomas?"

"It's a surprise. You're always organising them for me, so I thought…"

He did not finish the sentence but reached inside his jacket and handed the official two passports. The official checked, nodded, and handed them back.

"Have a pleasant trip, my lord," the man said and walked away.

"Come, my dear. We have a reservation. Don't worry. We'll be back late tonight."

Maggie dutifully ascended the stairs where she was greeted, "Welcome aboard, Lady Raynham. Lord Raynham."

She entered the cabin and things became clearer. In an elegant space of leather and polished woods, on the back of grey and cream upholstered chairs were woven the initials "SE."

"SE. Stanley Einhorn," she pointed.

"Yes. It's Stanley's plane. He's letting me borrow it."

"For an evening where? Reykjavik? Yekaterinburg? Tbilisi?"

That made Thomas' mouth twitch.

"No. Like I said. Be surprised."

Maggie hesitated.

"What? Are you the only one who can plan a surprise?"

There was a pause.

"If you don't like where we're going, we can come right back. Word of honour. But… I'd still like to surprise you."

Maggie sighed.

"All right."

The hostess escorted them to two comfortable seats that were more like armchairs. With seatbelts.

Maggie looked around curiously She had never been on a private jet.

The plane taxied and took off.

"Well, it's nice not to have to go through security," Maggie conceded.

Thomas nodded. He was clutching the arms of his chair. Thomas was a nervous flyer. In fact, by Maggie's count, this would be only his ninth flight.

The plane reached cruising altitude. The hostess came out with a bottle of champagne and some crystal flutes and set them on the table between them.

Thomas poured. They touched their glasses together in a silent toast and drank.

Maggie looked out the window. The plane was flying over water. They were heading east. To Europe?

The hostess returned with a cart holding toast. And caviar. A very large container of caviar. And it was her favourite type. Not Beluga, but Osetra.

"Oh my. Did you arrange this?" she asked Thomas. Caviar had been notably absent from the Beaumatin table.

"No."

"Compliments of Mr Einhorn," said the hostess.

"Ah." That made more sense. Although how did Stanley know she preferred Osetra?

Thomas was looking at the golden-toned eggs suspiciously.

"Have you ever had caviar?" she asked.

"Er, no."

"Really? Well, you survived sushi. And you don't have to use chopsticks."

Thomas' mouth twitched again and Maggie felt her defences crumbling. She put a small amount of caviar on a piece of toast and handed it to Thomas.

"It's salty. And when you bite down on an egg, there's a bit of resistance, then it pops and it's, er, liquidy. I find it quite irresistible."

Thomas had the piece of toast halfway to his mouth.

"Do you?"

Thomas' eyes gleamed.

Oh dear. This was just so unfair.

Thomas ate.

"Hm. Interesting. All right. Your turn."

He piled caviar on some toast and said, "Ah...."

"Thomas..."

"Open."

Maggie did, but Thomas had been over-generous with the caviar. A blob fell and stuck to the boddice of her dress.

They looked at it. Thomas shook his head. He extended a finger, deftly lifted up the eggs, and brought his finger to her lips.

"Here."

Maggie shook her head, but Thomas persisted. She hesitantly stuck out her tongue. Thomas deposited the eggs, then pulled her to him and kissed her.

Maggie felt as though all the nerve endings in her body were exploding like tiny firecrackers. She flushed and knew that Thomas had noticed.

At least it seemed he was not about to ask for a divorce, she consoled herself. But she was also aware that she was being manipulated. Like she had been manipulated into moving into Beaumatin. And agreeing to the marriage instead of a less contractual relationship. And giving up her cosy Oxford flat for the Hereford Crescent townhouse. And resigning the Appleton fellowship and accepting the Weingarten chair so she would spend less time away from her husband.

She wondered what she was being manipulated into now. Was it merely to return to her husband? Or was it to reduce her work even further? Or to give up her career altogether? Well, that was not going to happen. He had married Professor Margaret Spence Eliot and that was who she was going to remain. Besides, this trip was Stanley's doing and she was certain he would not have supported anything that would mean scaling back on her academic work or her role in his foundation.

Thomas was aware of Maggie's response to the kiss and then her withdrawal. But she hadn't recoiled. Or pushed him away. At that moment he knew he could win her back and have things return to the way they were before that insufferable Paley appeared.

He had finally admitted to himself that there was nothing romantic going on between them, despite Paley's seemingly ubiquitous presence in Maggie's rooms in Oxford and that damnable kiss he had witnessed. But what man wouldn't take it badly when a wife's former lover turns up and tries to insinuate himself back into her life? Perhaps he had over-reacted a bit. But it was only a bit.

He would have liked to kiss his wife again, but the plane was not an optimal place for love making. He would wait until they reached their destination.

They finished the caviar. And the champagne.

The plane landed and a helicopter was waiting. Maggie was not a fan of helicopters. She disliked the sensation of hanging in the air, which was quite different than an airplane's forward motion. But she decided not to wimp or whinge.

It was dark. All Maggie could tell was that they were flying over a city. Then over water. Then the helicopter landed. Another car was waiting and whisked them away into a warm night.

"All right, Thomas. Where are we?"

"Capri."

"Capri? The Isle of Capri? In Italy?"

"Yes. Stanley took Chitta here and they both enjoyed it. And isn't there some song. I seem to remember…"

Maggie knew the song. When she was ten her mother had given her a jewellery box that, when you opened the lid, a little ballerina twirled around in a circle while a music box hidden in the bottom played "The Isle of Capri." It had been one of her favourite things as a child. She still had it. It was in her dressing room at Beaumatin.

"And I thought, well, we never had a honeymoon. Not a proper one. There was that week at Beaumatin…"

"Yes. You taught me how to feed the chickens and collect their eggs."

The Greater Gloucestershire Galanthus Group

"And I found out you didn't know how to boil one."

"But my poached eggs were impeccable," Maggie reminded him.

They pulled up in front of an impressive hotel. The driver took out two suitcases and handed them to a waiting bellhop.

"I thought you asked me to dinner."

"Yes, I did. I know you like Italian food. But I didn't know if you'd want to wash first. Or change. Mrs Cook put some things together."

A manager in a grey uniform appeared.

"Lord Raynham. And Lady Raynham. Welcome."

They were escorted to a luxurious suite. There were several bouquets of flowers and another bottle of champagne waited in a cooler.

Maggie went through some doors and out onto a large terrace that overlooked the sea. A nearly full moon shone down and lights from the town danced on the surface of the water. She heard the sound of a champagne cork popping, then Thomas appeared carrying two flutes. He handed one to her.

This is so unfair, she thought again. She should never have agreed to come.

"So Stanley organised this?" she asked, to have something to say.

"Er, yes. In fact he came to talk to me. He was aware of how I felt about Paley. And the resulting, er, difficulties. He spoke of... disruptive technologies. And what happens when something completely new enters an economy. Like the combustion engine. Or the microprocessor."

"Like impact of the automobile on blacksmiths? Or word processing on typewriters?"

"Quite. And how these technologies can have destabilizing effects. That could not be anticipated."

Thomas took a sip of champagne.

"Anyhow, he seemed to think I married you was because at some level I wanted some disruption."

"More than pie, sheep, and the history channel?"

"Yes. More than pie, sheep, and the history channel. Since I was not going to climb Mt Kilimanjaro or motorcycle through the Pampas."

Thomas had once told her that having to take on responsibility for the barony after the death of his older brother meant giving up his dreams about doing those, and many other, things.

"You can climb Mount Kilimanjaro in a week. Ten days if you want to do some safari-ing…"

"Yes. Well. Perhaps. But Stanley's point was, that I hadn't been prepared for the extent of the disruption you caused. And Paley certainly was destabilizing."

Well, at least he wasn't saying he'd been an idiot and was sorry, Maggie thought.

"And did Stanley say for how long one should anticipate these… destabilising episodes?"

"No. He said every disruption was different. Sorry."

The Greater Gloucestershire Galanthus Group

"But things eventually do stabilise?"

"Er, yes. Or at least that's what I gathered."

Maggie considered this.

"Stanley also said... Well. He was of the opinion that, when I'm not in some state of destabilisation, that I, er, take you for granted."

Maggie looked surprised.

"Do you think I do? Take you for granted?"

"I don't know. I never thought..."

"He said as an example, that I didn't know your favourite flower."

"You mean in the gardens?"

"No. He meant if I were going to give you a bouquet."

Maggie laughed. "In fact, my friends know I don't like bouquets. What is that Stones' song about dead flowers? And Bear the cat eats them."

"Or what music you like. Or movies."

"Well I would have enjoyed seeing Skyfall with you. Or the production of Twelfth Night with Stephen Frey. Or the David Hockney exhibit that was at the Royal Academy."

Maggie paused. The building and terrace wall were still throwing off some warmth from the day. It was a beautiful night. And Thomas was standing close and she could smell his citrusy-spicy aftershave.

"Dinner?"

"Um, I'm afraid the caviar rather ruined my appetite. Unless you...."

"No, I'm all right."

He paused.

"I meant what I said. About being able to go back. Shall I call for the car or should I tell the captain that he and the crew can stand down for the night?"

Maggie thought. It had been a long trip and she was not looking forward to repeating it all again in reverse. And it seemed wanton to not stay and see Capri in the daytime. Where it would doubtless be warm and sunny. She could really use some warm and sunny.

Maggie suppressed a sigh. When she had fled Joshua, she had let her head rule her heart. And that had been the right decision, she was certain. Was she going to let her head rule her heart now?

Thomas saw a look of deep sadness cross his wife's face. But it passed and finally she said, "It's late. And now that we're here, it seems foolish not to see the island during the day. It's supposed to be quite wonderful. So perhaps you should tell the captain...."

Thomas, who had been unaware of how tense he was, relaxed. He wanted to kiss her. He wanted to kiss her and then take off her dress and then... But he would wait. It was not that late.

He went to call the pilot. He remembered overhearing Maggie tell Anne that Paley had described himself as an egocentric, manipulative bastard.

Well, Thomas thought, the Barons Raynham were also egocentric, manipulative bastards At least the good

The Greater Gloucestershire Galanthus Group

ones were. The ones who did the most for the barony. He made the call, then smiled in anticipation as he went back to join his wife.

Susan Alexander

THE GREATER GLOUCESTERSHIRE GALANTHUS GROUP

CULPABLE ACTS

SUSAN ALEXANDER

"A Scotsman, an Englishman, and an American go into a forest..." sounds like the beginning of a joke, but the punch line is far from funny. The trio were going to poach a rare snowdrop in the woods of a Gloucestershire landowner. When the men are discovered trespassing, they panic, and tragedy ensues.

It is snowdrop season in the Cotswolds and Maggie Eliot has her hands full with events at Beaumatin, her husband Thomas's estate, as well as with her husband, who is grumpy about having to give tours and be sociable with garden visitors.

Then an old friend of Thomas is brutally killed. The police are stymied, so Thomas uncharacteristically joins forces with his wife to identify a murderer. Is it a stranger? One of Beaumatin's snowdrop tourists? Or someone closer to home?

About the Author

A native New Yorker, Susan Alexander currently lives in the Grand Duchy of Luxembourg. She has had a non-linear career path that has included working as a professional musician, being ordained as a Presbyterian minister, heading derivative and fixed income research at a Wall Street firm, founding a web site and web application development company, and lecturing to Britain's Hardy Plant Society's Galanthus Group. In 2018, she earned a PhD in Human and Organisational Systems. Her books are informed by her life experiences.

Susan enjoys writing about women who have led complex and interesting lives, their relationships, and the choices they have made.

Website: www.alexander.lu

Facebook: https://www.facebook.com/SAlexanderAuthor

Printed in Great Britain
by Amazon